What a killer story! A miracle child and a serial killer collide in *Fearless*, a breakneck pace thriller that entrances and enthralls! With a relentless pace and raw, wounded characters, *Fearless* kept me up late into the night—I could not read fast enough. Dellosso is a writer to be reckoned with!

—RONIE KENDIG
Award-winning, best-selling author of the
Discarded Heroes series and *Trinity: Military War Dog*

Mike Dellosso's *Fearless* packs an emotional punch. His engaging characters and riveting plot pull the reader right into the story. He's a true craftsman!

—TOM PAWLIK
Christy Award–winning author of
Vanish, Valley of the Shadow, and *Beckon*

Mike spins a tale that combines suspense and compassion, intrigue and hope, by weaving in a remarkable visitor's gift into a situation of pain and loss. Born of fire but created in love, this is a ride that will keep readers wondering until they turn the final page. *Fearless* will challenge your faith and your courage!

—ACE COLLINS
Best-selling author of *The Yellow Packard*
and *Darkness Before Dawn*

MIKE DELLOSSO

REALMS

Most CHARISMA HOUSE BOOK GROUP products are available at special quantity discounts for bulk purchase for sales promotions, premiums, fundraising, and educational needs. For details write Charisma House Book Group, 600 Rinehart Road, Lake Mary, Florida 32746, or telephone (407) 333-0600.

FEARLESS by Mike Dellosso
Published by Realms
Charisma Media/Charisma House Book Group
600 Rinehart Road
Lake Mary, Florida 32746
www.charismahouse.com

Scripture quotations are from the Holy Bible, New International Version. Copyright © 1973, 1978, 1984, International Bible Society. Used by permission.

This is a work of fiction. The characters in this book are fictitious unless they are historical figures explicitly named. Otherwise, any resemblance to actual people, whether living or dead, is coincidental.

Cover design by Justin Evans
Design Director: Bill Johnson

Visit the author's website at www.MikeDellosso.com.

Library of Congress Cataloging-in-Publication Data:
Dellosso, Mike.
  Fearless / Mike Dellosso. -- First edition.
    pages cm
  ISBN 978-1-62136-241-8 (trade paper) -- ISBN 978-1-62136-242-5 (ebook)
  I. Title.
  PS3604.E446F43 2013
  813'.6--dc23
                              2013003046

First edition

13 14 15 16 17 — 987654321
Printed in the United States of America

For Laura, Abby, Caroline, and Elizabeth—

Innocent eyes see the soul.

Acknowledgments

ALL THANKS TO my God and Savior, Jesus Christ. Without Him any attempt to do anything would be futile.

Big thanks to my wife, Jen, for always cheering me on, giving advice, and supporting this crazy writing thing. Thanks to my four daughters for lighting up my life and giving what I do some purpose. They play a bigger role than they think they do.

Thanks to my parents for their constant prayers and steadfast support. They believe I can even when I don't.

Also thanks in abundance go to...

- ◇ Les Stobbe, my wise and sage-like agent: his advice and guidance is like gold.

- ◇ My editors, Adrienne Gaines, Lori Vanden Bosch, and Deb Moss: without them I'd be a sloppy kid with mussed hair and wrinkled clothes propped in front of an audience to look like a fool.

- ◇ The sales and marketing team at Charisma: they do some marvelous stuff.

Lastly, many, many thanks go to my readers. Thank you for your support, encouragement, and prayers. I'll be back!

Just a Word...

IN JAMES CAMERON's 2009 hit *Avatar* the alien race greets each other with the words "I see you." During the course of the movie we learn that those words mean more than they appear to mean at first. To the Na'vi "I see you" is so much more than acknowledging that an individual is present; it is to look into their soul, to see them for who they really are, their character, their passions, their hurts and fears and joys and dreams.

Interestingly native tribes in South Africa use the same greeting. It's quite powerful when you think about it. We are a busy people, working, playing, texting, surfing; our minds are constantly occupied. Yes, we're surrounded by people we never really see. Oh, we see they're there. They get in our way in line at the grocery store, cut us off on the highway, give us the wrong amount of change at the fast-food joint. But do we really see them? Mostly, no.

How radically it would change our lives if we saw those around us as not just bodies populating the landscape of our life, but as people with lives, with struggles and victories, as husbands trying desperately to provide for their family and wives exhausted from working and parenting and running here and there, as employees striving to do their best in a system that keeps expecting more for less.

What if we really saw those around us? What if we looked into their eyes and found the soul of them? How important would every connection be? Every word spoken? Every action portrayed? And what if others knew that when we looked at them we saw so much more than a body taking up space, that we saw them as a precious creation, a person made in the image of God. A person.

I want to see people, really *see* them.

Chapter 1

JAKE TUCKER COUGHED in a half sleep, a raspy, dry hack that burned in his lungs. He was dreaming of drowning, of being pulled into murky, dark waters by some unseen hand. Above, through ripples of water, he could see the sun, a blurry orb, disjointed like pieces of a jigsaw puzzle and fading quickly. His lungs tightened, felt as if they would burst. Water pressed around him. He flailed his arms and kicked his feet, but it did no good. He sank farther and farther away from the surface, away from that tiny wriggling light. He coughed again, and in his dream he could take the pressure in his chest no longer and sucked in a mouthful of water, welcoming the cold liquid and the death it would bring. It rushed down his windpipe and into his lungs. He tried to inhale again, tried to draw oxygen from the water, but he was paralyzed. Suffocating.

Jake Tucker hacked, a forceful bark that brought up a wad of phlegm, and awoke. Thick, acrid smoke filled his living room. He'd fallen asleep on the sofa while watching the evening news and…and what? He'd been waiting for something. Something to cook. But what? Panic seized him.

He rolled to the floor where he found a layer of cool, fresh air. Pulling it in through his nose, he coughed again, expelled soot and smoke from his lungs. The kitchen was engulfed in flames. Wicked things as tall as a man and angry, they clawed and licked at the doorway to the living room, blackened the jamb and molding. The linoleum peeled and melted, curled around the edges.

But what had he been cooking? What had caused the fire?

Jake thought of heading for the front door, but there was

something he needed to get, something he was forgetting. He drew in another breath and hacked again.

Yes, Jovie, his cat. He'd put her in the cellar but couldn't remember why. The cellar door was in the kitchen, though, the kitchen that was now an inferno. But he couldn't just leave her down there. She was family to him. Pushing to his knees then his feet, Jake pulled his T-shirt over his nose and mouth and stumbled through the smoke. He struck his knee on something hard. The coffee table. He was moving in the wrong direction.

The fire roared like a living beast hungry for the flesh of man, but it sounded like it was all around him. It was spreading fast, growing, gaining strength, sucking the oxygen from the air. Oxygen he so desperately needed. He wheezed, coughed. His eyes burned and watered. But still he felt his way through the gloom. Sweat droplets dotted his forehead and cheeks now, soaked his shirt. The temperature in the house rose exponentially, slowly baking him.

Over the raging flames he heard a low meow. Jovie. She was just on the other side of the door. If he could only make his way to her. He tried to follow the sound of her yowling but the smoke and fire were so disorienting he repeatedly came back to the same wall, the one with the family photos on it. His parents and grandparents. His siblings. Marta, his wife, his long-mourned wife. And Raymond, his son. Dear Raymond.

Jake leaned against the wall. His mind was slowing, trudging through mud. His chest felt like it was in a vise. Pressure grew around his lungs and heart, squeezing his ribs until they hurt. The pain, a deeply intense ache, radiated down his left arm and up into the left side of his neck and face.

"Raymond!" But Raymond couldn't hear him. He was three thousand miles away in California. "Raymond, I'm sorry. Please."

He coughed again and this time brought up some blood. The pressure in his chest worsened, like someone was standing on him. His left shoulder blade felt like it was being ripped from his back.

Still Jovie meowed, over and over, rhythmic, like seconds ticking off time on a clock. The charcoal smoke swelled around Jake; the heat built. He dropped to his knees and tried to crawl to the sound of Jovie's cries. His eyes burned and watered so badly he couldn't see a thing.

Raymond was on his mind, though. His son, Raymond. He'd never see him again. Never...

The eggs. Yes, that was it. He'd put eggs on the stove to boil then went to lie on the sofa and watch the eleven o'clock news. The pot must have burned dry and started the fire.

In one last moment of semi-clarity Jake Tucker almost laughed at the irony of it all. Done in by a pot of eggs.

He fell to his side and rolled onto his back. A ceiling of smoke hung above him like a phantom. Maybe it was a ghost; maybe it was the angel of death come to take him over to the other side where he could see Marta, hold her again, tell her face-to-face all the words he'd spoken to her photo over the past five years.

Somewhere in the distance but not too far Jovie still wailed. But her holler faded quickly as if she was on a boat drifting away into the fog, farther and farther away, so far that he could no longer hear her. Jovie.

The weight on his chest had increased, and his left arm had numbed. He couldn't feel the left side of his face either.

Then the swirling smoke began to change colors, red and white and blue. It flashed and stuttered, red-red-white-blue, red-red-white-blue. His mind fixated on it, on the colors, the rhythm. They must be the colors of heaven. The gates were opening and welcoming him home, bidding him come near and see his Marta.

Jake coughed again; his chest spasmed. Smoke was such an awful thing to inhale. He had to remember to turn the stove off next time. He still couldn't remember why he'd put Jovie in the cellar. He couldn't hear her anymore.

Something in the house cracked. Sounded like wood busting,

splintering. A hideous sound. But he didn't open his eyes. He was being pulled under, just like in his dream, but instead of fighting it he had succumbed to it. There was no way out now. This was how it was going to end. And how it would all begin.

Suddenly he felt a presence there with him and opened his eyes. A face materialized out of the smoke, hovered over him. Small, soft, white…the face of an angel. Blue eyes that seemed to glow from their own light. Hair the color of flax and pulled back off her face. A girl. A young girl, just a child. She smiled at him and placed her hand on his chest. Her smile was sweet and innocent, the smile of a child who's never known the worst of this world. Oddly, in the midst of such chaos, such hellfire, she showed no signs of fear.

When she spoke, her voice was meek, the voice of all that is pure and right. "Mr. Tucker, you can't go yet. Raymond needs you."

Raymond. His son. His dear son. How did she know about Raymond?

"He loves you." She smoothed his hair with her hand. "He needs his father."

She had freckles across her nose, a spattering of them shaped like a butterfly.

"Tell Raymond you love him. Tell him how much you love him. Tell him you forgive him."

Her hand lifted from his head, and she faded from view. She was an angel, had to have been. His time had arrived, and he was about to be ushered into eternity by this precious little angel.

In the distance, so far away, he heard a faint knocking, then more wood breaking. The house was falling apart around him, but he didn't care anymore.

"Live, Mr. Tucker. Live. God has given you life."

He heard his name. A man calling him. Muffled. Another angel. They were coming to get him, coming to give him eternal life. A strong hand wrapped around his ankle and pulled. Something went over his face, something cool. He was floating now, breathing in the clean, fresh air of the heavens. His chest no longer ached, and the numbness was gone in his arm and face. He felt new again. Whole. Young.

Chapter 2

J IM SPENCER SLIPPED on his jacket and pulled his ball cap snug on his head. He walked lightly into the bedroom so as not to startle his sleeping wife from her deep sleep. Sleep didn't come easy for her anymore, and when she managed to find it, he hated to disturb her. But he needed to this time.

Through the darkness of the room he crept, the only light being that from the hallway slipping in past the cracked-open door. The shades on both windows were black and pulled, blocking even moonlight from filtering into the room. To find that elusive sleep, Amy needed it dark.

Jim stopped at the bed and stroked his wife's hair. "Hey, babe. Amy."

She stirred, moaned, but did not awaken. Her sleep was sweet and deep this time. Again he felt a prick of guilt for disturbing it. He thought about just quietly exiting the room and slipping out of the house unheard, but if she awoke and found him gone, she might panic. She was prone to panicking lately.

Again he combed his fingers through her hair. It was soft and still carried the faint smell of the shampoo she'd used that morning. Peach. "Amy. Babe. Wake up for a second."

Her eyes fluttered, stuttered, and finally opened. She squinted at him and pressed her lips together. "What is it time?" Her words were jumbled and slurred, the language of weary travelers just arriving from the land of slumber.

"Almost midnight. Hey, you awake?"

She rubbed her eyes with both hands and pushed her hair from her face. "Yeah. What is it? Is something wrong?" Already the panic was there.

"Doug Miller called. Jake Tucker's house is on fire, and he wants my help."

"Wants your help? Why?"

"I don't know. He said he'd fill me in when I got there."

Amy extended her hand to him as if reaching out from a pit that housed a creature whose tentacles were wrapped around her ankles, and he took it. "Poor Jake," she said. "I hope he's okay. Be careful."

"I will." He leaned in and kissed her on the forehead. "You try to go back to sleep. Sorry to wake you."

He turned to leave, but she didn't let go of his hand. "Be careful, Jim. Come back to me."

And there was the fear, the uncertainty that had such a tight hold of her. She'd already lost so much.

Jim slipped his hand from her grip hoping those tentacles didn't win the struggle and pull her into the lost darkness of despair for good. He stroked her cheek. "Don't worry. I'll be back home before you know it. You try to go back to sleep, okay? And don't worry, okay?"

"Mm-hm." She rolled toward him and slipped her hand under the pillow.

Jim crept out of the room, wishing sleep upon his wife, wishing the sandman to pay her another visit, but he doubted it. If this was anything like an ordinary night, she'd lie awake in bed and allow her mind to conjure torturous thoughts of what was lost and what could have been. Should have been.

Downstairs he grabbed a Coke from the fridge and left, locking the door behind him. At his truck he looked back at the house. On the second floor the bedroom light was already on. She'd given up so quickly.

Jake Tucker lived on a gentleman's farm about a mile outside the town of Virginia Mills. It was a two-hundred-acre, fully functional dairy farm until five years ago when Jake sold all but fifteen acres to some contractor with big dreams and dollar signs in his eyes. What the contractor didn't and couldn't know was that the housing bubble was about to burst and he'd be out millions, with land to sell and houses to build but no one with enough money or guts to buy either. As it was, one half-built home stood on the road to Jake's, a skeletal reminder to all who passed of the woes of the economic crisis. The rest of the land was staked and graded but as barren as the moon's pocked surface.

Jim could see the flames a mile away. The sky above the horizon flickered with the orange glow of the fire and the red, white, and blue strobes of the emergency vehicles, a morbid light display anyone would be happy to miss. As he neared, he got a better view. The house was mostly engulfed now, huge tongues of fire a story high clawed at the sides of the building, licked at the night sky. Oxygen was what it craved, and out here, where the September air was fresh and cool, it had its fill. The flames churned and writhed as if they were alive, a living beast rising from the pit of hell and devouring Jake Tucker's home. In some perverted, macabre way, it was a beautiful sight, hypnotizing even.

Men scurried to and from, barked orders, worked the trucks, the tanker…it was a chaotic waltz with each partner dancing his part perfectly. Four men manned two hoses, but despite the steady streams of water, the inferno showed no signs of surrendering any time soon. It had grown too strong, too confident, too hungry. Its ravenous appetite was not yet satiated.

Stopping the truck behind a police cruiser, Jim killed the engine and got out. He'd known Jake ever since he was a kid, saw him at church every Sunday. Now he wondered where Jake would live. There was no saving the house, not after such fire damage.

Doug Miller, the chief of police, approached and greeted him. "What gives, Spencer?"

Jim dipped his chin. "Chief. How're things going?"

Miller's face was flat, emotionless. He turned and watched the fire with glassy-eyed enchantment, his face changing colors in rhythm with the cruiser's flashers. Red-red-white-blue. He was a big man, broad shoulders, thick neck, mid-sixties, with a mustache and crew cut that said he was all cop. "They're gonna lose that house. Shame too. It's been in Jake's family for three generations."

"What about Jake?"

Miller continued with his fixation on the flames. "They put him in the rig and took him to County General. No need to, really. He was fine. He was black as an alley cat from all the smoke and soot, but once he coughed it all up, he was breathing just fine. Nothing much to get excited about."

The flames gyrated and twisted, caught in the last throes of agony or passion; either would fit. The house was just a shell now, blackened bones of wood beams and posts. The beast had picked away and devoured anything of substance. The western side of the second story floor cracked, broke, and collapsed. An explosion of sparks shot up into the air then cooled and faded within seconds.

Finally Miller pulled his eyes from the inferno. "Except for one thing."

"It's always the one thing."

"There was a girl in there with him."

"A girl?"

"A child. Says she's nine."

Jim didn't remember Jake ever saying anything about grand-kids. He looked around the area and found the girl, wrapped in a blanket, sitting on the running board of one of the fire trucks. Tina, a volunteer EMT with the station, sat beside her, holding Jake's cat. "That her?"

Miller turned toward the girl. "Yep. Louisa. Least that's what she says her name is."

"Is she okay?"

"Physically she's perfect. Medics had her on oxygen for a while.

Just took her off. She can't remember her last name, though. Doesn't know who her parents are or if she even has parents."

"Amnesia from smoke inhalation?"

"I've seen stranger."

"What did Jake say?"

"He said she was in there with him, but that's the first time he's ever seen her. He thought she was an angel; can you imagine that? Poor old-timer thought he was gonna kick it."

Jim looked at the girl again. She was a cute kid, blonde hair, soft features. Sitting next to the fire truck she looked small, lost, and lonely. "I sure hope you don't think Jake was…you know."

Miller shook his head. "Naw, not Jake. Anyone else and I'd look at them cross-eyed, but not Jake. He's as straight as straw, always has been. If he says he doesn't know where she came from, his word's good enough in my book."

"Good. 'Cause I'd have to go rounds with you if you suspected him of that."

Miller was back to watching the fire. "I'm glad you could come, Spencer. I called you because the kid needs a home for the night, until we can sort this out, find out who she is and who she belongs to."

"And you want me to take her?"

"You used to take in foster kids, didn't you?"

"Yeah, but that was before—"

"You think Amy will be all right with it?"

Would Amy be all right with it? Jim had no idea. She could go either way. Bringing a little girl home could push Amy further toward that edge of utter despair, or it could be just the lifeline she needed to pull her back from the edge.

"Can't someone else do it?" Jim said. There had to be another option.

"Sure they could, but I wanted to ask you first. You and Amy were my first choice."

"Why am I not flattered by that?"

"Will you take her?"

Jim hesitated. It wasn't a matter of if it was right or wrong; he knew what the right thing to do was. And it wasn't a matter of not having room; they had plenty of space in their house. It was Amy. She was so fragile now, so wounded. Her emotions were frayed and raw, and something like this, bringing a child home, could do irreparable damage.

Jim watched as Tina combed the girl's hair back and put her arm around her shoulders. The girl leaned into her and closed her eyes.

Jim cleared his throat. "Okay. Until you get to the bottom of this." Even as he said the words, another lump formed in his throat.

Miller slapped him on the shoulder. "Great. I'll get all the paperwork in order and stop by your house in the morning."

Jim left Miller and walked over to the girl. Tina smiled at him and nodded.

"Hey, Tina. How's it going?"

"Just fine."

Jim knelt in front of the child. Strangely she smelled of burnt wood, but there wasn't a mark of soot or a smoke stain on her. She opened her eyes and lifted her head, looked at him. Her eyes were large and round, the bluest Jim had ever seen, but they weren't childlike. Innocent, yes, even guiltless, but mature and knowing, as if with them she could look past his weak exterior and see the true state of his soul.

"Hey, sweetie," he said. "Louisa, right?"

She nodded. "Hi." A yellow and white cat, dusted with soot and ash, poked its head out from behind the blanket. The girl stroked the cat's head between the ears. "And this is Jovie."

Jim scratched the cat's cheek. "Hi, Jovie. Louisa, I'm Jim Spencer. You can call me Mr. Jim. I was just talking to Chief Miller over there, and we both think it would be a good idea if you came home with me and my wife and spent the night at our house tonight. Does that sound all right?"

She turned her face toward Tina as if seeking her approval. Tina smiled and squeezed Louisa's shoulders. "It's okay. He's a good guy. And his wife, Miss Amy, is a sweetheart. They'll take good care of you."

Louisa smiled and nodded at Jim. "Okay. Can we take Jovie too?"

"Sweetheart," Tina said, "Jovie is going to come home with me. I already told Mr. Jake I'd take care of her. She'll be happy at my house. I have another cat she can play with."

The girl ran her hand over the cat's blackened fur one more time. "She won't like getting a bath."

"I know," Tina said. "But she needs one. She's filthy, isn't she?"

Louisa nodded.

Jim took her hand, mouthed "Thank you" to Tina, and led Louisa back to his truck. "You ever ride in a truck before, Louisa?"

She shrugged.

"Well then, this might be your first experience riding high." He hoisted her up and into the passenger seat. "There you go. Put that seat belt on, and we'll be ready to roll."

They were both quiet on the drive back to Jim's house. The only sound was the hum of tires on asphalt and the soft country tunes flowing from the radio. Louisa eventually fell asleep. Her head lulled from one side to the other then finally rested against the seat belt.

When they arrived home, Jim carried her inside and laid her on the sofa. He then went to the second floor hallway closet and got her a pillow and blanket. When she was comfortably situated and asleep on her side, he went back upstairs and into the bedroom. The light was off, and Amy had somehow found sleep again. He set his alarm for just after sunrise so he could be sure to get up before Amy. He didn't want her to wake up, stumble down the steps to get breakfast, and find Louisa on the sofa. If he got up first he could warn her, explain what happened, and pray for the best.

If it were a fait accompli, surely Amy would welcome Louisa into their home. She would have to. Wouldn't she?

After stripping out of his clothes and slipping into his pajamas, Jim got into bed next to Amy and spooned his wife, his hand on her hip. She stirred a little and moaned, a pathetic sound of sorrow and loss. He had no idea if she dreamed anymore or what she dreamed about; she never talked about it. But if she did dream, he supposed her night visions were anything but pleasant and fantastical. No princesses and magical unicorns for her.

He brushed her hair to the side and lightly kissed the back of her neck before settling back onto his pillow. It didn't take him long to slip into the warm waters of sleep. But the dreams that found him there were disjointed and violent, filled with flames and writhing bodies. Several times he awoke (or maybe he wasn't awake, he couldn't tell) and thought he saw Louisa standing in the corner of their bedroom. One time he even said her name out loud. But each time he was quickly pulled back under by sleep's firm grip.

At 3:12 a.m. Jim startled, snapped awake by something in his dream. To his right Amy rolled to her back and mumbled something incoherent. She was sleep-talking. She raised an arm and thrashed at the air, grunted from the effort, as if fighting off some unseen attacker. Then she began to weep. Jim had never seen her cry in her sleep before. She spoke again, and this time it was almost comprehensible.

Jim rolled to face her. "What is it, honey? Say it again." He spoke quietly so as not to wake her.

Tears seeped from Amy's closed eyes, trickled into her blonde hair. She whimpered, "I've lost my way."

She said it a few more times, each time more declarative than the previous, as if trying to convince her dream visitor that as strange as it sounded, it was indeed true. Jim did his best to soothe her. He combed her hair with his hand, kissed her cheek and forehead. Eventually she settled back into a comfortable sleep, and eventually Jim followed her…

Where he was met once again by the angry tongues of fire.

Chapter 3

THE SUN HAD barely peeked above the horizon Monday morning when the man wheeled his truck in front of the farmhouse and shut off the engine. The farmer and his wife should be up and about; in fact, they had probably been awake for the past few hours, preparing for a day of labor and satisfying toil. She had no doubt cooked him a scrumptious breakfast of ham and eggs, maybe some fruit on the side, oranges and grapes. He would need his energy if he was going to put in a full day's work.

The man got out of the truck and eyed the barn. It was everything a barn should be. He did a 360-degree turn, taking in the panoramic view of the land, the homestead, the barn and other assorted outbuildings. He'd spent time on a farm just like this one when he was a kid; that's why he'd chosen this particular property. It reminded him of the only peace he'd felt in the storm that had been his life. Plus not a single neighbor was in sight. The farmhouse sat square in the middle of two hundred acres, only accessible by the dirt lane that ran a straight half mile from the paved road. As far as he could see were cornfields and pastureland. The corn was high as a man and brown as dirt. Above the dry tassels the sky was bright and varying hues of clear blue.

He stood by the open car door for a moment, closed his eyes, and drew in a deep breath. The aroma of dirt and cut grass and aged hay reminded him of those days when he ran free on the farm, free of the violence, the torment, the hatred. But then it too was taken from him.

He closed the truck's door, and the sound brought the farmer's wife to the porch. Clare Appleton. She was a tall, lean woman, older than sixty but younger than seventy, and looked to be in fantastic health. Her skin was as smooth as any forty-year-old's, and her hair, as white as a cloud, was pulled off her face and fastened in a bun high in back of her head. She wore a knee-length plain dress and a flowered apron. Holding a dishcloth in both hands, she cocked her head to one side and said, "Hello, there. What brings you out at the crack of dawn?"

The man liked the sound of her voice. It was nothing like his mother's. He walked down a stone path to the porch. "Good morning, ma'am," he said. "Sorry to drop by so early, but I figured you'd be up. Beautiful morning, isn't it?"

"Every morning is beautiful." Her smile was warm and inviting. She must be a wonderful grandmother to some small children somewhere. "For every morning brings the chance to start anew, to put the old behind and set a new course."

The man smiled. This was no ordinary farmer's wife. She was also a philosopher.

"Right you are," he said. "Always looking forward."

"There'll be no regrets in this house. Not as long as I'm living in it, anyway." She finished drying her hands and tucked the dishcloth into her apron. "What can I do for you?"

"Name's Mitch Albright. I just moved in down the road apiece, bought the old Sanstead farm, and I haven't a clue what I'm doing. I was wondering if I could ask your hubby some questions, tap into his well of knowledge."

"Well, it's nice to meet you, Mitch. I'm Clare." She motioned toward the barn. "Bob's sharpening some tools. You're welcome to talk to him. I think you'll find him more than willing to share whatever he's learned over the years. Be careful; he likes to wax eloquent now and again, and if you get him going on politics, you may just be here longer than you'd like."

"How long have you been farming this land?"

"Bob was born here, right in this house. So I guess you could say he's been working the land since he was old enough to hold a hoe."

The man forced a laugh, and to his ears it sounded remarkably genuine. The woman showed no sign of seeing past his façade. "Thank you, ma'am." He nodded and turned away from her.

The barn, he could see as he approached, was a magnificent structure, much larger than most in this part of the state. The foundation and both end walls were constructed of sturdy fieldstone. Atop it, at the peak of its roof, sat an ornate cupola with a dairy cow weather vane that currently pointed northeast. The barn looked to have been recently painted a dull sandy color, trimmed out with forest green. The same colors as the farmhouse. The man walked up the earthen ramp to the large front doors. One was open, and inside he heard the churning of a grinding stone, the gritty hum of metal being sharpened. He stood by the door and waited for the noise to stop. When it did, he knocked twice and entered.

The barn was perfect in every way. Neat, cleanly swept, and cavernous. One half was stacked nearly to the ceiling with bales of hay, barley, and straw. Dust particles floated in the air, riding imperceptible currents as easily as plankton takes to the motions of the sea.

Bob Appleton was in the far corner of the barn, in an area set up as a small machine shop. Hand tools hung on pegboard walls. A workbench ran the length of the area, at least twelve feet long, and on it was the sharpening stone and an assortment of other table machinery. The space was organized and orderly, a testimony to the farmer's pride in what he did.

Bob looked up, set down the blade he was sharpening, and removed his safety glasses. "Howdy. Can I help you?" His voice was raspy and dry, as if to speak caused him great strain.

The man approached and extended his hand. "Are you Bob?"

"Sure am. Do I—"

"No, you don't know me. I met your wife by the house. Lovely woman. Name's Mitch Albright. I bought the Sanstead place and am new at farming. Was wondering if I might pick your brain for a bit."

Bob smiled wide, and his eyes crinkled into many-toed crow's feet at the corners. "Sure thing." When he straightened to his full height, he was an imposing man of at least six feet two. His broad shoulders and thick chest spoke of a lifetime of hard labor and earth-forged strength, but his warm eyes and easy smile said it was a gentle strength, restrained. This man loved what he did. Farming was his life, his passion, his purpose. He was confident yet humble, and because of that humility and the fact that he reminded the man so much of his own grandfather, he, Mitch Albright, would spare Bob's life.

"I love your barn," the man said.

"Just had it painted last year. Woulda done it myself, but I'm gettin' too old for that now. It was easier just to pay someone to do it. A bunch of college kids did it over the summer. Took 'em near the whole summer to get it done too."

"They did a beautiful job. I hope you paid them well."

"Not well enough," Bob said. "For the work they did I didn't think they charged enough, so I gave 'em all a little extra. You shoulda seen them smile."

The man, Mitch, liked Bob the farmer more and more all the time. "And the animal stalls are below?"

"Yep. We don't keep animals anymore, though. Used to. Horses, cows, goats, you name it. Now we just farm the land. Corn, barley, soy beans."

"And that pays the bills?"

"We don't have many bills to keep up with. The farm's been in my family since before I was even a thought, and the equipment, what little we have, is all paid for. Our son is a lawyer in Chicago. Partner in a big firm. I think he feels bad he's not here to help tend the land, so he does what he can, or what eases his conscience, by funding it." Bob rubbed his hands together. "Hey, why don't you fire some farming questions at me and I'll do my best to answer what I can."

"Good enough. How about starting with the tools here? What are the necessities a budding farmer needs?"

Bob walked over to the workbench and ran his hand along the surface. The look in his eyes was one of pride and contentment. Here was a man who loved what he did with his hands, who took great satisfaction in his work. He and the bench were old friends and had no doubt spent countless hours getting to know each other. Most of the hand tools dangled from the pegboard in orderly fashion but a few—a hammer, a wrench, a couple screwdrivers—lay on the bench. These were the ones that got used the most.

"A good work area is essential," Bob said. "And a variety of tools." He pointed to the pegboard. "You see here we have hammers in various sizes, mallets, an assortment of screwdrivers and wrenches, all the usual stuff."

The man pointed to a table saw standing next to the workbench. "And what's that?"

"That?" Bob looked at him incredulously. "Boy, you really are green, aren't you?"

Up until that moment, until that comment, the man was actually having second thoughts about what he had come to do. He could always find another farm, another place of solace and rest while he completed his task. This region of the state was dotted with farms. But that one remark burned him, ignited a fire that could not now be extinguished. He would spare Bob's life because he believed the old farmer to be truly a humble man as Mitch's grandfather was, but he would have to pay for his condescension, his disrespect.

The man laughed. "Yeah, I guess I am. Can you show me how it works?"

When Bob turned to the table saw and bent to hit the switch, the man grabbed the wrench from the workbench and brought it down on the back of the farmer's head. It landed squarely with a solid *thunk*, and Bob dropped like someone had kicked his legs out from under him. He lay on the floor of the barn, motionless.

On the pegboard, next to the hammers, was a wall-mounted handheld two-way radio, no doubt Bob and his wife's way of communicating between the barn and the house. The man lifted the radio and depressed the talk button.

"Uh, hello?"

A couple seconds later, "Yes?"

"Hi, uh, it's Mitch. I think you should come out here, to the barn. Bob's fallen over."

"Oh, dear…"

The radio went dead, and less than a minute later Bob's wife appeared in the doorway, flour splashed across the front of her apron. She scanned the barn, found them, and ran to where her husband lay on the floor. Her eyes were wide and frantic.

"What happened?"

"I don't know," the man said. "We were standing here talking, and he suddenly clutched his chest and went down, hit his head on the saw there."

"Oh, dear lord." She dropped to her knees next to her husband, and when she leaned over him, Mitch Albright slipped the wrench from his back pocket and gave her a matching head wound. She went limp and collapsed on top of Bob.

The man smiled and looked around the barn. Yes, this farm would do perfectly.

His name, of course, was not Mitch Albright.

Chapter 4

JIM SPENCER SHUT off the alarm before it even rang. He had been in a light sleep, and his internal clock knew the time to awaken was near. Muted rays of light slipped past the edges of the dark shades and cast the room in a dusty glow. He listened but heard nothing. The house was quiet.

He thought of Louisa, the enigma who suddenly appeared out of nowhere and saved Jake Tucker's life. Who was she? Where had she come from? Perhaps she'd been abandoned on Jake's farm minutes before the house went up in flames. It was sick, even unbelievable, but stranger things had happened.

But there was another option, one Jim didn't want to seriously entertain but nevertheless had to because it kept knocking on the door of his mind. She may be what Jake thought she was: an angel. It was absurd, unbelievable, and worthy of a visit to the asylum for even giving it weight…but there it was, a possibility.

Whoever she was and wherever she came from, she was here now, in their house, on their sofa, and he needed to explain to Amy what had happened before she went downstairs.

He rolled toward Amy and found her on her back, eyes open and staring at the ceiling.

"Hey, you. Good morning." He kissed her on the nose. "You're awake already."

She turned her head toward him and smiled. "Good morning. I didn't hear you come home last night."

"I know. I think I've mastered the art of walking on air. You were sleeping, and I didn't want to disturb you."

"What happened? Is Jake—"

"In the hospital getting checked out. He'll probably be released today."

"He's okay then?"

"Miller said he'd be fine. Just got a few good lungfuls of smoke."

"And his house?"

"Gone. They couldn't save it. Everything gone."

"Oh, how sad. Poor Jake."

Jim sighed. "Yeah. For now I imagine he's just glad to be alive, but once that wears off, he's gonna be hit with reality."

"I can't imagine losing everything we have." She stopped abruptly and folded her arms over her abdomen. A protective position, Jim knew. Her motherly instinct subconsciously kicking in. It already felt like they had lost everything.

Jim propped himself on one elbow. "Amy, something strange happened at the fire."

"Stranger than poor Jake losing everything in the middle of the night?"

"Much. There was a little girl in the fire with Jake."

"What little girl? Who?"

"That's the strange part. Nobody knows. She just showed up."

"Just showed up." If she was trying to hide her disbelief, she didn't do a very good job of it. Convincing Amy the child might be an angel stranded on earth would be as difficult as proving to her that Sasquatch was not only real but also a distant relative on her dad's side of the family. "Was she hurt?"

"Not at all. Jake said he never saw the girl before. It was as if she dropped from the sky."

"Like an angel." The sarcasm in her voice made Jim abandon any idea of posing that as a viable option for her appearance.

"No. She's real, all right. Flesh and bone. Cute little thing too. She's nine, but that's all we know. She couldn't tell us where she's from or who her parents are. Can smoke inhalation cause memory loss?"

Amy shrugged. "I guess. Carbon monoxide can."

"Miller asked me to take her home for the night."

Amy closed her eyes.

As if on cue the bedroom door opened, and there, standing in the doorway, backlit by the light of the hallway, was Louisa.

Amy opened her eyes and the child came forward, moving across the floor with small, even, determined steps, as if she were walking down the center aisle of a church spreading flowers before a bride. She kept her eyes on Amy the whole time. Those blue, piercing eyes cut through flesh, sinew, and marrow and examined the soul.

Amy's first intuition was to push back into the headboard, maybe even pull the covers up for some sense of protection or barrier. But the girl was so young and delicate, so innocent, she was hardly a threat. Her blonde hair was mussed from sleep and her dress wrinkled. Such a beautiful little dress, white with tiny blue flowers. But what grabbed Amy's attention more than anything were those eyes. She'd never seen such a striking shade of blue. She was a remarkable child, indeed, and in fact looked exactly how Amy had imagined her own daughter.

That thought sent waves of prickles up and down Amy's arms, and her flesh dimpled.

Jim must have noticed her response, for he put a hand on her arm and said, "Honey, this is Louisa. She's nine. Louisa, this is Miss Amy."

The girl, Louisa, stood beside Amy, her arms at her sides. If ever an angel came in human flesh, this is her, Amy thought.

She suddenly had a lump in her throat, and she had to struggle to swallow past it. "Hello, Louisa."

Louisa didn't smile, but her eyes seemed to glow with some queer sense of recognition. "Miss Amy."

Then the child lifted her hand and placed it on Amy's abdomen, low, below the navel, and closed her eyes. Her touch, the feel of her hand, so light and gentle, rendered Amy as useless as if she'd been struck by a bolt of lightning. She wanted to push Louisa's hand away, tell her that area, that blessed, cursed, area was off limits, but she couldn't move, couldn't even speak. There was something special—Mystical? Magical? No, it couldn't be—about the child's touch, something that sent involuntary shivers along Amy's body.

Louisa suddenly snapped her head up and opened her eyes. There was such hurt in them, such pity. Tears pooled along the bottom lid. "You're hurt," she said, and her voice quivered like a windblown leaf.

Amy wanted to say yes, she was hurt, and wounded, and scarred. She had the sudden urge to shout it, to release all the pent-up emotion, the fear, the great sense of loss she'd carried around for the past six months. She wanted to take this child, this Louisa, in her arms and hold her, but she couldn't; she was still paralyzed, still mute.

All this time Jim said nothing. Amy barely noticed he was there except for his hand still on her arm. He seemed just as transfixed by what was happening as she was.

Louisa kept one hand on Amy's abdomen and smeared tears across her face with the other. She sniffed. "You are loved, Miss Amy. He adores you so much."

Amy found her voice, but that was it. The rest of her felt heavy and awkward. "Who?"

"God. He hurts with you, but His love is bigger than the hurt. You have to believe that."

Amy didn't know what to say. She was again struck mute not by any physical malady but by mere ignorance. She believed once that God loved her, but now she didn't understand His way of showing it. Now she felt abandoned, left in some wilderness to fend off the wolves and cold and hunger by herself.

"Do you believe it?"

Still Amy said nothing. She couldn't answer. She wasn't sure if she believed it or not.

Louisa tilted her head slightly to the left, and the corners of her mouth curved upward ever so gently. "There's still life in you."

Amy didn't feel alive; she felt dead, like she'd perished with her baby daughter and now walked the earth as a zombie, trapped in her body but not really living.

Then suddenly Amy's strength returned, her ability to perform voluntary actions, and she was seized by a feeling of panic. Quickly she pushed Louisa's hand away. "Jim."

Jim jumped up from the bed and walked around to the child. "Louisa, honey, let's you and me go downstairs and get some breakfast, okay?"

Louisa nodded. Jim ushered her from the room, leaving Amy alone with a weird burning in her abdomen. It was not uncomfortable but odd enough that it caused her to rub the area. The girl had affected her in ways she could have never imagined. There was something about her, this Louisa, something peculiar yet attractive, odd yet oddly familiar.

Something that put an eel of uneasiness in Amy's stomach.

Chapter 5

LOUISA CHOSE WAFFLES and vanilla ice cream for breakfast, and Jim didn't argue. It was, after all, one of his favorite combinations. While the waffles toasted, he got the ice cream from the freezer and set it on the counter.

"Now this is a good choice," he said to Louisa. "Not the healthiest, but I'd imagine it's better for you than a couple of doughnuts and a large latte, and people eat that for breakfast all the time."

While they waited for the waffles to finish, he couldn't help but think about what had just occurred in the bedroom. Louisa, this girl who seemingly appeared out of nowhere, was a true enigma. What she'd said to Amy had given him goose bumps. Was it that obvious to someone else, even a child, that Amy was still licking her emotional wounds? He was around her every day, so he was sure on some level he'd grown accustomed to it, even immune to it. And Louisa was certainly no ordinary child. She was mature well beyond her years. What must she have already gone through in her young life to give her that kind of insight?

The bell on the toaster oven rang. He opened the door and slid the waffles onto a plate. "All right, hot out of the toaster, the best way." He divided them onto two plates, two apiece, and scooped a heaping amount of ice cream on each. "The warmth from the waffle will melt the ice cream just a little and soften it. Why don't you find a seat at the table and I'll get you a fork."

Louisa sat on a chair while Jim fished a fork from the drawer. He put the plate in front of her. "There you go, Mr. Jim's famous ice cream waffle breakfast. You won't find a better-tasting breakfast in all of the state of Virginia."

Louisa smiled and eyed the waffles hungrily. "Thank you."

"You're very welcome."

Jim got his own plate and a fork and joined her at the table.

Louisa looked up from her plate. "Will Miss Amy be joining us?"

Jim paused. "Not yet, sweetie. She'll come down a little later."

"Can you say grace?"

Again Jim hesitated. Ever since Amy's miscarriage prayer seemed different, forced, even useless. Like words spoken in an empty room with no one around to hear them.

He forced a smile, said "Sure," then quickly prayed, thanking God for the food, for Jake's safety, and asking him to please help them find Louisa's parents.

When he said "Amen," he lifted his head and found Louisa staring at him. "What is it, sweetie? Is something wrong?"

"No. I just wanted to watch you pray."

For no apparent reason the goose bumps returned to Jim's arms. Had she caught a hint of his faltering faith in the sound of his voice? Could she see past his propped-up exterior to his wounded spirit? "How did I look?"

She shrugged. "Normal."

"Good. Normal is good, right?"

When she didn't answer, Jim said, "Eat your breakfast, sweetie, before the ice cream melts too much and all you have is a gooey, soggy mess. Then I'd have to get you a spoon to eat it with, and waffles aren't made for spoons."

Louisa wasted no time digging into her breakfast. Midway through the mound of ice cream Jim said, "Louisa, do you have any memory of your parents at all?"

She paused, and a distant look overtook her eyes. They focused on nothing in the room but rather something in her mind, some far-reaching memory bank that was now as empty as an abandoned vault. The fork hovered over the plate, dripping melted ice cream. Finally she refocused on Jim and shook her head. "No. I can't remember a thing."

"You don't remember how you got to Mr. Jake's house?"

"No."

"Where you got that pretty dress?"

"No."

"But you remember your name is Louisa and that you're nine years old."

She thought a moment. "I guess so."

"Well, hopefully Chief Miller will be able to find something out."

She cut off a huge piece of waffle topped with ice cream and shoved it into her mouth. After chewing and swallowing, she looked at him with those intensely blue eyes, eyes that seemed to be hiding something, a secret of sorts, and said, "Yes. Hopefully."

Again the goose bumps were there, running patterns up and down Jim's arms. Why wasn't this child more upset? Shouldn't she be spooked too? Or did amnesia not only take away memory but also emotionally paralyze its victim?

Louisa took another bite of her waffle, chewed, swallowed. "Will you have to go to work today?"

"No. I'm taking the day off. I work here at home, though. I write books. Most people wouldn't call it work at all, but it is."

"What kind of books?"

"Books for grown-ups. Love stories. Not the kind you see in the grocery store—" He remembered who he was talking to. "Nice love stories."

He hadn't always been a full-time writer. For the first ten years of their marriage he'd worked as a mechanical engineer and wrote on the side. He was able to put out twelve books in that time, but none of them had garnered any national attention. Sales were respectable enough that the publisher kept the contracts coming, but there was not a best seller among the lot. Then a movie producer in Hollywood found his books and fell in love with them. One after another she optioned his stories and found homes for them, mostly at Hallmark and Lifetime. It was nothing to make him rich, but it was success like Jim had not seen before, and when he'd gotten a couple movie deals under his belt, enough money started coming in on a regular basis that he could quit his engineering job and write full-time.

"Does Miss Amy work?"

"She did. She was a teacher. But she's taking this year off."

"How did Miss Amy get so hurt?"

The question did not take Jim by surprise. He expected she would ask it sooner or later and thought it would be sooner. "Well, this past April she got pregnant. Miss Amy had always wanted to be a mother, but for some reason it just didn't happen. Finally, after we'd been married for fifteen years, it happened, so as you can imagine, this was a very special baby." He had never told the complete story to anyone, and here he was spilling it to a nine-year-old. "She was a girl, and we were going to name her Olivia."

"Olivia is a beautiful name."

"Yes, it is."

He paused and pushed melting ice cream around on the plate with the fork. This next part was the hardest. Amy had her wounds, certainly she did, and they were raw and oozing still, but he was also hurt. He'd wanted a child too, and the thought of having a daughter, a little girl to spoil and cuddle, had put him on another level of happiness. But when the miscarriage happened and he saw the needless suffering Amy endured, such sadness overcame him that it plunged him beneath dark waters and held him there. He cried out to God at first, begged for mercy, for any relief. He needed air; they both did. But there was only silence.

After a month of begging an absent God and watching his wife descend deeper and deeper into a pit of depression and isolation, Jim gave up on seeking help from above. It wasn't there and wasn't coming any time soon. If anyone was going to help Amy, it would have to be him. He had to be the strong one.

"Well, uh, a woman is pregnant for nine months while the baby grows inside her, right?"

He nodded and pushed forward to the awful end of the story. "After three months the baby died. Miss Amy got really sick, and they had to do an operation. The doctor told her she would never have another baby."

Tears ran thin trails down Louisa's soft cheeks. "I'm sorry," she said. "I'm sorry that happened."

"So are we. Anyway, that happened two months ago, and Miss Amy's not been herself since."

"And you haven't either?"

The girl saw things most adults missed. "No, I suppose I haven't."

Chapter 6

AMY NEEDED TO take a shower. After her encounter with Louisa she felt tense and thought a good dousing of hot water might help to massage her nerves and wash away the deep stress. She was not angry with Jim for bringing the girl home. He would have been a jerk not to. She needed a place to stay, and they were, after all, foster parents. Or had been, anyway, up till her miscarriage. Until this morning she had it in her mind that they'd never take another child in. They'd seen so many hurt kids come through their home, heard so many nightmares. Amy doubted she could ever spend herself emotionally for a child again. She felt like a dishrag now with nothing left to wring out of her.

She turned on the shower water and adjusted it to the right temperature then stripped out of her pajamas. Immediately steam started to build and envelop her in a warm, moist blanket. Stepping under the hot stream of water, she closed her eyes and let it cascade over her face and body. Instantly her muscles relaxed, but the thought of the girl was still there, the image of her and those brilliant blue eyes and that freckled nose and flaxen hair imprinted on her mind's eye.

Amy turned away from the water and opened her eyes. The image vanished. She proceeded to shampoo her hair and work it into a rich lather. Sun-ripened peach was her favorite fragrance, and the aroma filled the bathroom, hung in the steam. She tried to think of something else, anything other than Louisa, but her mind kept returning to the girl, like a television set with the same show on every channel. How did she know about the miscarriage? Or did she know? She merely said that Amy was wounded. And it probably didn't take a psychotherapist to determine that by looking at her. Depression is often recognizable by someone's appearance, the deadness in the eyes, the lack of will or emotion. But she'd placed her hand on Amy's abdomen when she said it, over her wounded and damaged uterus. The uterus that could no longer sustain life. The uterus that killed her baby. Olivia.

Grabbing the bar of soap, Amy worked up a rich foam in her hands then scrubbed her forehead, cheeks, and chin. Keeping her eyes closed, she stuck her face under the water to rinse.

She thought she heard the bathroom door open and close. Pulling her face out of the shower's stream and brushing away the excess water, she opened her eyes and listened.

"Jim?"

The bathroom was quiet, but she felt a presence in there with her. She sensed eyes on the shower curtain and thought, if she listened real close, that she heard a rustling. The girl. Louisa was in the bathroom with her. She knew it, felt it, sensed it. Where was Jim?

"Louisa?"

But no answer came. Amy found herself afraid for no reason in particular. Fear, like an unreachable itch, scratched beneath her skin. Louisa was just a girl. A child. Innocent and vulnerable. And yet Amy was too afraid to open the curtain. Minutes ticked by, and she did not move. The water ran off her body in thick rivulets and was hotter than usual, but still she felt chilled. Steam clouded the shower and bathroom.

Once more, "Louisa, is that you?"

And again no answer came.

Eventually the water started to cool, so Amy turned down the cold water. She wasn't ready to get out yet.

Finally she mustered enough courage to take a peek. Slowly, as if to do it quickly would replay some gruesome scene in an old horror flick, she peeled back the curtain and found the mirror above the sink. Normally the reflection provided a full view of the rest of the bathroom, but now it was fogged into a hazy opaqueness. Slowly still she pushed the curtain aside farther and scanned the room. It was empty. The sink and toilet stared back at her with dumb indifference.

Amy cursed her irrational fear and went back to her shower. She still needed to rinse away the shampoo. Backing into the water, she closed her eyes and let the water massage her scalp, washing away the foamy lather she'd worked into her hair. Again, the image of the girl was there, that face like an angel's, those thoughtful, penetrating eyes, the butterfly pattern of freckles that stretched from cheek to cheek. It loomed and hovered like a phantom. The lips moved and the words "There's still life in you" echoed through Amy's mind. What did that even mean? The girl had said it while her hand rested on Amy's...

She felt a hand on her abdomen. Amy jumped and snapped her eyes open. She thought she saw a tiny hand pull away from her and disappear through the curtain. Foamy shampoo inched down her forehead and tickled her eyebrow. More ran down her back, hugging the curves of her body.

The girl was there. In the bathroom. Anger flared in Amy— how dare the vagrant touch her while she was showering—but fear as well. Again she found herself unable to open the shower curtain. It might as well have been an iron wall. By now the water was turning cooler again, and when she tried to twist the cold-water knob more, she realized it was turned off as far as it would go. She had to do something quickly or she'd wind up taking a frigid shower or standing there with shampoo still in her hair. Casting aside the visions of murderous shower scenes or cryptic messages drawn on steamy mirrors, she threw the curtain open, fully prepared to confront the girl in the nude. The bathroom was empty.

Holding on to the corner of the shower stall, Amy leaned out and opened the closet door, thinking maybe Louisa had hid in there. Only towels, washcloths, sheets, and dirty laundry. Had she slipped out of the bathroom that quickly and quietly? Or had Amy imagined the whole thing? She'd ask Louisa when she saw her. If there was one thing her experience with kids had taught her, it was that children were terrible liars, and Amy would be able to tell if Louisa was hiding the truth.

Cursing herself again, Amy pulled the curtain closed, quickly finished rinsing her hair, and shut off the water.

She stood there shivering while the last of the water and shampoo circled down the drain. The only sound in the bathroom was the soft plunk of water droplets as they slipped from Amy's body and hit the shower floor.

But for Amy the chill she felt was not merely due to the cold water she'd finished rinsing in. This was an irrational cooling, birthed from nothing of this world, nothing of flesh and blood, but rather of spirit and things that lurk in darkness, feed on fear. It was the same chill brought on by bogeymen and monsters under the bed, by things that hide in shadows and exhale icy breath down the back of necks. For some reason unknown to her she wasn't sure she could trust this mystery girl that wound up in their care. This Louisa from the fire.

Chapter 7

A KNOCK AT THE front door pulled Jim Spencer away from the breakfast table and the last of his waffles and ice cream. Chief Doug Miller was there, a wad of papers in hand. He nodded and furrowed his brow and looked past Jim into the house. "Spencer. How did the night go?"

"Just fine. Louisa slept like a log on the sofa. Did you find anything out?"

Miller shook his head. "Nope. Mind if I come in?"

Jim stepped aside. "No, not at all."

Miller entered, and Jim closed the door behind him.

"Would you care for some waffles and ice cream?" Jim said.

Miller looked at Jim as though he'd just offered him spaghetti and meatballs for breakfast. "No, thanks. Already had breakfast."

"Coffee and doughnuts?"

"Don't I wish. Tea and parfait. The wife makes me eat it."

"Ouch."

"I brought the paperwork," Miller said. He hesitated, glanced around the living room. "You mind if you need to keep the girl a little longer?"

"I had a feeling that was coming. How much longer?" Jim didn't mind keeping her, but it was Amy he was concerned about. He knew her encounter with Louisa had left her shaken.

Miller dipped his head and smoothed his mustache with one hand. He eyed Jim through his bushy eyebrows. "Indefinitely?"

"Indefinitely. As in maybe another day, maybe a decade." Jim crossed his arms. A lump sat in the bottom of his belly. He wanted to say yes. It was the right thing to do, and Louisa seemed to be a charming, albeit odd, child. He doubted she'd bring any trouble upon his life, but he was less sure of Amy. The last thing he wanted to do was invite this sweet child into his home with the promise of security and provision and then have to turn her out if Amy couldn't cope. "I'll need to talk to Amy about it."

"How did she do with Louisa staying the night?" Miller seemed genuinely interested.

Jim shrugged. "I didn't tell her until this morning. It'll take her some time to get used to the idea, but I think she'll come around." He lowered his voice. "No one has come forward looking for their daughter?"

"Not yet. We've run all the databases. No kidnapping reports, no missing person reports, nothing."

"Have the inspectors gone through Jake's house yet?"

"You thinking she was there with her parents and they didn't make it out?"

Jim nodded.

"I was thinking the same thing. Stopped by the hospital this morning and saw Jake. He said he didn't have any visitors yesterday. None. Home alone the whole day. And he was pretty adamant that he didn't know who the girl was."

"So what, she just pulled a Star Trek and teleported there?"

"Seems like it, don't it?"

"I've seen a lot of interesting kids over the years, but this would definitely be a first."

"A first for science too."

"Is Jake okay?"

Miller nodded. "Physically, yeah. But he keeps going on about needing to get out of the hospital so he can call his son. You ever meet Raymond?"

"No." Jim had never even heard Jake talk about his son.

"Odd fella. Suspicious, you know. Real con artist type. He and Jake had a falling out some years ago, seems he conned his own father out of some money. Jake never forgot it."

"When will he be discharged?"

"This morning. Docs all say he's fine to go home. I don't think it's settled in yet that he doesn't have a place to call home."

"Where will he stay?"

"The Red Cross is putting him up in a hotel, the Giffords' place out on 34, until they can find him an apartment. But he said something about taking his insurance money and selling the land and settling down in a retirement home."

Miller paused and looked at the papers in his hand, leafing through them as one might absently flip through a stack of old bills. "Did the girl say anything this morning about her family? Her last name? How she got in Jake's house?"

"Said she couldn't remember anything. You think she's telling the truth? I mean, there's a possibility she's a runaway and pulling this amnesia thing to keep from being taken back home. Some kids endure some pretty harsh stuff and would do anything to get away from it." They had fostered some runaways, so he knew what he was talking about.

"I've had the same thing on my mind," Miller said. He nodded toward the kitchen. "Want me to talk to her?"

"Chief, if it's all the same to you, I think it would go better if I did it. The uniform can be intimidating to kids. Give her some time to get comfortable here, and then I'll broach the subject."

Miller stroked his hand over his mustache again. "Fine. If you find anything out, let me know. Any more information will help." He handed the papers to Jim. "Here. They should all be filled out. Sign them and drop 'em by the office sometime today so we can get things filed with the county."

"Will do." Jim saw Miller to the door and let him out. He closed it and studied the papers. All the routine forms. He'd filled them out so many times before. But never had he and Amy received a child under such bizarre circumstances.

Behind him a chair scraped across the kitchen floor, then

shuffled footsteps. Jim turned and found Louisa standing in the entryway between the living room and kitchen. She had one hand on the wall. "Was the policeman asking about my parents?"

Jim went to her and took her hand. "Here, come sit down with me, Louisa." He led her to the sofa, and they both sat. "Do you remember your parents?"

She shook her head. "I only remember helping Mr. Jake. He couldn't breathe, and his chest was hurting real bad."

"So what did you do?"

She shrugged. "Told him not to be scared. Then I told him that Raymond still loves him and needs him." She looked Jim right in the eyes, and her gaze made him uneasy. "He was very sad about Raymond, you know."

"How do you know Raymond?"

Again she lifted her shoulders and let them drop quickly. "I just do. I saw him."

"Where?"

Another shrug. "I just did."

Jake had photos of a younger Raymond scattered throughout the house. She must have noticed them. Jim wasn't sure how much deeper he wanted to probe, though. He was afraid of what he might find. He doubted Louisa was ready to talk, and he wasn't certain he was either. Not yet.

"Louisa, would you mind staying here with Miss Amy and me a little longer, until they find your parents?"

Louisa reached out her hand and laid it on Jim's. Her touch was soft and warm, and as much as he didn't want to, Jim couldn't help but think that this must be what it was like to be touched by an angel. "Is it okay with Miss Amy?"

"I'll talk to her, but I'm sure it will be."

"Okay then. As long as it's all right with her. I think she needs me. She's sad too."

Jim couldn't help asking. "And you, Louisa? Are you sad?"

She looked at the sofa and blinked several times as if the question had caught her off guard. "No. Should I be?"

"Do you miss your parents?"

Her eyes found his. "I don't remember them."

"Are you okay with being here?"

She nodded. "Yes. I think this is where I should be."

Chapter 8

THE MAN, MITCH Albright who wasn't really Mitch Albright, was in fact very skilled with hand and power tools alike. Most kids learned such skills from their old man, but Mitch's old man never bothered with teaching his son anything but how to duck and avoid. Mitch's grandfather had stepped in and filled the void; he taught Mitch how to measure and cut wood and hammer nails. Next to the work area in the barn was a stack of wood for farm and home repairs. Some of it was quality lumber, some old and warped. Bob had quite the stockpile. He was a resourceful old farmer.

Mitch gathered the wood he would need and put it in a separate pile. Then, after binding and gagging the still unconscious Appletons and tying them to a thick post, he headed to the house for a drink and snack.

The house was not your typical farmhouse. Mitch had been in plenty of farmhouses, and they all had one thing in common: they were cluttered. Most farm folk were so busy with keeping up with the land and animals they had little time left over for housekeeping. As a result, corners filled fast, and stacks of magazines and newspapers and empty boxes grew high.

Not so with the Appleton house. It was clutter-free and well organized. Clean too. None of the farm dust or dirt or manure made it past the front porch. The interior even smelled clean, like freshly washed linen. Clare had done a good job of keeping the farm odor out of their home by placing scented candles in every room.

In the rear of the house was the kitchen, a large area wrapped with natural wood cupboards and granite counter space. Gleaming pots dangled from a rack suspended from the ceiling.

An island sat beneath it positioned in the middle of the kitchen for easy access from any direction. Mitch opened the refrigerator and was amazed at the amount of food the Appletons kept on hand. He envied Bob for what he had. With an abusive father and disinterested mother, Mitch had learned to spend most of his time outside the house, fending for himself.

Retrieving ham, salami, roast beef, cheese, mustard, and pickles from the fridge, he quickly found a loaf of oat bread and assembled two sandwiches for himself. He would eat one now and save one for later. He would need plenty of energy for the project that awaited him. The sandwich was delicious, quite possibly the best he'd ever had, and he washed it down with a tall glass of Southern-style sweet tea, heavy on the sugar.

From there he explored the rest of the house and found it too to be meticulously cared for, finely furnished, and free of the farm outside. The second floor housed four bedrooms, one complete with a queen-sized canopy bed and an ornately carved armoire. The other rooms had been converted into a sewing room, a study, and a plainly furnished guest room. The hallway was decorated with a very large collage of family photos of the Appletons and their son. He apparently was married and had three boys. Very rambunctious boys from the look of the pictures. And one very attractive wife.

The second-floor bathroom was no different than the rest of the house, spacious, perfectly decorated, and clean. Not a spot of mildew anywhere.

Mitch liked this house, indeed, because it was more than a house; it was a home. And the more he explored it and enjoyed its comforts, the more it reminded him of his grandparents' home.

Returning to the first floor, Mitch found the cellar door in the hallway near the kitchen and opened it. Worn, wooden steps descended into the underbelly of the house. Cool air rose from the space and carried with it an earthy smell. The house was old,

probably early 1800s, and therefore the foundation was old, constructed of the same fieldstone found in the barn. To the right
was a light switch, so Mitch flipped it. Light illuminated the cellar,
revealing an unpainted concrete floor.

Mitch descended the steps and found the cellar in the same
order as the rest of the house. Storage bins were neatly stacked
and labeled along the far wall. A new hot water heater and small,
energy-efficient furnace sat under the staircase. The rest of the
space, which ran the full length of the house, was mostly empty
save for a washer, a dryer, an old exercise bike, and another workbench loaded with a complete set of hand tools. Two naked bulbs,
one on each half of the cellar, gave the area an almost prison-like
aura.

Yes, the house and barn were both perfect. Mitch pulled
in a deep breath and smiled. He loved this farm. It was everything he'd hoped it would be. He rubbed his hands together and
laughed with excitement.

Upstairs again, on the first floor, he went to fridge, removed
a can of orange soda, and popped the top. He took a long swig,
downing half the can at once.

Outside he heard the crunch of gravel under tires. Someone was
there, come to visit the Appletons. Quickly he exited the kitchen
and crossed the house to peer out a front window. A Honda Passport sat next to his truck, a man behind the wheel. Due to the
glare on the windshield, Mitch couldn't make out what the man
looked like. He sat there for a few seconds then got out of the
vehicle. Tall and lean, he was dressed nice in khakis and a blue
short-sleeved polo shirt with some kind of logo on the left breast.
He looked to be mid-twenties and carried a clipboard in one hand.
Standing by the Passport, he looked around and squinted into
the sun. A salesman, had to be. He glanced at the clipboard then
headed for the house.

Mitch realized he'd left the front door open.

Chapter 9

AMY STOOD AT the mirror, combing the tangles out of her hair. She was still a little shaken. Had she imagined the sound of the door opening and closing and the hand retreating from the shower? She'd never had hallucinations before. She was grieving, yes, but she wasn't crazy.

She placed a hand on her abdomen and thought of the daughter she should have had. Strangely, she thought of Louisa. The blonde hair and blue eyes. The freckles. The delicate features. She was everything Amy had ever imagined her own daughter looking like. But there was that feeling again, the sense of distrust and unease. Who was this intruder in her home? Where had she come from?

Amy scolded herself for being so cynical, so paranoid. She was a girl, nothing more. Someone's daughter who had either been abducted or lost or abandoned. She needed love right now, not some suspicious, grief-stricken woman giving her the cold shoulder.

Heading out of the bathroom and down the stairs, Amy couldn't help but hope that Chief Miller had found the girl's parents or at least solved the puzzle of who she was and how she wound up in Jake's burning house.

Louisa was seated on the sofa in the living room, Jim next to her. The girl's eyes widened when she saw Amy, and she said, "Good morning, Miss Amy."

Amy smiled. "Good morning, Louisa. Did you sleep okay last night?" She sat in a plaid upholstered chair across from the sofa.

Louisa followed her with her eyes. "Oh, yes. I slept real good."

"Did Mr. Jim get you some breakfast already?"

A smile stretched Louisa's mouth almost ear to ear, and her eyes flashed like the clearest aquamarines. "We had waffles and ice cream."

Amy gave Jim a sideways look. "Waffles and ice cream, huh? Wow, what a treat."

"Waffles and ice cream was a staple when I was growing up," Jim said. "Sure beats sausage cooked in lard and birthday cake. And it's a nutritious part of your daily diet. You know, vitamin D, good for the bones and teeth and eyes." He winked at Louisa.

"Louisa." Amy shifted in the chair. "Did you come into the bathroom this morning while I was showering?"

Louisa glanced at Jim then back at Amy. "No."

"Are you sure? I thought I saw you in there."

Again, the furtive glance toward Jim, and Amy couldn't help but feel the girl was hiding something. "No. I was in the kitchen eating my waffles and ice cream." She was lying, Amy was sure of it now. She *had* sensed her in there, seen her hand in the shower.

"Then why did I—"

Jim stood rather abruptly. "Amy, can I have a word with you in the kitchen?"

Without saying another word to Louisa, Amy stood and followed Jim into the kitchen.

He kept his voice low. "What's going on? What was that all about?"

"She was in there with me. While I was in the shower. She reached in and touched my abdomen again."

"What? You're sure?"

She paused—*was* she sure?—and knew immediately that her hesitation spoke louder than her words. "Yes. I'm sure. I was rinsing my hair and felt her hand on my stomach. When I opened my eyes, she pulled it back real quick."

"And you saw her in the bathroom with you?"

The fact that Jim felt it necessary to grill her annoyed Amy. He didn't believe her. "By the time I opened the curtain she was gone. She'd left the room."

Jim rubbed his jaw and closed his eyes. "Amy, she was with me the whole time. Here in the kitchen, eating her breakfast. There's no way she could have gone upstairs and sneaked into the bathroom without me seeing her."

"Were you with her the whole time?"

"Ye—" He stopped mid-word, dropped his eyes. "No. Chief Miller stopped by, and I was in the living room talking to him for a while."

"How long is a while?"

"Ten minutes, maybe. Not even that long."

"Long enough for her to sneak upstairs and come into the bathroom without you seeing her."

Jim pressed his lips into a thin line. "She said she didn't, though. Why would she lie?"

Now Amy was really annoyed. Jim not only didn't believe her, but also he was siding with the girl. "You're taking her side?"

"I'm not taking anyone's side, just trying to figure out what's going on here."

"What did Miller say?" Maybe changing the subject would cool them both down.

Jim looked toward the living room. "He hasn't found anything out yet. Asked us to keep her until he did."

"And what did you say?"

"I said I'd have to talk to you. Make sure you were on board with it."

"I'm not."

"Why not?"

Amy lowered her voice even further, to a whisper. "I don't trust her."

"She's a kid, for crying out loud, Amy. A little girl."

"I don't trust her."

"Amy, listen to yourself. She's a nine-year-old little girl. Who knows what she's been through? Her parents could be dead or halfway to Mexico by now. Or they could be worried sick about her. If she was our daughter, wouldn't you want someone like us to care for her? Okay, maybe she was in the bathroom with you, maybe she misses her mother and you look like her. Maybe she just wanted to be close to someone. She's been traumatized. I'm willing to overlook some odd behavior. Give it a try, babe. This might be just the thing we need to get us out of this funk we've been in."

He made sense. Amy hated to admit it, but he did. Maybe the girl used to sit in the bathroom while her mother took a shower. Maybe she longed for some kind of familiarity. Maybe Amy's paranoia and distrust were more a reflection on her than Louisa.

She nodded and forced a little smile. "All right. We'll see how it goes."

"Good." Jim kissed her lightly. "Thank you. I'm going to take her out and buy her some clothes while you get ready."

"Good idea."

He hesitated, eying her. "What do you think of putting her in the spare bedroom?"

She stiffened. By "spare bedroom" he had to mean the baby's room, since the other bedroom had been converted into his home office. "She seems fine on the sofa."

"But I want her to begin to feel at home here. The sofa seems so 'Hey, why don't you crash at our place for the night.'"

"She is crashing at our place."

"But she's a little girl, not some college buddy who dropped by while he was in town. She needs stability, consistency."

Amy pressed her lips together.

"Okay, okay," he conceded. "How about if I just set up a cot for her in my office?"

Amy nodded. "All right, but—"

Amy turned and found Louisa standing by the kitchen entryway, arms at her sides. "I'm sorry I upset you, Miss Amy. And I'm sorry about your baby." She smiled, but there was something about her grin that Amy didn't like, something...

No, she had to stop imagining things.

Chapter 10

THE SALESMAN KNOCKED on the open front door. "Hello?" Mitch didn't do anything. He stood in the kitchen with his back against the wall and waited as quietly and patiently as a lion bides his time in the tall grass. Maybe the guy would go away.

He didn't, though. He entered the house and stood in the entryway. "Hello? Anyone home?"

His voice was high and squeaked on "anyone." Still, Mitch remained quiet. He heard the salesman's feet shuffle along the wooden floor, heard him snort deep in his sinuses.

Again, "Hello? Anyone here?"

The footsteps retreated from the house, and Mitch heard the man's boots clop on the front porch, down the stairs. A thought came to him then: any salesman worth his salt wouldn't give up so soon. Mitch's truck was parked out front and the front door was wide open; the man would assume *someone* was home and go searching for that someone. He wouldn't miss an opportunity to give his precious sales pitch. He'd look in the barn next; it was the only logical place. And there he'd find…

Mitch grabbed a large knife from the countertop and ran through the house. He hit the porch and stopped. The salesman was already halfway to the barn.

"Hey!" he called after the man.

The man turned, shielded his eyes from the sun.

"They're not home," Mitch said.

The salesman talked as he walked. Dust stirred into little clouds around his feet. "Who are you?"

"Carpenter. Doing some work in the basement. Heard you calling, but it took me a second to get up the stairs."

"Are the owners home?"

"Naw, they went into town to get some groceries and run some other errands, I think."

"Bummer," the man said. "I was hoping to catch 'em." Reaching the porch, he stopped, his hands on his waist, and smiled broad, flashing some of the whitest teeth Mitch had ever seen. "Reel 'em in, know what I mean?" He winked.

"Sure. Hook 'em and reel 'em in. I know just what you mean." Mitch didn't like the salesman. Young, cocky, no respect for anyone. He knew the type.

The man stuck out his hand. He held a business card between his index and middle fingers. "Cody Wisner, EnviroPride. Could you tell 'em I was here? Give 'em the card there?" He was twenty-something, thick shock of brown hair, combed neatly to the side (too neatly). He was full of himself, too confident in his own ability to make a sale.

Mitch looked at the card. *Cody Wisner, Agricultural Consultant.* "Agricultural consultant, huh? You go to college for that title?"

"Sure did. Penn State. Nittany Lion through and through."

"Well, that's real nice."

Wisner hesitated, pointed at the card. "Give 'em the card, huh?"

Mitch forced a smile. He certainly didn't like this kid. "Sure thing. I'll set it on the kitchen counter and make sure they get it."

"Thanks, sport." Mitch found the arrogant salesman's smile annoying. "And just tell 'em I'll swing by again tomorrow."

"No problem."

Wisner turned to leave, but when he was midway back to the Passport, Mitch stopped him. "Wait. Agricultural…"

Wisner stopped, spun around. There was that plastic smile again. "Consultant. I consult, you know? Help farmers find the best fertilizers and pesticides. All natural stuff too, none of that chemical junk. Best products on the market."

"Yeah, whatever." Mitch left the porch and approached the

salesman. "I got one of those cards too. Just in case you ever need any carpentry done." When he reached Wisner, he went for his back pocket, but instead of retrieving a genuine cowhide wallet, he pulled out the knife from the kitchen counter and plunged it into the young salesman's stomach.

After dragging the salesman—Cody Wisner, Agricultural Consultant—to the backyard by his ankles and parking him in a shady area by the house, Mitch Albright stood over the corpse and tried to steady his shaking hands. They said the first kill was the hardest, but from there it got easier. For Mitch the killing wasn't hard at all. He was so empowered by adrenaline that it happened and was over before he realized what he'd done. It took a few minutes for Wisner to die, for the life to leak out of him, during which time Mitch made steady eye contact with his first victim. He relished the look of respect Wisner gave him, the reverence that was there until his final breath was drawn and exhaled.

Afterward Mitch went to the Passport and rummaged through the interior, removing anything that would identify it as Cody Wisner's. He'd have to ditch the vehicle, of course. He'd drive it to a remote spot on the farm and leave it there, out of view. By the time anyone found it, he'd be gone, leaving nothing behind but a mystery.

When he finished and returned, he thought for a moment that Wisner was still alive, that some small trace of life was still surging through the punk's veins, but it was only an illusion.

Wisner's head was cocked to one side at an odd angle, and his left eye was open and appeared to be fixed on his murderer. Mitch squatted and was about to shut it when the eye triggered a flash memory. Southeast High. Freshman year. Hands pulling at him, hitting him, messing his hair, finding the elastic band of his underwear and yanking, so hard it tore skin. For a week it hurt to sit. Using the bathroom was plain torture.

Closing his eyes, Mitch drew in a deep breath of clean, country air. There was nothing like it. It filled the lungs with oxygen and cleared the mind. Steadied the nerves. The memory eventually faded.

He'd leave Wisner's body here for now then return for it later. Tonight it would all begin and then continue for the next six days. The townspeople of Virginia Mills would have hell descend upon them, and when it was all over, when his mission was complete, he would be a respected man, not because of the clothes he wore or the car he drove or the job he had, but because of who he was. They would all respect him.

Returning to the barn, Mitch found Bob propped up against the post, groggy-eyed and confused like he'd had too much to drink. His wife, Clare, was still unconscious next to him. Or maybe she was dead; Mitch couldn't tell. He squatted before Bob and looked him in the eyes but didn't say anything. For a few long seconds Bob stared back. His eyes were glassy, and dried blood smudged his cheek.

Mitch removed the gag from the farmer's mouth.

"You okay, Bob?" Mitch said. "You look kind of confused."

Bob's eyes moved around the barn. "Wha–what happened?" Finally they landed on his wife. "Is she…"

"Dead? I don't think so. I didn't hit her that hard. 'Course, some people just have thin skulls." He reached over and found Clare's carotid with two fingers. A pulse was there, thin and thready, but there. "I guess she's got a thick skull."

"She's alive?"

"For now."

"What are you—"

"Doing here?" Mitch shrugged, looked around the barn. He was still impressed by its size and orderliness. "You're a respected man, aren't you, Bob?"

Bob didn't say anything. He appeared confused by Mitch's odd question.

"And you're respected not because you're an American farmer, not because you live a simple life and own acres of land and a beautiful house." He glanced at Clare. "Not because of your lovely wife. You're respected because of who you are as a man, as a person. I imagine you're honest and kind and selfless. Patient, hardworking, loyal. A real man of integrity. You were very quick to offer help to a new farmer who hadn't a clue what he was doing. I respected you, and that's why you're still alive."

Mitch tapped the sole of Bob's work boot. "For some of us respect doesn't come that easy."

He stood and withdrew the knife from his back pocket. There was still some smeared blood on the blade. "Now, I'm going to need both of you to come with me to the house. So if you don't mind, wake up your wife."

Bob hesitated, stared at Mitch with wary eyes.

"Come now, Bob. You and Clare were very nice to me. I don't want to hurt either of you anymore, but we need to do this. Now wake her up and let's go."

Gently, as if he were waking her from a deep nap on a Sunday afternoon, Bob stroked Clare's hair and rubbed her cheek. His actions were loving and tender, for that was the kind of man he was. Eventually her eyes fluttered open, and she stared blankly at her husband as if he were a stranger.

"Clare, darling, I need you to wake up," Bob said. His voice was soft and tight. He didn't want his wife to see him cry. Mitch was touched by his bravery.

Clare pushed herself to sitting, wincing more than once. Her head must have been killing her. She looked up at Mitch, confusion clouding her eyes, then found the knife in his hand.

He couldn't help but smile at her. She was such a lovely, beautiful woman. "Can you stand and walk?"

Clare's eyes moved to her husband. Bob nodded, stood, and helped Clare to her feet. "It's all right, darling. We need to go to the house."

Clare obeyed, but she wasn't all there. The blow to the head had short-circuited some neural pathways.

No one spoke on the walk from the barn to the house. The sun making its way up in the sky, swallows flitting around the barn's roof, a gentle breeze playing through the corn fields—it was a perfect day on the farm. Perfect for Mitch, not so much for the Appletons. Or for Cody Wisner, Agricultural Consultant.

When they reached the front door, Mitch allowed Bob and Clare to enter first. "Head for the cellar, folks, and go on down."

They obeyed without a word or struggle. They respected him.

Once in the cellar Mitch took a length of rope and tied them both to the thick leg of the workbench. "You'll need to stay here for a while." He looked at them both and found fear and uncertainty in their eyes. "Don't worry; I have no intention of hurting either of you. That's not why I'm here. In fact, up until an hour ago I was going to kill both of you, but you so impressed me with your integrity and respect for each other that I changed my mind."

His plan had been to remove the Appletons and inhabit their home while he completed his work. He knew them to be independent people with few friends and no family in the area. The farm would provide a secluded respite from this world and a comfortable escape to another one.

He smiled at them, a genuine smile, for he genuinely liked them. "And you live to love another day."

Bob lifted his head. "What are your plans for us?"

"My plans don't include you at all. They're much grander than one old couple living on a remote farm. But because I've chosen to allow you to live, it's going to mean more work for me. For the next week you and Clare will live here in the cellar."

"And then what?" Bob's voice quivered ever so slightly. He knew they were on borrowed time.

"Then…well, let's just get through the next seven days, and then we'll see where we are."

Chapter 11

ALICIA SIMPSON LEANED in close to the mirror and touched her left cheekbone. A dark charcoal shadow, rimmed in red, surrounded her bloodshot eye. The area below the eye socket was the color of raw meat and puffy. Derek had been at it again last night, and she was lucky he didn't break anything. She'd already called in sick, knowing there was no way that makeup could completely mask her black eye.

She opened the medicine cabinet and reached for the Oxy-Contin to ease her thumping headache. Closing it again, she faced her disfigured reflection and barely recognized the woman staring back at her. Her nose was slightly off-center, and the right side of her mouth drooped ever so slightly. Both the handiwork of Derek's temper. Booze always brought out the worst in him, and she didn't know when to keep her mouth shut.

Alicia set the bottle of painkillers on the sink. Her hand trembled and tears welled in her eyes. She wasn't sure how much more she could take of this. Her nerves were frayed like worn threads; she lived in fear of the man she thought she loved. Her mother told her two years ago that she could do better than Derek, that she needed to find a man who would love her and take care of her. But Alicia didn't deserve anyone like that. Not two years ago and certainly not today. No one else would want her now, not with all the baggage she lugged around. That was one thing about Derek; he looked past all that and said he loved her anyway.

So why didn't she feel loved? Was love supposed to be like this? She was scared and lonely. She hated her own reflection, the sound of her own voice. Her thoughts plagued her, thoughts of violence and shame and embarrassment. Thoughts of suicide. Is that the way love was supposed to be?

Derek told her he loved her, sure, when they were doing it, but that was the only time. When he was sober, he mostly read his books and kept to himself. When he wasn't home with her, he was out with his buddies—Rod, Buddy, and Jason—hitting the clubs and probably cheating on her. He'd come home smelling like alcohol, looking for a fight. And she, stupid woman that she was, didn't know how to keep her trap shut and just let him talk. She knew he didn't mean any of it when he called her a lazy whore, when he said she didn't respect him and never would. She would protest, defend herself, and that only got him angrier. Eventually the fists would start flying, and the next thing she knew she was lying on the floor in a puddle of blood with another broken bone or colorful shiner to add to her collection.

The OxyContin seemed to be calling her name, beckoning her to come and take part in its painless escape. It was her ticket out of this hell. She could down the whole bottle with a fifth of whiskey, fall asleep, and never wake up. How would Derek like that?

She slammed the cabinet shut, took one last look at her image in the mirror, grabbed the bottle, and headed for the kitchen. She was going to do it. It was time to end this nightmare.

In the kitchen, under the sink, she found the bottle of Jack Daniels. Derek always kept a healthy stash in the apartment. She unscrewed the cap and held the mouth of the bottle to her nose, drew in a long breath. The odor stung her nose but enticed her as well; it was a genie with the power to grant wishes in one hand and a double-edged dagger in the other. It was ironic, she thought, that the very vice that had caused her so much pain and heartache was the same thing that would bring freedom and rest. She took a swig, swallowed hard, felt the burn in the back of her throat. Immediately she started to warm, to relax.

Next was the bottle of pills. The top was one of those safety jobs, but it came off easily. There were a dozen or so left from last month when Derek knocked out three of her teeth. She told the dentist she'd been mugged walking home from work. With the whiskey a dozen should be enough to do the job. She dumped the contents of the bottle into her palm and stared at the pills. A cold sweat broke out on her forehead. She was really going to do this, wasn't she? She wasn't going to write any note pointing the finger at Derek, wasn't going to say good-bye to her mother. Wasn't going to pay the month's rent or turn off the appliances. It would be as if she existed one moment and didn't the next. That was it. And the sad thing was, with the exception of her mom, no one would miss her. She was totally expendable.

The pills loomed in her palm and suddenly looked the size of grapes. There was no way she could swallow all twelve at once. But if she separated them she might have second thoughts about finishing them off. She had to do it quickly, just toss them into her mouth, take a huge swig of the JD, and swallow at once.

But she couldn't. Something stopped her. Her hand trembled; the sweating increased. Her breathing grew shallow and rapid. She was panicking. She couldn't do it. She wanted to, oh, how she wanted to end this misery, but her will to survive was greater.

She looked around the kitchen trying to find something, any-thing, that would give her cause to stay this execution, but there was nothing of any worth, either monetarily or sentimentally. Everything she had she'd purchased with her own money. The refrigerator held no photos of good times with Derek, of cute nieces or nephews, of graduation photos or colorful child art-work. There was one magnet she'd picked up at the grocery store. Looking past the kitchen and out into the living room was no dif-ferent. No fond memories offered rescue. She saw Derek hollering at her, belittling her, hitting her. She saw herself, lying on the floor, hugging the carpet, covering her head, hoping Derek had had enough and didn't start kicking. Her life was meaningless, so why was this so difficult? She stared at the pills again, and they mocked her cowardice. She was too weak to even take control of her own death.

Alicia cursed and jammed the pills back into the bottle. She turned on the water from the kitchen sink and stuck her hands under it, cupped some of the cold liquid and splashed her face. She had to get out of there, go somewhere and think. Back to the bathroom she went to dry her face and cover the bruise with as much foundation as it would take.

She had to get out of the apartment, away from its destructiveness, even if for only a few hours.

Chapter 12

FTER PICKING UP a few outfits for Louisa at the local
JC Penney and running some errands of his own to the
hardware store and auto supplier, Jim took the child to the Red
Wing Diner for lunch. Their hot dogs were famous all over Rockingham County.

The diner was not unlike any other small-town eatery where
locals gathered to catch up on local news and gossip, where polit-
ical positions were waxed eloquently and world annihilation was
avoided on a daily basis. Booths populated the floor space, and
along the far wall was a counter that stretched from one end of
the building to the other. Beyond the counter were the soda, iced
tea, and milk machines, shelves of glasses and pitchers, and two
swinging doors with round windows in each. The place smelled of
cooking meat, frying oil, and onions.

Jim and Louisa stood at the entrance, her in her new jeans
and long-sleeve T-shirt. She looked more like a regular kid now
instead of an angel dropped from heaven.

The diner was slow this Monday, but already they'd caught
the attention of the few patrons. Jim knew most of the folks and
nodded hello to them. Word spreads fast in a small town, and
already most of Virginia Mills had no doubt heard of the little
girl who showed up at Jake Tucker's burning home. "Well, kiddo,
where do you want to sit? Take your pick."

Louisa surveyed the empty booths. "How about on the stools?"

Of course the counter was lined with barstools, and every kid
loved to spin on the stools. "Great idea."

They found seats at the counter, and Louisa immediately had to try the spinning action. They turned smoothly, without a single squeak. Someone had taken the time to grease them properly.

Within seconds Angela, the waitress, was there with two menus.

Jim waved off the menus. "No need for them, Angela. I'll have the Fat Boy platter, and Louisa here will have the hot dog special. Both with the largest, coldest Cokes you have."

Angela smiled big. A middle-aged, single mom, she'd worked at the diner for as long as Jim could remember. "Nice to meet you, Louisa," she said. "Your friend Jake was in here not too long ago. Just got out of the hospital and said he wanted some real food. He told me how you helped him last night. That was very brave of you."

Louisa shifted her eyes uncomfortably, glanced at Jim then back at Angela. "Thank you. He needed my help." She said it like she'd helped him carry the trash to the curb instead of kept him from the doorstep of death.

"Well," Angela said, "you're a hero in my book. This world could sure use more kids like you." She placed her hand on Louisa's and winked. "Jim and Amy will take good care of you as long as they need to. And as long as you're in town, the food in here is on the house."

She left to get the drinks, and Louisa turned to Jim. "What does 'on the house' mean?"

"It means you get to eat for free. You've got VIP status now. You're a celebrity."

"I'm just a kid."

"A kid who helped save Jake Tucker's life, and around here Jake Tucker is a legend. So that makes you a celebrity."

She thought about that for a second then said, "Do you think anyone will ask for my autograph?"

"You never know."

"If they do, I'll just have to sign my first name." She paused while she scanned the shelves beyond the counter. "On second thought, I don't think I want to be a celebrity. I'm just a kid."

Angela returned with the Cokes and set them on the counter. "Your food will be right up."

"Thanks, Angela," Jim said.

Louisa looked around the diner, spun a 360 on the stool, then said, "Mr. Jim, why is everyone looking at me?"

"It goes with being a celebrity, kiddo. Get used to it. Just be glad the paparazzi isn't knocking down the doors to get in here and snap pictures of you stuffing a hot dog in your mouth. That would be most unflattering."

She smiled and took a sip of her Coke. "What's a poppa rocksy?"

"Paparazzi. They're the people who make big money taking pictures of celebrities in embarrassing situations."

"Like stuffing hot dogs in their face?"

"For some that would be embarrassing. For others it's how they make a living."

She laughed. "That's crazy."

"You have no idea." Jim decided to take advantage of the relaxed atmosphere. "Hey, do you remember anything other than your name and age yet?"

She thought for a moment then shook her head. "Nope."

"Nothing? No memories of when you were younger, of school, of your mom and dad, movies, friends?"

"No. I try to think back, but there's nothing there to think about."

"What about foods? Any foods you know you don't like?"

She gave him a blank stare.

"How about asparagus? You like asparagus?" Jim thought if he could jog her memory about something, anything, it may open the door for more memories to start slipping through.

She shrugged.

"Broccoli? All kids hate broccoli."

Another shrug. "I probably don't like it."

He was leading her; he shouldn't do that.

"Okay, what about your parents. Do you know their names?"

"Mom and Dad?"

"Their real names, first names, pet names, anything."

"I don't remember if we have any pets."

Jim smiled. "Pet names are things your parents call each other rather than their real name. Like Pumpkin or Lovey or Cookie or—"

"Snickerdoodle?"

"Uh, yeah, sure. Did your parents call each other Snicker-doodle?"

Louisa shrugged again. "I don't know. I just like how it sounds. Do you think they're looking for me?"

"Of course they're looking for you. If you were my daughter, I'd be blowing the phones up calling newspapers and TV stations and everyone I could think of to find you."

"Then why did the policeman say he hasn't heard anything yet?"

She was an observant child, smart too. She didn't miss much. How could parents abandon such a child as this? And if they hadn't, where were they? They should be busting every outlet they knew to get the word out about their missing daughter. "Sometimes these things take time to get organized. He'll hear something soon; I'm sure of it." Only he wasn't sure of it, and the question nagged in the back of his mind: What if her parents never show up? What then? He and Amy couldn't have children, might she be open to the possibility of adopting…

"I do remember one thing," she said.

"What's that?"

Angela returned with two plates and put them in front of Jim and Louisa. "Here ya go, you two. Anything else I can get you?"

"Looks great, Angela," Jim said. "I think we're good. Thanks."

She walked away, and Jim turned his attention back to Louisa, ignoring the double-stacked hamburger with its special sauce on the plate before him. "What is it, Louisa? What do you remember?"

"My birthday."

Her birth date would be invaluable information for Chief Miller. A spark of hope lit in Jim, but with it came a shadow of disappointment. He wanted nothing more than for Louisa to be reunited with her parents, to be happily home again, but there was a part of him, pushed way back into a dark crevice of his heart where it would stay, that now hoped she wouldn't be claimed. She was everything in a daughter he ever wanted...

"When is it so I can send you a birthday card?"

"January twenty-first."

Jim's heart thudded, skipped, thudded again.

January twenty-first had been Amy's due date.

Chapter 13

SITTING BEHIND THE wheel of her well-used Nissan Sentra, Alicia still contemplated her own death. The pills took too much time, too much willpower. The thought crossed her mind to run her car into a tree. The stretch she was on was lined with tall, thick-trunked oaks and maples. It wouldn't take much to stomp on the accelerator, take the Sentra to eighty or ninety, and steer the car into a sudden, deadly collision with an immovable object. Thing was, though, she wasn't a good enough driver to spin the car so the driver's-side door met the tree, and knowing her luck, she'd hit it square on, deploying the air bags. She'd walk away with nothing more than some bruises and brush burns and a one-way ticket to the nuthouse.

She rolled down all four windows and filled the car with fresh, cool air. She was getting panicky again and needed to get her mind off of death. It served no purpose. A question surfaced then as it always did, like a whale coming up for air and making itself known. On the surface it was just a question, innocent enough, but like that whale, beneath the surface there was so much more to it, so much more to contemplate, so much more the very inquiry said about her as a person.

If life with Derek was so bad, why didn't she just leave him?

Yes, why didn't she?

Her answer came quickly as it always did: because he loved her and she loved him. It was complicated, their life, their love. He only beat her when he'd been drinking, and most of the time she instigated it, pushed him too far. She didn't know when to keep her mouth shut. The last time they talked about it, he apologized, told her how much he loved her and hated himself for hurting her, but that sometimes she had it coming. And she couldn't disagree. And the fact was, he could have left her at any time and found another woman, a better woman, more attractive, more successful. But he'd stuck with her because he loved her. She couldn't walk out on that.

And where would she go anyway? The thought of being alone ripped holes in her heart. She couldn't be alone. She didn't do alone very well. But nobody else would want her; she had nothing to offer. She lugged so much baggage around with her she'd scare off any suitor in a matter of minutes. And she couldn't move back in with her mother. For one thing, her mother now lived halfway across the country in Kansas with her new boyfriend. She was happy, finally, and Alicia didn't want to ruin that by intruding on her new life and bringing all her rain clouds with her.

And so she stayed with Derek.

At the next intersection Alicia turned the Sentra around and headed back to town. The vastness of the rural landscape, the openness, the aloneness, was giving her the creeps. She needed to be around people.

Ten minutes later she wheeled the Sentra into a parking space beside the Red Wing Diner. She wasn't hungry but needed a drink, and just to be around people, life. As she got out of the car, she spotted an elderly woman pushing a shopping cart down the center of High Street. Cars slowed as they passed her, but not one stopped to offer any kind of assistance.

Alicia knew the woman, Bonnie Bags. She'd been walking the streets of Virginia Mills pushing that same cart for the past fifteen years, since Alicia was in middle school. Bonnie wasn't homeless—she lived in a dilapidated mobile home just outside of town—but she was delusional. She spent her days wandering the streets, collecting other people's throwaways. She was crazy and she was alone—two things Alicia wanted desperately to avoid.

After waiting for one car to pass, Alicia crossed the eastbound lane of High Street and approached Bonnie. The woman was hunched at the waist and wore a tattered gray overcoat and worn leather Stetson. Wild, wiry, dirty gray hair, like unruly weeds in a neglected garden, climbed out from under the brim of the hat.

"Bonnie?" Alicia stopped the cart with her hands.

The woman looked up with gray, sad eyes. Her skin was so deeply rutted and creviced, the wrinkles looked like scars.

"Bonnie, you can't walk down the middle of the road like this. Someone's likely to not see you, and that wouldn't be good."

Bonnie seemed to understand but then said, "Sandra, where did you come from, dear? I thought you'd moved to Chicago? How's your mother?"

Alicia had no idea who Sandra was. She put her arm around Bonnie's shoulders. "My name's Alicia, Bonnie. Come, let's get you and your cart over to the sidewalk. These cars don't understand how important you are to this town, and we wouldn't want one of them getting in your way."

The old woman cracked a toothless grin and patted Alicia's hand. "You're a good girl, Sandra. You always were." She allowed Alicia to guide her through traffic and to the curb.

Once Bonnie Bags and her cart were safely on the sidewalk, Alicia dug through her purse for a five-dollar bill. She handed it to Bonnie. "Here, get something scrumptious and warm, maybe a hot coffee and piece of pie. And Bonnie, please stay out of the streets, okay? Streets are for cars; sidewalks are for people."

Bonnie took the five, stared at it, then stuffed it into her pocket. "Thank you, dear. I'll be sure to tell your mother what a good girl you turned out to be."

And then she went on her way, pushing her cart and mumbling to herself.

Alicia watched Bonnie go until she was out of sight then turned and entered the diner.

Jim took a bite of his hamburger and chewed it slowly, thought-fully. He barely tasted it, his thoughts all centered on this girl, this enigma, Louisa. He'd fostered enough troubled kids to rec-ognize the signs of negligent, even abusive parents. Louisa didn't show any signs of that, thankfully. Her hair and nails were neatly trimmed, her dress and shoes stylish and (he'd checked) of name-brand quality. And her demeanor was that of someone well treated and well educated, upper middle-class. Like an Elizabeth Smart. Could she have been kidnapped? But if so, then where were her parents?

He swallowed what he'd been chewing, washed it down with a gulp of Coke. Louisa was eating her hot dog. She looked so small and thin in her new clothes, so ordinary. But she wasn't ordinary, was she? Besides all the mystery of her identity, she seemed to know things a nine-year-old dropped out of nowhere shouldn't know. She acted like she knew about Amy's miscarriage even before Jim told her about it. How? And how did she know that Amy was suf-fering from depression? And then there was the strange behavior this morning. What had happened in the bathroom?

Taking another bite of the hamburger, Jim chided himself. She was a child, nothing more. An insightful, intelligent, beautiful child, yes, but still a child. There were plenty of nine-year-olds in the world with her features; actually, they came a dime a dozen. And it didn't take a psychoanalyst to see that Amy was depressed. As for the miscarriage, maybe Tina had said something before Jim even got there, knowing Miller would ask him to take the child home. And as for her odd behavior, like he'd told Amy, Louisa had been traumatized, ripped from everything familiar, stuck in a burning home, watched a man almost die, and lost her memory. He held no degree in child psychology, but he presumed a little odd behavior wasn't too unexpected after something like that.

Fact was, she was polite, quiet, thoughtful, and more well behaved than a lot of the men in Virginia Mills. Her parents were lucky people. If she was his child…

He stopped himself. Better to not entertain those kinds of thoughts.

"How's your hot dog?" he said.

Louisa looked at him, her chipmunk cheeks puffed out with food. She'd taken a huge bite and was having difficulty handling it.

"Blink once for delicious, two for 'tastes like dog food.'"

She blinked once and smiled.

"That's what I think. They have the best hot dogs in the whole county, maybe the state." He pretended to think then shrugged. "Probably in the country."

Louisa nodded her agreement. Finally, after she'd swallowed and drank some Coke, she said, "Maybe in the whole world. Thank you for the treat, Mr. Jim."

"You're welcome, Louisa. When we find your parents, don't tell them how you ate around me. Honestly, waffles and ice cream for breakfast, hot dog and fries for lunch. Terrible. And wait till you see what we're having for dinner."

"What?"

"Birthday cake and popsicles."

"Really?" Her eyes grew to the size of marbles.

"Uh, no. Not really. But maybe we can have cake after dinner."

"Oh, that sounds good too."

"Do you remember ever having cake before? Maybe for a birthday?"

She thought for a moment, her eyes focused on nothing in particular, then looked around the diner. "No." She stared past Jim, behind him, as if she'd noticed a familiar face she'd not seen in a long time. For a few long seconds she stayed fixated on something, then slid off the stool and walked away from the counter.

Jim turned and watched her. He didn't want to interfere right away; she may have seen something or someone that triggered a memory, and he knew how fickle memories could be. Here one second, gone the next, as fleeting as a flock of birds lifting from a tree and taking to the air. If Louisa was in some kind of state of retrieval, he would let her go and see what came of it.

She wove around tables and down an aisle then stopped at a booth where a young woman sat alone. Jim had seen her around town; she worked as a cashier at the Food Lion.

The girl came out of nowhere. One second Alicia was lost in thoughts about Derek and their life together, his violent tendencies, their future…her death, and the next second a child stood by her booth. Cute kid too. Deep, intelligent eyes. Smattering of freckles. Face like an angel. She said nothing at first, and oddly it didn't bother Alicia. There was nothing awkward about it. This was a child completely comfortable with silence, just like Alicia.

Finally the girl said, "You're alone, aren't you?"

Instantly Alicia knew the kid wasn't just speaking of her presence in the diner. She meant alone in the broadest and deepest sense of the word, alone like being the sole occupier of a deep and lightless valley where no life resided. And she was right, of course. Though she shared an apartment and bed with Derek, and though they occasionally had a conversation or went out to eat together, she was indeed alone, and her aloneness was a wound that would not heal. Her health, both mental and physical, had deteriorated as well. She suffered in solitude, cried in the dark of the night, longed for death…

There was something about this girl, though, that spoke of honesty and goodness, something that welcomed the truth, that said it was all right to remove the mask and reveal one's wounds. Through tight vocal cords Alicia said, "Yes. So very alone."

A tear formed in the corner of the girl's eye, and she lifted her hand, such a small, frail hand, and placed it on Alicia's. "You're never alone. He's with you."

Alicia was transfixed by the girl's gaze. Though the diner was filled with chatting patrons and scurrying waitresses, she paid no attention to any of it. It was as if a veil had been dropped around her and this remarkable girl and they had been shielded from the prying eyes of the others.

"Who?" she said.

The girl's hand was warm; it radiated a comfortable heat that relaxed Alicia.

"God."

God. Not once in her life had Alicia reached out to God. She supposed He was real, she had no cause to believe otherwise, but He was so distant, so "out there," and seemed so unconcerned with her problems. If God was indeed real, He was a wealthy grandfather who lived a continent away in a strange land and never bothered to extend His graces to those who really needed them. Why would she think of Him?

"God isn't bothered with me." She kept her voice low. "He doesn't know of my pain."

"He does know, and He hurts with you. He loves you more than you could ever love Him back."

She spoke like no child Alicia had ever encountered before. But the words she spoke, such words of comfort, warmed her and brought a spark of hope.

Alicia tried to say something back but found she was speechless.

The girl's eyes penetrated her, probed deep into her soul where no one had ever ventured before. Alicia was sure the kid saw every wound, every hurt, every fear there. She expected the girl to turn in repulsion, or laugh and deride her for her lousy life, but instead she said, "You're so full of light. You shine goodness and kindness. God wants to use you. He *will* use you. His love will heal your sores and give you new life and purpose. But you need to let Him…because if you don't…"

Something appeared in the girl's eyes then, shock and confusion. She knew something, had seen something. The innocence was gone, and Alicia saw something there that terrified her. Alicia yanked her hand away, slipped out of the booth, and bolted for the exit.

She had to find Derek.

Chapter 14

THAT EVENING AT dinner Amy said little. She was still upset about the shower incident and Louisa's refusal to admit she was in the bathroom. A strange child, indeed. On the surface she was a cute enough kid and seemed to possess a certain poise. She was polite (even in disagreement), gentle, and soft-spoken. Whoever her parents were, they must be a family of means and high standing in society. Louisa was obviously raised to be a child seen and seldom heard, yet encouraged to speak her mind when asked but in a respectful and dignified way. She did not appear to be smug or wise-cracking, nor was she uppity. Her manners and movements were refined and delicate, the stuff of cultural polishing. She'd no doubt lived a good life.

And yet there was a quality about her that went against the finely smoothed grain of the higher levels of society. She possessed humility, such humility, in fact, that it almost came across as contrived, only it was apparent that there was nothing phony about it. She cared more about the plight of others than for her own disheartening dilemma. She had eyes that could see past her own situation, her own wants and even needs, and focus on the heart of another—a rare quality for anyone, but especially one so apparently privileged in life.

Amy wondered why Louisa's parents hadn't shown up yet. A family with money would certainly have the resources and clout to bring a ton of attention to the disappearance of their daughter. She remembered the media attention the Smarts stirred when their daughter Elizabeth went missing. Where were the TV cameras, the news anchors, the crying mother and father pleading for the safe return of their sweet little daughter?

Something about this whole ordeal didn't sit right with Amy. Something was off. Louisa, while appearing to be nothing more than a precious girl lost or abandoned, was an oddity. Amy had a strange feeling about her, like Louisa knew more than she was putting on, like she was familiar in some weird way, or at least that the Spencers were familiar to her. She was more than just a lost child, Amy was sure of that.

Amy had made chicken Parmesan for dinner, and halfway through the meal a knock came at the door.

"Who could that be?" Amy said.

Jim put down his fork. "I'll get it."

He stood, crossed the house, and opened the door. Amy heard the familiar voice of Jake Tucker.

"Sorry to bother you, Jim. I know you folks are probably in the middle of dinner, but I was wonderin' if I might see the girl. Wanted to thank her in person for what she done."

"No bother at all," Jim said. "Come right in." The door closed. "How are you feeling?"

"Never better, actually. Doc says the old ticker is as strong as it ever was. Lungs are clear too."

A second later they both appeared in the entryway to the dining room.

Amy stood and hugged Jake. "Jake, it's so good to see you. Jim told me everything that happened. I'm glad you're okay, but I'm sorry about your home."

Jake shrugged it off. "Nah, that's just stuff; none of it really matters." He turned and looked at Louisa, and his face visibly brightened. "There she is." He knelt beside her chair. "You helped save my life, you know. Of course you know. Listen to me, talkin' like a fool of a old man."

Kneeling there with one hand on the table and the other over his heart, Jake Tucker looked to be thirty years younger and healthier. Full of life and vigor, he resembled a medieval knight bowing before his queen, offering her his undying allegiance.

He swallowed and cleared his throat. "I called Raymond." He paused and smiled as if awaiting her response, her praise, but she said nothing.

"We talked for nearly an hour," he said.

Amy glanced at Jim, caught his eye. He appeared to be just as in the dark as she was. She knew Raymond was Jake's son, though Jake had never talked about him. And she knew they had some kind of falling out quite a few years ago. In a small town nobody had secrets.

"We *talked*." Jake said it like a miracle had taken place right there in the little village of Virginia Mills. A solitary tear spilled from his eye and tracked down his cheek, following a laugh line to his jaw. "He asked for my forgiveness, and do you know what I did?"

Louisa smiled. It was a genuine smile, honest and pure, and for an instant Amy caught herself adoring the girl. Apparently she knew something of Jake and Raymond's relationship, but how?

"I forgave him. Yes, I did. Then I asked him to forgive me. After all these years that wall came down. And you know what? He's comin' to visit me next month." Jake cupped Louisa's small hand in both of his and shook it. He was a big man with big farmer hands that swallowed hers. "My Raymond is comin' home."

Louisa smiled, and her blue eyes seemed to flash like splashes of the purest cerulean water. "You're a good man, Mr. Tucker," she said. "And God has a lot more for you to do."

Jake stood and released Louisa's hand. He looked at Jim, then at Amy. He smoothed his shirt, massaged his hands. There were tears in his eyes. "Folks, I'm sorry for interrupting your dinner, really. I just had to see Louisa. If there's anything I can do, anything to help find her family, please let me know."

"Won't you stay?" Amy said. "We have plenty."

"Thanks, but Angela over at the Red Wing said I could eat there for free anytime I want until I get settled in somewhere again. I told her I'd be there tonight, and she's expecting me."

"With a hearty appetite, no doubt."

Jim saw Jake to the front door. When the two men left, Louisa slipped from her seat and approached Amy. The set of her jaw, the posture of her lips held no expression, but her eyes were wild and expectant. Momentarily Amy thought of getting up and joining Jim and Jake in the living room. She didn't want to be alone with the girl.

At Amy's side Louisa reached out and placed her hand on Amy's, the same hand that rested on her abdomen just this morning. It was warm and soft. The girl said nothing, but her eyes spoke volumes. There was no fear in them, not even a trace, but rather uncertainty, a questioning that was both profound and awful. She'd been ripped from her family, survived a burning house, placed with total strangers, and had heard nothing of any kind of search effort to find her. Looking at her like that, Amy felt something she hadn't felt toward another person for six months, an emotion reserved only for herself: pity.

She put her free hand on top of Louisa's. "You don't have to be a—"

Her words and the pity were clipped short by a sudden brilliant vision of all her life could have been. Should have been. Herself standing in a nursery, the nursery they'd set up, with a child, a baby, *her* little girl. She was holding her and rocking her. Singing her a lullaby while she kissed her velveteen skin. She looked so happy, so content, like she had everything she needed in life. All her sorrow and remorse and hurt were gone.

She ripped her hand away and stood abruptly. "Help me clear the table."

Her voice was cold.

Chapter 15

Having spent the day securing the cellar, boarding the windows, and constructing a small room in one corner that would become the Appletons' home for the next week, the man, *the* Mitch Albright, took one final stroll through the large farmhouse before heading out. The sun had set an hour ago, and the soft glow from table lamps and floor lamps in each room gave the place a very homey feel.

Yes, this was a place Mitch could call home. It was everything he ever wanted in a home, and certainly more of a home than the rotten apartment he currently resided in. He imagined himself sitting by the fireplace, reading a good book, maybe smoking a cigar, with his dog sleeping on the floor beside him. Nobody would bother him here; nobody would disrespect him. In fact, if he allowed himself to, he could almost imagine that this was his home, that Bob and Clare were his grandparents, that they'd not been killed in a terrible car accident, that it had all been a horrible misunderstanding and they were here, on the farm, waiting all these years for their Mitch to return. And now fate had drawn him back to the place where he belonged, to the farm where he should have been properly raised, where he should have been loved and respected.

After touring the house and fantasizing about his lost life regained, he locked all the doors tight and went around back. The body of the salesman was still there. Mitch had every intention of transporting the salesman to another location, but when he took hold of the man's hand, he found rigor mortis had already set in. He'd overlooked that detail. He could try to drag it to the barn, but the thought of moving the cool, stiff corpse that distance turned his stomach. He would improvise, leave the body where it was until morning, then bury it. He hated to waste a perfectly good victim, especially one as disrespectful as Cody Wisner, Agricultural Consultant, had been, but there were plenty of other victims out there, waiting to be taught how to respect.

Rounding the house, he unlocked the Passport with the remote keychain, and the car's lights flicked on. He got in behind the wheel and shut the door. It was a nice vehicle, indeed, and went well with his new home. Wisner had hung one of those pine tree air fresheners from the mirror, and it gave the interior a nauseatingly outdoorsy aroma.

Mitch started the Passport and shifted it into drive. He slipped the knife from his belt and balanced it in his hand, remembering the feel of plunging it into Wisner's abdomen. He couldn't say it was an enjoyable feeling; it wasn't, and the slippery texture of the blood on his hands was unpleasant, but it was invigorating. He was no stranger to being in a position of authority, but a *position* alone doesn't guarantee respect. Actions bring respect, and holding someone's life in your hands is the ultimate catalyst for respect.

He drove the Passport around the back of the house and down a dirt lane that wound through the cornfield to a small pond on the far end of property near a tree line where acres of wooded land began. He maneuvered the vehicle into the woods and killed the engine. Then he threw the keys into the pond. From where he stood at the water's edge, the Passport was barely visible. From the house, with the stalks of corn blocking all view of even the pond, it would be impossible to spot the vehicle.

Amy was already in bed by the time Jim climbed in next to her.

"Louisa's all tucked in on the cot," he said. "I left the bathroom and hall light on for her, told her if she needs anything to just call for me."

Amy rolled over and faced him. "Does she strike you as odd?"

"Aren't all nine-year-olds a little odd?"

"Were you odd?"

Jim gave her a sideways glance. "Nine-year-old boys are the oddest, simply out of their minds. They live in a world totally of their own making."

"It's more than that, though," she said. "There's something about her I can't put my finger on."

"There's a lot about her that's odd, but look at what she's been through. I'd act odd too, I think. There is no road map to adjusting to what her life is right now."

Amy had considered that, of course she had, but wasn't convinced that was all it was. Up until the incident at dinner she may have agreed with Jim, but that strange touch, that vision of herself holding a baby in the nursery, changed everything for her.

She was now certain what she'd seen was a vision of either what could have been or what would be. And since she had been told she'd never bear a child again, it had to be what could have been. And Amy was also certain the girl, this Louisa, had produced the vision. She didn't know how or why, other than to torment Amy with the life she missed out on, the blessing that should have been.

"Jim…"

Jim, who'd been lying on his back, turned and faced her. "What is it?"

She wanted to tell him about the vision and almost did, but then thought better of it. Jim already knew she was struggling emotionally since the miscarriage; this would only confirm that she'd gone loopy and needed professional help. But she didn't need a shrink. Or did she?

Instead she said, "Hold me?"

Jim scooted close and put his arms around Amy, their legs

intertwined. She rested her head on his chest. They lay like that for a long time before Jim tilted her head back and kissed her on the lips, nose, forehead. He found her lips and kissed again, gently at first, then harder, deeper, with more passion and need. At first she let him, even joined him, then suddenly pulled away. She wasn't ready to give herself to him, not in that way, not yet. Even after two months...not yet.

Chapter 16

OZY'S BAR SAT two miles outside the Virginia Mills town line on a seldom-used road lined with farmland and marshes. It was a one-story, wood-sided building built in the seventies during a time when the lumber mill employed 80 percent of the town's men and 80 percent of them needed to wind down after a shift of hard labor and toil. But in the late nineties, due to cutbacks and a merger, more than half the workforce was laid off and forced to either find employment elsewhere or pick up and move their family. Cozy's remained open, but it was never the same again. Gone were the pool tournaments, the drinking competitions, even karaoke night. Now a handful of patrons frequented the place, guzzled a few beers, dropped their money on the bar top, and then headed home to marriages that were falling apart.

Billy Cousins was one of those patrons. A big guy with broad shoulders and a deep chest, he'd worked at the mill for the past ten years as a green chain puller. A week ago he was moved to second shift because of a scuffle he'd gotten into with another of the first-shift guys and had made it a habit to stop by Cozy's on his way home, throw back a few Budweisers, and pick a fight or two. Most of the guys worked swing shifts, alternating months between first and second, but Billy had been permanently buried on second with no hope of ever working first again.

With his big mouth and attitude to complement it, Billy was a troublemaker and proud of it. He'd been in more brawls, spent more nights in the town jail, and taken home more shiners than anyone at the mill. And this was a badge he wore with honor.

Monday night, after work, he headed to Cozy's the same time he always did, took his seat at the bar, and ordered a Bud.

"Tough day at the mill today?" Ernie, the bartender, said as he slid the glass to Billy.

"Nah. Ain't never a tough day there. That place can't beat me." He took a swig of beer, wiped his mouth with the back of his hand. "If anything, I work too fast for 'em. The chain can't keep up with me."

Ernie leaned an elbow on the bar top. "How're you liking your new home on second?"

"Me? I love it. They thought they was punishin' me or somethin' by stickin' me there for good, but they was doin' me a favor. I get to stop by this sorry 'stablishment every day now and see your ugly mug, toss back a few, go home when the wife is sleepin' so I don't have to listen to her yapper, stay in bed till noon, then get up and do it all over again."

"Sounds like a real life."

Billy shrugged, took another gulp of beer, and licked his lips. "Works for me."

"You're not going to give anyone a hard time tonight, are you? I don't want to have to call the cops again."

Billy didn't like what Ernie was implying. "You sayin' I started that last fight? 'Cause I didn't. Blevins, he threw the first punch, you saw him. You was standin' right there."

Ernie wiped the bar top with a towel. "After you mouthed off to him for a solid hour, called his wife, mother, and daughter every name in the book."

"Hey, any man that can't take a verbal banterin' ain't much of a man. Blevins proved that much. 'Sides, everything I said was true enough." He looked around but didn't see the older man. "He ain't here tonight?"

"Nope. I don't think he'll be back for a while. 'Til things settle down again."

"You mean 'til I settle down."

"That's one way to look at it."

Billy smirked and took another long sip. There were a dozen other patrons there, some at the counter, some in booths. Most were from the mill, guys Billy knew and worked with every day. And most of them disliked him.

The tinny sound of the eighties-style jukebox playing Billy Joel's "It's Still Rock and Roll to Me" filled the bar. Billy hated that song. Really hated it. It reminded him of his high school days, and those were times he'd rather forget. He was smaller then with wild, tangled red hair and usually wound up the brunt of jokes after being stuffed in somebody else's locker.

He swung around on his barstool and stood. The song had produced memories, the memories had produced feelings, and feelings had ignited in him an anger that begged for a fight. His fists tightened. "Who put this song on?"

When Mitch Albright pulled into Cozy's parking lot, he wheeled his truck around to the back, parked along the grass barrier, and killed the engine. The vehicle's cabin was quiet save for the methodical tick of cooling metal. On the drive here, just a fifteen-minute trip, he'd thought extensively about the victim and how things would play out. If the night went the way it usually did, he was in there now, stirring up trouble. Eventually he'd either get thrown out or grow tired of his own big mouth and leave, but not before swinging around the back of the building to take a leak.

And that's when Mitch would approach him, when he was most vulnerable, most inhibited, and most likely to be taught a valuable lesson in respect.

He rolled down the window, grabbed the pine tree air freshener from the mirror, and tossed it out of the car. The smell was beginning to annoy him.

Billy Cousins was in the mood for a fight. He hadn't come into Cozy's like that, but that song, that blasted song, had done it to him. It was the song playing when he suffered the worst humiliation imaginable, when Becky dumped him in front of all the guys. He was the laughing stock and the butt of every joke for the rest of the school year. And he'd gotten into plenty of fights because of it too, which eventually found him expelled from school. He never did finish, which is why he was stuck working second shift as a green chain puller at the age of forty-eight. All because of that song.

He positioned himself in the middle of the bar. "Come on, you cowards, who put this song on?"

Nobody moved, but all eyes were fixed on him. They knew he was upset and hungry for violence, and they all feared him, something that only excited him more.

"Now just calm down, Billy," Ernie said from behind the bar.

"Shut up, Ernie. One of ya'll put this song on. You know I hate it. Who was it?"

A few of the men glanced at each other then back at Billy. "Was it you, Ed?"

Ed Polowski, a fifty-something saw operator, looked across the booth at Joe Harding and shook his head in disgust.

"Well, was it?"

Ed stared sharp eyes at Billy. He was a small but hard man with wiry muscles and a bushy mustache. But he wasn't the fighting type; Ed was a family man. "Leave it alone, Billy."

Billy didn't work on Ed's line but never cared for him. He approached the smaller man's booth and put both hands on the tabletop.

From across the room Ernie said, "That's enough, Billy, you hear?"

But Billy didn't hear, didn't care. "Did you put this song on?"

Ed readjusted his weight in the booth, ready to protect himself if needed. "I said leave it alone."

Billy hit the table with both hands and spilled beer from Ed's mug. "I ain't gonna leave it alone 'til you own up to it."

As smooth as if he'd been sitting on glass, Ed slid from the booth and was on both feet in front of Billy. He only came up to Billy's chin and gave at least fifty pounds away. Ed straightened his shoulders, but Billy didn't miss the flecks of fear in his eyes.

"I'm not looking for a fight, Billy."

"Well, you found one, little man."

"Billy, back down or I'm calling the cops." Ernie again. His voice was high and tight.

Billy smacked Ed on the side of the head with an open hand. The smaller man tipped sideways but caught himself on the table. Joe Harding was to his feet in an instant, as were four or five other men.

"That does it, Billy," Ernie said. "If you don't walk out of here right now, I'm calling the cops." He had the phone in one hand and his billy club in the other.

Billy threw up both hands. "Okay. Fine. I'm outta here. No need for this lousy bar anyway." He knocked over a chair on his way out.

Outside the air was cool and clean, but Billy's temper was still hot. He rounded the back of the building. He had to take a leak.

Billy Cousins was a first-rate troublemaker. Over the years Mitch had had his own share of run-ins with the brute. He had no respect for anyone, let alone Mitch. He was a big guy with a bigger mouth and liked to throw both around. So when Mitch saw Billy come storming out the bar and head around the back of the building, he was more than ready to do what he'd come to do.

He waited a minute or so to give Billy time to find his spot and get in position, then he exited the truck and entered the shadowed darkness behind the bar. None of the yellow light from the lamp outside the door made it to the back of the building. Billy was there, back to him, legs spread in a wide stance, one hand on his hip, filling a coffee can from three feet away.

Mitch approached Billy at an angle. "Hey, Billy Cousins, how's it going?"

Billy turned his head, found Mitch. "What are you doin' here?"

"Looking for you. What are you up to?"

"Tappin' a kidney, what's it look like? What, you want to see how a real man does it instead of squatting like you girls do?"

"You're a pretty funny guy, you know it? But you got one problem."

"You think? What's that?"

"You have no respect for anyone."

"Get lost."

With catlike quickness Mitch retrieved the knife from his belt and plunged it into Billy's lower back, into his right kidney, and twisted.

Billy arched his back but didn't make a sound.

Without a word Mitch yanked out the knife, raised it, and slit the big man's throat.

Billy gurgled once, twice, dropped to his knees, then went face first onto the asphalt, a puddle of urine widening out from his hips.

Mitch stood over him. He hated the slick feel of Billy's blood on his palm, between his fingers, on the handle of the knife.

Chapter 17

STARTLED FROM A deep sleep, Alicia Simpson sat up in bed, panting like she'd just run a hundred-meter dash. Sweat stuck her nightshirt to her chest and matted hair to her forehead. Her sheets were wet too. The air in the room felt cool as a cave against her damp skin.

Moonlight snuck past the venetian blinds, casting bars of lunar blue across the bed and floor. The room was quiet, as was the outside world. The clock on the dresser said it was 2:12 a.m., and she was alone. Derek hadn't come home.

She wiped her forehead and tried to think, to remember his work schedule. He worked swing shift and she could never keep track of when he was working which shift. And he was rarely around anymore to tell her.

Alicia got out of bed, went into the bathroom, and started a warm shower. She felt gross after doing all that sweating and needed to wash off and change clothes before going back to bed.

Under the stream of warm water she tried to remember her dream but couldn't. It was there, just out of reach, like a dropped treasure just below the surface of water, just beyond an arm's length. At times it would inch closer, moved by a subconscious undertow, and she felt it against her fingertips, but then it was gone again, deeper, pulled away by a forceful riptide. But the emotions were there, lingering like the dampness after a quick rain. There was a feeling of urgency, of needing to do something or talk to someone. She still felt as though she needed to talk to Derek, but she wasn't sure if that was it or not.

After her encounter with that girl in the diner she'd rushed out and tried Derek's cell, but he didn't answer. Hadn't answered all day. When the girl touched her, she'd had a vision of some sort flash through her mind. She didn't know what to make of it but knew intuitively that Derek was in trouble, that something horrible was going to happen. The girl knew it too; Alicia saw it in her eyes, the astonishment and violation of her innocence.

That must have been what her dream was about, Derek and her needing to find him.

Alicia stuck her face under the water. Was she going nuts? When she saw the girl in the diner, she'd been contemplating suicide, her mind fixated on death and Derek. It wasn't a stretch to believe she'd imagined the whole vision thing, the surprise in the girl's eyes. The poor girl had probably seen the desperation and terror in Alicia's eyes and was only responding to that. Derek was fine; he was more than capable of taking care of himself. Her worrying was only a by-product of her own suicidal tendencies.

She pulled out of the shower's stream and dashed the water from her face. She hadn't realized it before, she was so fixated on her dream and the cold sweats it had produced, but the thoughts of suicide were gone. It was strange, and she barely knew what to make of it. It was nothing tangible, like waking up one morning and realizing your nose is gone, but definitely noticeable.

She no longer wanted to end her life.

Chapter 18

POLICE CHIEF DOUG Miller hated early mornings, and 4:00 a.m. was definitely early. He'd been dragged out of bed by a phone call. A body had been found behind Cozy's Bar. Billy Cousins had been murdered. Didn't surprise Doug—that guy had it coming sooner or later. He'd made enough enemies over the years to form a small army. The suspects would be plentiful. What did surprise Doug, though, was the murder itself. Virginia Mills was Mayberry RFD when it came to violent crime. Break-ins, yes, occasionally. Some drug trafficking and domestic assault, of course. But murder? Not so much.

After kissing his wife and telling her to go back to sleep, he'd be back home in a few hours, Doug hopped in his pickup and headed for Cozy's.

Fifteen minutes later he was standing over the body of Billy Cousins. The big guy was on his back, skin as pale as paper, neck cut from ear to ear like he'd grown a second mouth—a gruesome sight. Dried blood formed a ring around his body. The whole area smelled of stale urine.

By the Dumpster Officer Peevey talked to Ernie James, the bartender.

Jerry Frizetti, the county coroner, stood next to Doug, nursing a coffee in a paper cup. He was a large man with a heavy brow and narrow, deep-set eyes. His shirts usually carried a smattering of coffee stains, and he was never without a necktie, loose in the knot, that hung around his neck like a noose. Frizetti held a coffee in one hand and a wrapped fast-food sandwich stuffed in his shirt pocket. "Haven't seen anything like this around here for a while, huh?"

"I would have liked to have kept it that way," Doug said. "How come you don't have that just-pulled-out-of-bed look about you?"

"Sometimes—" Frizetti sipped his coffee. "—sleep eludes me."

"Maybe it's all the coffee; ever think of that?"

"It's decaf."

"I didn't know you drink decaf."

"That's 'cause I never told you. Doc told me to get off the caffeine last year, and the wife, she makes sure I listen. Wants to keep me around for some odd reason."

"Must be the money," Doug said, then motioned toward the corpse of Billy Cousins. "Billy was a piece a work, but no one deserves to go like this. What do we got?"

Frizetti handed his coffee to Doug. "Here, hold this." He rounded the body, squatted next to it, his big form nearly folding in half. He lifted the right side of the corpse. "Stab wound to the right kidney. Lacerated neck, deep too, hit both jugulars and carotids and almost went through the trachea. Then this…" He lifted Billy's shirt to reveal a series of large lacerations across his chest and abdomen forming the letter R. "Best I can tell, Cousins here came out back to relieve himself, someone came up from behind, got him in the kidney, cut his throat, then went to work on his chest."

Doug didn't like this. Too strange, too vicious. The only other murders he'd ever dealt with had been straightforward, open-and-shut cases. This one was like something out of some crime TV show. And he hated those shows. "How long's he been dead?"

Jerry stood, took his coffee back, and stared at the body of Billy Cousins. "Hard to tell here. No more than three, four hours. Rigor mortis is just starting to set in. Peevey's talking to Ernie now. He was first to respond. Should be able to give us more details on a timeline."

"Peevey."

Peevey looked up from his steno pad.

"A minute when you're done."

Peevey said something to Ernie, shook his hand, then headed toward Doug and Jerry. "We're done."

"You got his statement?"

"Every word of it." Peevey stopped at Billy's head and put his hands on his hips. "Billy here came in the bar after his shift at the mill. Ernie said he was his usual self, loud, stirring up trouble. Upset about some song playing on the jukebox. Got in Ed Polowski's face about it, tried to start something, but Ed didn't take the bait. Joe Harding was sitting with Ed. Ernie threatened to call the police. Billy finally gave up and left. That was a little before midnight and the last time Ernie saw or heard from Billy. Until the bar closed and he finished cleaning up and headed out here to dump the garbage. That was about two thirty. Bar closes at two."

Doug smoothed his mustache. "How many were in the bar when Billy left?"

"Ernie said he remembered thirteen other men, no women."

"And he can name them all?"

"Every one of them. Said they're all regulars, either mill workers winding down or townies looking for a night cap."

Doug said to Jerry, "You said he had to be dead at least three hours, right?"

Jerry nodded. "It's rare for rigor mortis to set in sooner than that."

"So he would have had to have been offed shortly after he left. Anybody leave shortly after him, Peevey?"

Peevey checked his steno pad. "Nope. But Jude Fabry came shortly after midnight, sat in the corner, drank a few beers, and left before closing."

"Jude Fabry? Don't think I know him."

"He's new in the area. Works second at the packaging plant in

Jefferson. Lives out off 807. I talked to him once. Quiet guy but seemed nice enough."

Doug would have liked to believe this case was that easy, pin it on the new guy, but something told him it wasn't. He also would have liked to think they could narrow down the suspect or suspects to one or a few of the thirteen, but he couldn't be sure of that either. But it was certainly a place to start. "Okay. Peevey, I want your full report by noon. I'll get forensics in here to comb the place. Don't touch or move anything until they're done, then the body's all yours, Jerry. Get me the examiner's report as soon as the autopsy is done. I'm going home and getting back in bed." He turned to leave, stopped. "Did anyone tell Billy's wife?"

"Not yet," Peevey said.

Doug had half a mind to tell Peevey to do it but knew it would go better coming from him. "I'll do it." All in all he loved being a cop, but there were aspects of the job he just hated. Telling a wife—even the wife of a jerk like Billy Cousins—that she was now a widow was one of them.

He returned to his car and found Jackie Hale, police reporter for the *Harrisonburg Daily News-Record*, standing behind the yellow police tape. Doug lifted the tape and passed beneath it.

"Jackie Hale, star reporter, you're up early today."

Jackie looked like she too just climbed out of bed. Usually a woman who appeared to take plenty of time to primp in the morning, she had no makeup on and her hair was pulled back in a sloppy ponytail. Jackie followed Doug to the car. "Who is it, Chief?"

"Billy Cousins. What, do you have your scanner right next to your bed or something? Or do you just never sleep, waiting up all night for something exciting to happen in Rockingham County?"

"Ditano called me," she said.

Victor Ditano was the editor of the *Daily News-Record* and a man Doug rarely got along with. "Oh, so Vic's the one who never sleeps, huh. Not surprised there."

"What happened to him?"

"To who?"

"Cousins."

Doug reached his car and opened the door. "Murdered."

"How?"

"Stabbed."

"How many times?"

"Hard to say. I didn't take the time to count."

"So multiple times?"

"I didn't say that."

She scribbled something on her notepad. "Any suspects yet?"

"You know I can't comment on that."

"Any apparent motive? Was there an altercation in the bar? Did Cousins have enemies?"

Doug sat in his cruiser. "Cousins saw everyone as an enemy."

"That's a lot of suspects to weed through."

"An awful lot." He closed the door and started the engine, glad to leave the reporter and her probing questions far behind.

Chapter 19

AMY SPENCER AWAKENED with a start. She'd had another nightmare.

Jim slept peacefully beside her. The darkened room was cluttered with disjointed, misplaced shadows. But there was something wrong, something odd about the way the shadows were positioned. In the far corner of the room, next to her dresser, a dark figure occupied the space. The visitor's face was shrouded in darkness, but Amy instinctively knew who it was. She said the girl's name out loud—"Louisa"—but the child did nothing.

She closed her eyes a moment, and when she opened them, Louisa was next to her bed, at her head. She had both hands on the mattress, almost touching Amy's shoulder. The bedroom door was cracked open, and a bar of light from the hall slanted across the girl's face. Those blue eyes captured the light and appeared to glow from their own inner source.

"You're afraid," the girl said in a wondering voice.

Amy thought to nudge Jim, awaken him and let him take care of this, but she didn't. Instead she said, "Louisa, why are you in here?"

"You're afraid." Her voice was small and seemed to get lost in the room.

Behind Louisa the shadows on the walls and ceiling moved, they writhed and gyrated, as if they were alive and growing more anxious by the second.

"Why? Why am I afraid?"

Louisa turned her head slowly and glanced out the window then back at Amy. "He's coming, isn't he?"

"Who's coming?"

"You don't have to be afraid. Fear has no real power."

"Afraid of who? Who's coming?"

The girl shook her head, backing away, then disappeared through the open door. Amy sank back into her pillow, and an inexplicable cloud of fatigue engulfed her. Once again she drifted to sleep.

Moments later Amy started awake, but this time to the sound of a baby crying. She lay in bed for a moment, listening to the sound, so foreign and distant, alien to their home. Was it a baby? Or was it Louisa, lying on her cot? Or perhaps a stray cat outside.

The crying grew louder, urgent, desperate, and now she could tell it was definitely that of an infant. It came from another room in the house, the nursery, just across the hall.

Amy threw off the covers, not caring if she disturbed Jim, and crossed the bedroom in four steps. Darkness hid the corners, but her eyes had adjusted enough that she could see Louisa was not in the room with her. She and Jim were alone. The depth of that thought suddenly struck her as profound. They were alone. They had no child. But the crying was still there and increasing in volume by the moment. The baby sounded to be in pain or terribly afraid.

Amy opened the door and welcomed the light of the hallway. Across the way, in the nursery, the crying became muffled, as if someone had placed a hand over the baby's mouth. *Her* baby's mouth. She no longer cared that every ounce of reason said it couldn't be her baby because she had no child. To her the child in her nursery *was* her baby, her little girl, Olivia. And something was wrong.

She dashed across the hallway, pushed open the nursery door, and found Louisa standing next the crib, both hands in it and holding something over the baby.

"Get away from her!" Amy cried, rushing across the room.

Louisa yanked up what she was holding (Amy saw it to be a pillow) and stumbled backward.

As tears sprung to her eyes and blurred her vision, Amy pushed the girl out of the way and looked into the crib.

A baby was there, just a newborn, wrapped tightly in a pink blanket. By the light of the nightlight in the room Amy could see the baby's skin was pale blue and that she wasn't breathing. "What did you do?" she screamed at Louisa.

Louisa dropped the pillow and backed away.

Amy reached into the crib and scooped up her baby, her precious Olivia, and held her limp, lifeless body tight. The tears came in a torrent, sheets of them like the worst summer storm…

And suddenly she was awake, in her own bed, in her own room, the morning sun slipping past the shades, brightening the walls. And though she was awake, she still quaked and felt a heaviness in her chest.

She pushed back the covers, swung her legs over the side of the bed, and sat up. The feelings and emotions stirred by the dream remained, lingering like the after-tingle of an electric shock. She had to check the nursery, had to see for herself that it was indeed only a dream.

The nursery was across the hall, just like in her dream, and still decorated and furnished to welcome their new arrival. Jim had wanted to sell the furniture—the crib, changing table, dresser, glider rocker—or at least put them in the attic, but Amy would have none of it. For several months the room had remained unchanged, a brutal reminder of what could have been.

Amy crossed the hall and opened the door of the nursery. The smell of new linens and baby stuff greeted her, the aroma of new life. Sunlight hit the windows at just the right angle, causing the yellows and pinks in the room to glow, as if the light came from within and from outside. Farm animals danced across the wall, the pig holding hands with the cow, the sheep with the horse.

She'd painted it herself shortly after discovering she was pregnant. Amy walked to the crib and looked in, still feeling the fright
and despair and utter horror over what she'd found there in her
dream, but it was empty, of course, occupied only by a neatly
folded stack of baby blankets and a stuffed pig. Picking up one of
the blankets, she put it to her face, felt the softness, breathed in
the newness of it…and heard a floorboard creak behind her.

Amy turned, expecting to see Jim there but found Louisa
standing in the hallway watching her.

Louisa took a step forward. Her face was flat, but her eyes were
alive. She looked around the room as a child would after entering
a candy story for the very first time and appeared to almost smile.
"Don't change a thing, Miss Amy. It's perfect."

Chapter 20

ITCH ALBRIGHT WAS in a rather good mood come morning, despite his lack of sleep and nighttime activities. In fact, he was in such a good mood he thought he'd make some coffee and toast and take the Appletons breakfast. While the coffee was brewing, he explored more of the expansive farmhouse and found himself in the study. There three of the four walls were lined floor to ceiling with bookshelves. Two overstuffed chairs, each with an ornately carved side table and upholstered footrest, sat on a braided rug in the center of the room. A footstool was available to reach books on the top shelves.

At closer inspection Mitch found most of the shelves stocked with the classics—Dickens, Alcott, Austen, Shakespeare, first editions of all of Jack London's works—and reference books of every kind and size. Of particular interest was the sizable collection of books on horses and horse racing, with particular interest in Secretariat. The wall without bookshelves was dedicated solely to this fascination with horses. Paintings and photos nearly covered the entire wall, many of Secretariat, the great champion of 1972 and 1973.

From the kitchen a soft chime sounded, signifying that the coffee was ready. Mitch left the study, put the bread in the toaster, and prepared three mugs of steaming coffee. When the toast was done, he placed it and the coffee on a tray along with sugar and cream and three spoons, and headed down to the cellar. In his pocket he carried a bottle of Tylenol he'd gotten from the medicine cabinet in the bathroom.

Bob and Clare were in the room he had constructed for them and made no sound as he came down the steps. Previously Mitch had carried three chairs to the cellar and arranged them in a triangle of sorts with a small table in the center. It was there that the three of them would sit and enjoy their coffee. He placed the tray on the table and unlocked the door to the room. The Appletons sat on one of the cots Mitch had provided for them, holding each other. On their faces was a look of fear and worry.

"Good morning, folks," Mitch said, trying to sound cordial and nonthreatening. "Would you care to join me for some coffee and toast?"

The two looked at each other, then Bob spoke. "What are you going to do with us?"

"I told you already, Bob. Nothing at the moment, except maybe enjoy a cup of coffee and some light conversation. Come, join me. I promise I won't bite." He held out his hands, palm up. "And look, no wrench."

They hesitated a moment before Clare broke away from her husband and walked toward Mitch. She was a brave, confident woman. Bob wasn't far behind her.

The Appletons sat in two of the chairs and Mitch in the third. He served them their coffee and offered them Tylenol, which they both took with a pleasant "thank you."

Mitch sat back in his chair, sipped at his coffee, and said, "I noticed you admire horses and the classics. A nice combination, if I must say. For farmers you seem to be very cultured."

Clare spoke first. "Are most farmers you've met not cultured?"

A bold volley, Mitch thought, and he liked Clare even more than he had before. She had spunk and knew how to wield it without coming across as bumptious or condescending. "Most are—" Mitch thought for the correct word. "—uncomplicated."

"Is that another way of saying they're simple?"

"Maybe. But not as in stupid. I meant only that they either don't have the time or the interest in seeking out such things as the classics and horse racing."

Clare tilted her head and fingered the napkin in her hand. Mitch didn't miss her quick glance toward the staircase leading out of the cellar. "You don't know the farmers we know. Most are very cultured, learned men, but as you said, they're uncomplicated. They do like to keep life simple, as it should be. Too much clutter wreaks havoc on the soul. We have our interests outside the farm, but I'm afraid we're not nearly as diverse as you may think. Bob likes his fiction, yes. When he isn't doing something around the farm, he has his nose in one of those books. And we watch little, if any, television." Remarkably, she appeared to be of sound mind again. The fog from yesterday's concussion had cleared.

"Jack London is my favorite," Bob said.

Mitch smiled, genuinely. "*White Fang, Call of the Wild, The Sea-Wolf.* I loved them all." He looked at Clare. "Then you must be the horse fanatic."

"I like to read and learn," Clare said.

Bob set his mug on the table. "She can't get enough of learning. Anything really, but especially those horses of hers."

"I grew up on a horse farm," Clare said. Again she glanced at the staircase on the far side of the cellar, and her hand found her husband's. "Worked in stables all my life. When I was a child, horses were my passion. I guess I never outgrew it."

Mitch knew Clare was only biding her time, engaging him in conversation to distract him or maybe make some kind of genial connection, but he didn't care, for he enjoyed talking to the Appletons. They were polite, courteous to each other, didn't interrupt, and respectful. "They're amazing beasts, aren't they?"

Clare's eyes squinted shut a little, and the corners of her mouth curled up. She was digging way back in her memory vault. "'Do you give the horse his strength or clothe his neck with a flowing mane? Do you make him leap like a locust, striking terror with his proud snorting? He paws fiercely, rejoicing in his strength, and charges into the fray. He laughs at fear, afraid of nothing; he does not shy away from the sword. The quiver rattles against his side, along with the flashing spear and lance. In frenzied excitement he eats up the ground; he cannot stand still when the trumpet sounds. At the blast of the trumpet he snorts, "Aha!" He catches the scent of battle from afar, the shout of commanders and the battle cry.'"

She sat back in her chair, tears pooling in her eyes. "That's from Job, chapter thirty-nine. I memorized it as a girl and would repeat it to myself every day."

"It's beautiful," Mitch said.

Clare sighed, swept her hand over her eyes, and smiled at her husband. With that one look Mitch saw how much she loved him, adored him even. "And the greatest of all horses, racehorses mind you, was Secretariat."

"The Triple Crown winner."

"Yes, the champion of champions. I saw him in person once, up close. He was a beautiful beast. Gorgeous and strong. His time of two twenty-four at the Belmont Stakes will never be touched. He did the impossible."

Mitch said nothing. He was enjoying his time with the Appletons so much he nearly forgot the reason he was there, his mission.

Clare continued. "Did you know his heart weighed twenty-two pounds? It was perfect. *He* was perfect. His will to win should be an inspiration to us all."

The three sat in silence for a full minute, Clare obviously soaking in the memories of her childhood, her love for horses.

Finally Bob spoke. "What are you doing, son?"

The fact that he called Mitch "son," a term of endearment in any culture, loosened Mitch's inhibitions. "I'm getting something I've been missing my whole life."

"And what's that?"

"Respect."

"By holding us hostage?"

"I told you yesterday, Bob, this isn't about you and Clare. This is about me earning the respect due me."

"You must have had an awful childhood," Clare said. "I'm sorry."

"Yes, I did, but don't be sorry for me, Clare. I don't want pity. Respect is something to be earned, and I never bothered taking the time to earn it before. It's just as much my fault as anyone's."

"But now you plan to earn it?" Bob studied Mitch with those thoughtful, kind eyes.

"Yes. Seven is the number of completion, right? In the Bible? So after the seventh one, my mission will be complete, and I will have earned the respect of everyone, maybe even of the world."

"After the seventh what?" Clare said.

Mitch didn't want to say anything more. He didn't want to be one of those killers who bragged about his exploits. He wasn't looking for fame or infamy, wasn't seeking attention or publicity. He simply wanted to be respected. Really respected. Not just given lip service or compulsory admiration.

A great sadness overcame him then. Because he'd opened his mouth and told the Appletons about his mission, his desire to earn and gain respect, he would now have to kill them too. He loathed the thought of it. "Nothing, Clare," he said, forcing a smile. "Let's talk more about your horses. Why don't you have any here on the farm? I'm very interested in that."

Chapter 21

"CAN I TALK to you for a minute?"

Amy stood in the entryway to the kitchen, towel wrapped around her head, arms folded across her chest. It was the first Jim had seen of her this morning since she woke him saying Louisa needed breakfast. Jim had left the bedroom then heard Amy get in the shower a few minutes later. He could tell by the way she woke him, by the way she practically ordered him to get "the girl" breakfast, that she was in some sort of funk this morning. Not unusual, though. The past few months she'd experienced a lot of funks.

Now, standing in the doorway, Amy did not look upset. The set of her jaw, the lines on her brow, the dip of her mouth showed more fright than anger. The look chilled him. What was she afraid of? Louisa?

Steeling himself, he poured Louisa more milk and said, "Sure."

"Alone? In the office?"

Jim paused. Alone and in the office could only mean one thing: it was about Louisa. "Sure thing."

He followed her to the room. She closed the door behind them and leaned against it. "I want you to find her another home."

Her statement didn't surprise Jim as much as it should have. "Why?"

She began to pace the room. "Do I have to have a reason?"

"Reasons are good for explaining yourself, especially when you give an order like that."

"I guess 'because I said so' won't work?"

"I'm not three."

She stopped pacing but worked her hands as if she were kneading an invisible clump of clay. "She scares me, Jim."

"*She* scares you or *you* scare you?"

"*She* scares me."

"She's a nine-year-old kid."

"She's more than that."

"More than a kid?"

"More than...I don't know." She unwrapped the towel from her head, let it drop to the floor, and sat on the desk chair. Wet, clumped tendrils of hair hung to her shoulders.

Jim knelt before her and put his hands on her thighs. "She's a good kid, Amy. Really. She has a good heart."

"I had a dream about her last night."

"Okay."

"She killed our baby. Murdered her. With a pillow."

"That's more like a nightmare. Don't you see what this is? Somewhere deep inside you feel like Louisa is trying to replace our baby, be the daughter we lost. She's not, Amy. She's a lost, scared little girl, that's all. If she does anything odd, don't you see why? Look at what she's been through."

"A fire."

"The whereabouts of her parents unknown."

"Stuck with strangers."

"In a strange town." Jim stood. "Look, if it will make you feel any better, I'll take her down to the police station and talk to Doug Miller, see if they've gotten any leads on who she is or where she came from. Okay?"

Amy kept her eyes down and nodded.

Jim lifted her chin, looked her in the eyes. "Okay?"

She smiled. "Yes."

He kissed her. "But what?"

"What?"

"Your mouth said yes, but your eyes said 'but.' Yes, *but.*"

"I just…" She started with the kneading again. "I just have a feeling something bad's going to happen, and it's going to center around her."

"You think you're dreaming omens and prophecies now?"

"No. Nothing so Hollywood. Just a feeling. Please, can't we at least try to find her another home?"

Jim took her hands in his. "Amy, she's been through so much already. She's just getting comfortable with us. To shuffle her off to yet another home, who knows what kind of further psychological damage it could cause the poor kid. Her whole world's been turned upside down. She needs some stability, some consistency. Who knows what she's going to find out once Doug locates her parents. She needs to be as emotionally strong and prepared as possible for whatever news awaits her."

Amy forced a smile.

Jim knelt again. "Babe, listen, we've been so focused on ourselves the last few months because we had to be. Healing had to take place. It's time to start looking outward again, start giving again." He knew she'd grieved longer and harder than he had and that she'd resented him for that in the past. But he had grieved in his own way, and still did. His wounds weren't totally healed yet either. But he knew it was time to move on. "This child needs us."

She nodded. "You're right."

"Can I get that in writing?"

"You better have a good lawyer."'

Jim stood and kissed the tip of her nose then her lips. "As soon as we're ready, I'll take her and head down to the police station, see what's going on."

Chapter 22

ALICIA SIMPSON AWOKE with that feeling of urgency in her joints again. She had to get up, had to move. The clock said it was nearly 9:00 a.m., but that couldn't be right, could it? She checked her watch. It was right. She had to be at work in fifteen minutes. The alarm never went off. She was glad now that she'd taken a shower earlier.

After throwing on a pair of khakis and a pullover, she slipped into her sneakers, brushed and pulled her hair back into a tight ponytail, applied makeup to hide her lingering bruises, and almost swallowed an apple whole. Done in ten minutes. Five minutes to get to the Food Lion in time to punch in at nine. A glass of orange juice went with her in the car.

On the way to work Alicia thought of Derek and how he never came home last night; she thought about their relationship, the smiles they'd shared, the tender moments, but also the violent ones, the bruises, the pains, the excuses. She thought of ways to escape, reasons to leave him for good. She thought about the girl, the survivor from the fire at old Jake Tucker's, and her touch and the feelings it had produced, the confusion in her eyes. She thought about work and what Mr. Eysler, her manager, would say if she was late to her register.

But never once did she think about suicide.

She got to the grocery store just in time, punched her card, donned her apron, and took her place on the front end behind a register. Business was slow, as it always was on a Tuesday morning. Customers filtered in, filtered out, made small talk as she scanned their items, smiled, said good-bye, have a nice day. But Alicia's mind wasn't on her job today; it was on the girl and

the look in her eyes. Strange too, because she thought she'd settled that matter during her early morning shower. The girl had
probably seen the desperation and fear in Alicia's eyes and had
been confused by it. But there was something more to it than
that, more than mere confusion. There was something about her
touch and the vision that had accompanied it, the image of Derek
frozen in a wide stance, facing a dark figure, obscured by shadows,
but menacing, obviously intending harm, possibly murder. It
wasn't her imagination, or was it?

At eleven thirty Alicia took her first break and went outside to
sit on one of the three benches along the store's front and enjoy
some fresh air. Maybe it would help clear her mind. The air was
unusually humid for September. Low clouds formed a rippled
canopy over the region. Rain was on the way.

Not more than a minute or so into her break Jake Tucker
drove past, found a parking space, and climbed out of his truck.
Alicia had seen him there before, plenty of times. He was a regular, as was every other local, and friendly enough, but she could
tell he held an underlying sorrow at bay. But he seemed different
today, lighter on his feet, more erect, younger…something. He
seemed *better*, happier.

When he reached the front sidewalk, he met Alicia's eyes and
nodded, and she smiled and waved. The automatic front doors of
the store slid open with a dry scraping sound, but right before Mr.
Tucker walked through she called to him.

He stopped, turned, smiled kindly. "Yes?"

Alicia stood, smoothed her apron, and took one step forward.
"Do you have a minute?"

His smile grew. "Sure, Alicia. What is it?"

Alicia was surprised he knew her name until she remembered
the name tag she wore on her apron. He'd probably seen it a hundred times or more. They both stepped away from the doorway

and moved closer to the benches. Alicia twisted her hands, shuffled her feet.

"What's the matter? What is it?" Mr. Tucker's eyes were warm
and inviting. She didn't need to fear him or be embarrassed.

"The girl, uh, the girl from the fire."

"Louisa."

"Yeah. Did she, like, did she touch you at all, I mean, did she put
her hands on you at any time?" What an awfully strange question,
and for a moment she thought he'd turn and walk away from her.

Mr. Tucker put his hands in his pockets and tilted his head to
one side. "Why do you ask?"

"Well, I, um, yesterday I…"

He touched her arm lightly. "It's okay, you know. Just tell me."

"Yesterday I was in the Red Wing, and she was there with Jim
Spencer. She came up to me and, like, put her hand on my hand
and, I don't know, something happened."

"You saw something. A vision?"

"Yes." She said it so fast it nearly came out twice. She thought
he'd ask what she saw, but he didn't, which relieved her because
she wasn't ready to share that with anyone. She had to process this.

"And felt something too?"

Unbidden, tears welled in her eyes and would have spilled
down her cheeks if she hadn't dashed them away first. She was
surprised by the sudden wave of emotion that washed over her,
but his confirmation meant she wasn't going nuts, that something
really had happened between her and the girl in that diner. She
couldn't speak past the lump in her throat, so she nodded.

Mr. Tucker squeezed her arm. His touch was gentle but firm,
full of excitement and childlike wonder. "She did touch me. Put
her hand directly on my chest and quieted my heart, eased the
pain that was there. I saw Raymond, my son, too. Saw him just as
clear as I'm lookin' at you here. He was smiling at me, arms open,
tears in his eyes. And I was filled with such a feelin' of relief and

joy and…weightlessness, as if I'd been filled with helium like one of those balloons and just lifted off."

"Who is she?"

"Louisa. But other than that, beats me. But I know she's special. God has His hand on that little girl."

Alicia smiled and had an urge, which she resisted, to give Mr. Tucker a hug.

They said their good-byes, and Mr. Tucker turned and entered the store. Alicia dropped down on the bench, wiping more tears from her cheeks. She wasn't going crazy, that was good, but the fact of the vision was still there. Derek was in trouble. Spiders of unease tickled her arms and the back of her neck.

And stranger yet, she was now convinced the girl had seen the vision too.

Chapter 23

JIM AND LOUISA met Chief Doug Miller at the front desk area of the county police station. It was a new building tucked away on Route 11 between a stretch of farmland and an Omaha's Feed store but centrally located in the county, north of Harrisonburg. The station employed more than a hundred patrol officers to serve and protect the 75,000 residents of Rockingham County.

After shaking Jim's hand, Miller said, "Have you ever been here?"

"Nope. First time and hopefully my last."

"As long as you're here for the right reasons, no need to worry."

"I guess if you find yourself behind bars, you know you came for the wrong reason."

Miller smiled under his mustache. "You'd be surprised how many we get who don't even know why they're here or how they got here. Come with me."

They followed him through the reception area, down a short hallway, and into an office area with cubicles and desks arranged neatly in two rows. Miller's office was off to the left in a separate room. They went in, and he picked up the phone on his desk and punched a button.

"Cindy? Could you come in here for a second, please?" He placed the phone back in the jack and smiled at Louisa. "How are things going for you, young lady? Are the Spencers treating you okay?"

"Just fine, Chief. Mr. Jim and Miss Amy are taking real good care of me."

"Good. Good. Have you remembered anything more other than your name and birthday?"

She shook her head, and the ponytails Amy had fixed earlier whipped back and forth. "Nope."

"Well, I'm sure it will come to you soon enough. Hey, how would you like a grand tour of the building? You can see the jail cells and where we keep the dogs. There may even be one here you can meet."

Louisa's mouth stretched into a wide grin. "Sure. I'd love that."

"Great."

Just then Cindy, a young, thin officer appeared in the doorway. "Chief?"

"Cindy, would you please show Miss Louisa around the place, give her the grand tour, hide nothing from her, share all our secrets."

Louisa looked at Jim and smiled. "Boy," Jim said. "You're really getting the royal treatment. Must be something special, huh?"

Louisa took Cindy's hand and allowed the officer to lead her away. Miller closed the door behind them and turned to Jim. "How's it going?"

"She's a great kid. No problem at all."

Miller sat behind his desk. "All right, so how's it going?"

"You mean with Amy?"

"With Amy, with Louisa, with you."

"Well, Amy still isn't sure about the whole thing. Louisa has moments of…odd behavior around her."

"Odd?"

"She knows Amy had a miscarriage, and she seems a little fixated on that. I think it just creeps Amy out a bit. She told me this morning she wanted me to find Louisa a new foster home until all this was settled."

Miller shifted in his chair. "Do you want me to get Children and Youth to find another family?"

"No. We talked, and Amy understands that wouldn't be best for Louisa. The last thing she needs right now is to be jostled around from home to home. She needs some semblance of order, consistency."

"I agree. How about her memory? Anything coming back?"

Jim shook his head. "No. Nothing. How 'bout on your end? Any luck?"

"Nothing but dead ends and non-starts. No missing persons that match her identity, no reports of abductions that fit her. I ran her first name and birthday through our system and came up with nothing. At least not around here. Unless she isn't nine and the year is off, but it can't be off by more than a year or two either way. Or…"

"Or what?"

"Or Louisa isn't her real name. Maybe she made it up, or it was her doll's name or cat's name, and since it was in her head, she assumed it was hers."

"What about posting her picture?" Jim said. "You know, sending it out through your databases and networks, getting it on the news."

"I already put it in the system. I'm not too hopeful about that, though. You know how many kids are reported missing every year?"

"It's gotta be thousands."

"Try hundreds of thousands."

"So what about TV?"

"And have every pervert in a hundred-mile radius showing up to claim her as his long lost darling daughter? I don't want to put her through that. Not like that." He lifted a pen and scribbled something on a piece of paper. "I've been thinking; maybe it would do her good to talk to a psychologist. You know her better than anyone here; what do you think?"

"Honestly? I don't like it. I don't think she's ready for someone to go probing around in her head, asking her a hundred questions she can't answer. She's a sweetheart, but she's fragile, you know?"

"I figured you'd say that, so I took the liberty to talk to Dr. Willows, a child psychologist the county uses from time to time.

She said there are two main reasons a child would get amnesia: physical trauma—blunt force to the head—or emotional trauma. She suffered no physical trauma that we know of, so we have to assume this is emotional. Something happened to that girl that she doesn't want to remember, so she's forgotten everything."

"Which is why I want to take this gently. Whatever it is she's going to remember isn't going to be pleasant, and the remembering itself will be traumatic for her."

Miller stroked his mustache and nodded. "Agreed. How about getting her out in public more, take her to the store, the gas station, the school. Maybe something will jog a memory, and that will kick in more memories. A domino thing. Kind of ease her into it. In fact, I can call the elementary school in Virginia Mills and arrange it so she can meet the kids during recess."

Jim liked it. Meeting other kids might just be the catalyst to trigger a memory, a feeling, anything. Something to get the ball rolling. He had hoped that her remembering her birth date would trigger such a reaction, but it didn't happen. "Yeah, okay, arrange it for this afternoon."

"Great." Miller scribbled more notes on his paper. "I think they have recess at two o'clock. I'll double-check, let them know you're coming, and give you a call back."

"What if you never find her parents?" It was something Jim had wondered more and more about as time passed and there was no word on anyone looking for Louisa.

Miller shrugged. "Then she becomes a ward of the state, an orphan."

"How much time do you allow to pass?"

Another shrug. "A lot. We'll exhaust every avenue we have three or four times before giving up. Her parents may have been in an accident and are in some hospital in a coma right now. They may be dead. Or they may have abandoned her and fled to Canada or who knows where. If we can get to the bottom of who she is, then we can get somewhere. I won't leave any stone unturned. But understand, in a case like this there may be family members that will want to take her in, aunts, uncles, grand-parents, who knows."

Miller's comment about Louisa being taken in by family members triggered a wave of longing. Was he falling in love again with this new possibility of a daughter, only to have her ripped from his life?

"Spencer."

Miller had said his name. Jim pulled himself from his thoughts, that weight of loss and sorrow still dangling from his neck. "Yeah?"

"Are you all square with that? It may be weeks, even months."

"Uh, yeah, sure. Absolutely. As long as it takes." *May it take a lifetime*, he prayed.

Chapter 24

OFFICER PEEVEY STEERED his cruiser into the gravel driveway outside Jude Fabry's trailer. It wasn't much to look at, but it wasn't falling apart either. The aluminum skirting was all still in place, that was something, and it looked like Fabry had at least attempted to keep the lot clean and free of clutter. There was not a single upholstered chair or broken-down car in the front yard. He lived on a stretch of mostly abandoned road. Only a handful of trailers occupied cleared-acre lots. Behind them was woods, and across the road barren field ran all the way to the horizon.

Shutting off the engine, Peevey grabbed his steno pad from the passenger seat and exited the car. Gravel crunched under his feet as he made his way to the small front porch. Overhead the sky was gray and seemed to hover like a blanket about to fall and smother him. Peevey didn't like interviewing people. He wasn't a talker by nature and found most people to be anything but forthcoming with information.

He climbed the steps to the porch and rapped on the door, a flimsy, foam-core and plastic job. All was quiet inside. It was a little after noon, and he suspected Fabry was still sleeping off his buzz from early that morning. Again he knocked, this time harder.

Now he heard stirring inside, a grunt, then, "What?"

"Jude Fabry, it's Officer Peevey, Rockingham County Police."

"Ah. Okay. Just—just wait a sec."

Peevey checked his watch out of habit. Inside he could hear shuffling, heavy footsteps moving away from the door and into a deeper part of the home.

He knocked again. "Mr. Fabry. Open the door. I need to talk to you."

The footsteps moved closer. "I'm comin'."

The door opened and Fabry was there, hair mussed, glasses tilted at a weird angle on his nose, eyes squinting into the daylight. Jude Fabry was not a young man, but neither was he old. With his leathery, sun-thickened, and creased skin, his yellowing eyes and raspy voice, it was difficult to put an age on him, but Peevey guessed he was in his late forties or early fifties.

The interior of the trailer was dark and hazy. The shades had been pulled to keep daylight out, either because it worsened Fabry's hangover or because he'd rather live in darkness where the nicotine stains were concealed.

Fabry dragged the sleeve of his sweatshirt across his mouth. "Yeah?"

Peevey looked past Fabry and did a quick survey. "May I come in, Mr. Fabry?"

Fabry appeared uncomfortable, nervous. "Uh, yeah, sure. There a problem?"

Jude Fabry had moved into the area a little over a month ago. Gossip around town had it that he came from Ohio, where he caught his wife in bed with his brother. Not waiting for an explanation or an apology, he threw some clothes in a duffel and high-tailed it out of town, drove all night until he found himself in Virginia Mills. Butch Oldroyd told Peevey that Fabry called him and offered to buy the trailer on the spot, with cash. A week later he'd landed a job at Fresh Valley Foods in Broadway.

Once Peevy was inside, Fabry closed the door and turned on a small table lamp that cast a tent of dirty light onto a dusty table. Old smoke hung in the air like a fog. The place reeked of used cigarettes.

"You want to sit?" Fabry said, motioning toward the sofa.

"Thanks, but I'll stand." Peevey opened his steno and removed the pen from his pocket.

Retrieving a cigarette from the coffee table, Fabry pushed it into his mouth. "You mind?"

"Actually, I do."

Fabry pulled the cigarette out and tossed it back onto the table. He sat and grabbed at his hands. They were both trembling. Like most chain smokers, Fabry was thin and his muscles wiry. His movements were hesitating and anything but fluid.

"Mr. Fabry, where'd you go after work last night?"

Fabry looked up like he was surprised Peevey would ask such a question. He scratched at the side of his nose. "Is somethin' wrong?"

"Not yet. Where'd you go?"

"Uh…" Fabry shifted his eyes over the floor, back and forth, as if searching for the answer in the fibers of the carpet. "I went to Cozy's."

"What time did you get there?"

Fabry blew out. "Jeez. I don't know. I finished my shift at eleven, went to the bathroom, filled the truck at the station, had a bite to eat, then headed over. After midnight, I guess."

"And what did you do there?"

He shrugged. "Downed a few beers. Why? That a crime?"

"Only if you drove home drunk."

Fabry shook his head hard. "No way. I only had two beers. I did the hard stuff when I got back home here."

"Are you hungover now?"

"Yeah. Pretty bad too." He pointed at the pack of cigarettes on the coffee table. "Can't I have just one?"

"I'd rather you didn't. How long did you stay at Cozy's?"

"I don't know, a couple hours, I guess."

"Do you know Billy Cousins, Mr. Fabry?"

"That loudmouth who comes in Cozy's?"

"That's the one."

Fabry nodded and wiped at his mouth again. "You mind if I get a Coke? My mouth tastes like something crawled in it and died last night."

"After you answer the question."

"I know who Cousins is, yeah. Know the type too. Loudmouth punk. Can I get that Coke now?"

Peevey nodded. "Did you ever have any run-ins with Cousins?"

From the small kitchen area Fabry said, "'Bout a week ago. I was mindin' my own business, you know?"

"At Cozy's?"

"Yeah. Well, he comes over and asks for a smoke. I tell him to get lost."

"And what happened?"

Fabry rounded the counter, can of Coke in his hand. He took a long swig. "Nothin'. He shot his mouth off some, cursed me pretty bad, but didn't mess with me. He likes the sound of his own voice, makes him feel good about himself."

"And that's the only time you ever had contact with him?"

"Nope." He took another drink of the soda and licked his lips.

Peevey shrugged. "You care to share what that means?"

"When I left Cozy's, I noticed my front driver-side tire was flat. Didn't think nothin' of it at the time. Put the spare on and the next morning took it to Arnold's for a new tire. Guy there said someone slit the old tire, that's why it'd gone flat. I couldn't have seen that in the dark."

"And you think Cousins did it?"

Fabry shook his head, tightened his jaw. "Nope. I *know* it was him. Confronted him too. 'Course he denied it, got that big mouth of his goin'. What was I gonna do? I didn't have no proof or nothin' so I had to let it go."

"Did you talk to Cousins last night?"

"Nah. Didn't see him there."

"Do you remember what time you left?"

Fabry rubbed his hands together then ran his fingers through his hair. "I guess it was around two. I think it was. Yeah, that sounds 'bout right."

"And what did you do then?"

Fabry shot Peevey a wide-eyed look. "Why? What's goin' on? Why all these questions? What happened?"

"Where did you go when you left?"

"I came here, like I said. Had a few more drinks, maybe a bunch more, watched the TV 'til I fell asleep. Didn't wake up 'til just now when you came knockin'."

"Can anyone corroborate that? Did you call anyone? See anyone?"

"'Course not. It was two in the mornin'. What's goin' on? Somethin' happen to Cousins?"

Peevey glanced around the trailer. The furniture was old and well used, the carpet worn, but it looked clean and uncluttered. At least Fabry wasn't dirty. He was a drunk, but he wasn't a slob. "He was murdered outside Cozy's last night, Mr. Fabry."

Fabry nearly dropped his soda can. "Well, I'll be—"

"Mr. Fabry, do you know anything about that?"

Fabry's eyes were wide and his jaw hung nearly to his chest. "Wait a sec." He looked around the room, scanned the floor again. "You think I had somethin' to do with this? You think I killed him?"

"I don't think anything. Not yet, anyway. I'm just asking questions."

"Well, don't ask no more," Fabry said. "I ain't got nothin' to do with this." He stood, still a little wobbly from his bingeing last night. "And I ain't answerin' no more questions. I can't say he didn't have it comin'. Lord, everyone knows he had it comin', sooner or later. Man had more enemies than Hitler. But I didn't do it."

"Any ideas who did, then?"

Fabry rounded the coffee table and headed for the door. "You got a wife, girlfriend, Peevey? Maybe a sister?"

Peevey didn't say anything. Fabry was agitated and hungover, and he'd let him have his say and leave. He'd gotten what he came for anyway.

Fabry opened the door and squinted at Peevey. "A girlfriend. I bet you got a sweet little girlfriend. Maybe she done it. Now I'll ask you to leave my home."

"Very well." Peevey wanted to grab the drunk by his neck and pin him against the wall. Maybe take his baton to the back of Fabry's legs. But he didn't. The last thing he needed was for this piece of nothing to bring up accusations of brutality. As he left, he turned and nodded at Fabry. "Thanks for your time, Mr. Fabry. And just know, whoever murdered Cousins may be coming after you next. We'll be watching you just in case."

Chapter 25

THE CLOUDS HAD finally parted without giving up one drop of rain, and the sun hung high in the sky when Jim and Louisa walked onto the playground behind the Virginia Mills Elementary School. The playground was an open area backed by acres of fallow field, leaving the children and the school vulnerable to winds that blew across the landscape.

Recess was in full force when Jim and Louisa arrived, and children chased one another here and there, swung on swings, and huddled in small groups.

Two teachers stood duty over the children, standing close, talking intently to one another like two hens clucking out a continuous thread. They appeared barely aware of the near chaos playing out around them. When Jim approached, they both looked up. One, the taller and older of the two, smiled warmly and said, "Hi, you must be Jim Spencer and Louisa. I'm Mrs. Haversly, and this—" She motioned to the younger, shorter teacher, a woman with deep green eyes that bent into crescents when she smiled. "—is Mrs. Kellam." She shook Jim's hand then stuck out her hand to Louisa. "And you must be Louisa. I heard you were coming by to meet our children."

Louisa took her hand and shook it but didn't say anything. Jim wondered what she was thinking. On the way to the school he had explained where they were going and why. He figured she was an intelligent enough girl to understand the reasoning behind having her mingle with some children her own age. She seemed agreeable to it but not thrilled. He imagined in her own world— *her* family, *her* school, *her* church—that she was outgoing and friendly, but in a stranger's world she tended to shy away from crowds, preferring one-on-one interactions.

Mrs. Kellam offered Louisa her hand too. "Louisa, I teach third grade here. You see that group of girls over there?" She pointed to seven girls huddled by the corner of the building. "They're all third graders too. Why don't you come with me, and I'll introduce you."

She took Louisa's hand and led her away. Jim watched as they neared the group of girls and Mrs. Kellam made the introductions. The girls seemed to welcome Louisa openly, pulling her into their little circle.

"That seemed to go well," Mrs. Haversly said. "Chief Miller filled me on what happened. Has she remembered anything at all?"

"Just her name and birthday, and we can't even be sure they're right. No way to verify anything."

Mrs. Kellam came back and, rubbing her arms, said, "I think she'll be okay. That's a nice group of girls."

"Hopefully it triggers something for her," Mrs. Haversly said. "Poor girl. Ripped from her family and stuck in a strange place with no memory. Must be terribly frightening for her."

Jim watched Louisa interact with the girls as he small-talked with the two teachers. He noticed she kept glancing to her left and followed her eyes. There, in the breezeway between two wings of the building, sat a girl in a wheelchair, a blanket over her legs, reading a book.

"Who is that girl?" Jim said, motioning to the wheelchair-bound child.

"Audrey," Mrs. Kellam said. "I told her she didn't have to come outside, that it was too breezy, but she loves to read and watch the other kids play."

Mrs. Haversly leaned in a little, as if sharing something secretive. "She has muscular dystrophy, poor child. She's been in that chair most of her life and will never get out. Good mind, though, very smart girl."

Again Jim watched as Louisa glanced at Audrey and finally pulled away from the huddle of girls and headed toward the breezeway and the girl in the wheelchair. The two teachers had their back to the school and didn't notice what was unfolding.

"We have assistance for special needs children," Mrs. Haversly said. "But Audrey's parents don't want her getting any special attention; they want her engaged with the other children. And Audrey seems to thrive here."

"Do the kids accept her?" Jim asked, only half paying attention to Mrs. Haversly. His focus was on Louisa. She'd reached Audrey and stood beside her.

Mrs. Kellam cleared her throat. "At first they kept their distance. I don't think they knew quite how to treat her, but when they saw she was just like them, with the same likes and interests, only she was bound to a wheelchair, they warmed up to her."

Louisa knelt on the concrete next to Audrey's wheelchair and placed one hand on the girl's knee.

"It took some time," Mrs. Haversly said, but Jim barely noticed her talking, so intent was he on what was transpiring in the breezeway. "But…" Her voice faded away.

Louisa stood and pulled the blanket from Audrey's legs. The girl scooted herself to the edge of the seat, placed her feet on the ground, one at a time, and pushed up, as if standing on stilts for the first time. Mrs. Haversly was still going on, but Jim heard only the rhythm of her voice, no distinct words. Audrey stood on wobbly, bent legs at first then steadied herself. She looked at Louisa with wide eyes, and Louisa smiled and nodded. Like a newborn foal on untested legs, Audrey took one step then two then three. With each step her eyes and smile grew wider.

From the group of children by the corner of the building one of the girls screamed, "Mrs. Kellam! Audrey!"

Chapter 26

BEFORE JIM EVEN heard the car door open and shut, before he heard the knock on his front door, he knew who the visitor was. He'd been expecting him.

After the incident at Virginia Mills Elementary School—the *miracle*—he'd swept Louisa from the chaos and rushed her back to his home. He still couldn't believe the signals his own eyes had sent to his brain. The girl, the invalid, Audrey, had walked. She'd stood on her own two legs and walked. Mrs. Haversly said she hadn't walked ever, not one step, went right from the stroller to the wheelchair. Muscular dystrophy had ravaged her muscles and twisted her legs into unusable appendages. But she'd walked today. Oh, did she walk, laughing and smiling the whole time.

On the way home Jim kept asking Louisa what she'd done, how she'd healed Audrey, but the girl seemed to have no idea, kept saying she just prayed for her, that's all. She felt bad for Audrey, for the way her legs looked, the way they wouldn't work properly, so she prayed that God would give her legs strength.

When the knock came on the door, Jim's head was still spinning, his palms still sweaty. He'd heard about this kind of thing happening, but usually it was in some tent meeting in Florida and a sweaty, double-breasted suit was pacing the stage, waving his arms, and hollering for people to come forward and be healed, be healed, "be HEALED, I tell ya, in the name of a-Jaysus, be healed!" He heard of people going forward claiming a healing, maybe even walking on shaky legs a few steps, but reports were that it mostly didn't last. A surge of adrenaline, the power of persuasion, wishful thinking—whatever it was—gave the poor victim a temporary healing, a moment of freedom from his affliction, before sending him back into that dark dungeon a few short days or weeks later.

But this was different. He had no scientific or medical reason to think so, but Jim knew, just *knew*. Audrey's healing was complete; the girl could walk and would walk for the rest of her life.

The knock came again, and Jim knew who it was: Chief Miller, come calling to ask what all the hubbub at the school was about.

Jim looked at Louisa, sitting on the sofa, and smiled. "It'll be all right."

Amy was gone when they'd arrived home, and Jim purposely did not call her cell phone and fill her in on the events that had transpired. He'd rather tell her in person.

He stood and crossed the room, opened the door.

"Afternoon, Jim," Miller said. "Mind if I come in?"

"I'd act like I didn't know why you were here if I thought you'd buy it."

"But we all know why I'm here."

Jim opened the door wider and allowed Miller to enter. "Have a seat. We've been expecting you."

"I suppose you have." He smiled at Louisa. "Hello, Louisa. How are you?"

The girl smiled back. "Just fine, Chief."

Miller sat in the wingback chair and interlaced his fingers. "I was just at the Murphys' house. They'd just gotten back from taking Audrey to the doctor."

Neither Jim nor Louisa said a word. An uneasy feeling that felt a lot like guilt sat in Jim's gut, and he didn't like it. They'd done nothing wrong. Louisa had done nothing wrong. Praying for someone was not a crime. *Healing* someone was not a crime. It was a gift, a great, precious gift. Audrey's life would never be the same. A world of opportunity now awaited her.

Miller smoothed his mustache. "Mrs. Murphy said Doc Adams nearly fell over when he saw Audrey walk into the exam room."

"I bet he did."

"Said he couldn't explain it, but she seemed to be cured. I don't need to tell you that muscular dystrophy doesn't just go away."

"No, you don't. I'm too familiar with it," Jim said. When he was a kid, his cousin had muscular dystrophy. He'd died of respiratory failure at the age of nineteen, a slow, progressive death. "There's no cure."

"And yet we have Audrey here. Cured."

"Do you believe in faith healing?"

"You mean the laying on hands and speaking in tongues type?"

"Not exactly, but something like that."

Miller shrugged. "If you would have asked me that question yesterday, I would have told you no, that it's a bunch of hype. But now I'm not sure what to think."

"And that's why you're here."

"That's why I'm here."

They all sat and looked at each other for a few long uncomfortable moments. Finally, Miller stroked his mustache and said, "What's your side of the story, Louisa?"

Louisa shifted in her chair but never took her eyes, those brilliant blue eyes, from Miller. "I felt sorry for her, so I prayed for her."

Miller glanced at Jim than back to Louisa. "You prayed for her. That's it."

"Sure." She said it like there couldn't possibly be another explanation. Like praying for someone and then having that prayer answered instantaneously was the most common thing in the world, like she could pray for gold to fall from the sky and moments later the heavens would open and all the gold in Fort Knox would come plummeting down.

"And then Audrey just got up and walked," Miller said.

"She didn't need the wheelchair anymore."

"No, I suppose she didn't."

As if she sensed there was still some disbelief in Miller, she said, "With God anything is possible, Chief."

Miller tented his hands in front of his face. "I'm almost ready to believe that."

"So what happens now?" Jim said, still wrestling with that inexplicable feeling of guilt.

"Nothing. The Murphys are ecstatic. Audrey is giddy with joy, can't stop walking, even tried running outside."

"But..." Jim knew there was more to Miller's visit than just wanting to hear Louisa's side of the story. Why did her account even matter? Audrey's walking, even *running*, was proof enough.

Miller stood, smoothed his shirt. "The Murphys would like to keep this quiet, and frankly I agree."

"Gonna be kind of hard to keep it quiet, isn't it? People are going to notice something's different about Audrey. Then there's all the children at the school, the teachers."

"I know. Some we can't do anything about. But let's not go announcing to the world that we have a faith healer in our presence." He winked at Louisa. "Huh, kiddo? You know how folks can be. Before long we'll have pandemonium on our hands. People camping out on your lawn waiting for the miracle child to exit the house. We'll do our part to downplay it as much as possible, at least try to keep it contained. And you two, maybe just lay low for a couple days, huh?"

Jim winked at Louisa and smiled. "We can do that."

Chapter 27

HAILEY'S TRUCK STOP and Wayside Diner was an oasis of sodium and fluorescent lights along a dark and barren stretch of Interstate 81. Built in the 1970s, it hadn't changed much. The owners, Deb and Wayne Hailey, put little money back into their business, but the long-haul truckers and hungry locals who stopped there didn't seem to mind. The man—Mitch Albright— had eaten there twice, and both times his intestines had rebelled in a most unpleasant way. He would not set foot in the diner this time; that's not why he was here. He'd driven the five miles from Virginia Mills for two reasons: One, to fill his new vehicle, an unclaimed Explorer he'd pulled from the impound lot, with gas. And two, to teach Clint Efforts some respect.

Efforts was an over-the-road trucker who'd become a regular at Hailey's, stopping there for dinner, sleep, and a chance to use his big mouth on his way from Savannah, Georgia, to Bangor, Maine, and back again. He made the trip once a week, stopping at Hailey's two times. Mitch and Efforts had crossed paths a couple times, and each encounter had proved that Efforts was a blow-hard know-it-all who didn't respect anyone.

That was about to change.

The Wayside Diner, which sat adjacent to the truck stop, was wrapped in filmy plate-glass windows. Inside, the turquoise and white décor, the paneled walls, and the off-white linoleum were outdated, but for a place like Hailey's it remained accept-able. Efforts was in there, jawing away to the waitress, a thin-as-a-broom, attractive brunette who couldn't have been more than twenty. Efforts probably thought he was hitting on her, impressing her with his stories of the open road, life in a big rig. Mitch had heard Efforts had a wife and kids in Georgia but rarely saw them. Didn't respect his family either.

Mitch pulled the Explorer around the back of the diner to the gas pumps, filled the tank, paid with cash in the little convenience store, then parked where he could keep an eye on Efforts. He left the SUV running and heat flowing. When the sun dipped behind the horizon and darkness moved in, the temperature had plummeted into the forties.

A little after eleven Efforts finally finished his meal and attempts to woo the young waitress, dropped some money on the table, paid for his food at the register, and left the diner. Mitch watched with keen interest as the middle-aged trucker walked across the asphalt lot to where the rigs were parked. A line of them sat along the far end of the lot, parking lights glowing, generators humming, chrome glistening like polished silver under the dull sodium vapor light from the parking lot lamps. Inside each one a long-haul trucker took his mandatory six hours of rest before heading out again.

Efforts walked up to his blue and white International, picked at his teeth with a toothpick, glanced back at the diner as if waiting for the cute waitress to follow him to his cab, then turned his face toward the night sky. Mitch wondered what the bearded man was thinking, what thoughts of grandeur were swirling through his self-absorbed mind. A minute later Efforts looked back at the diner again then swung the driver's side door open and stepped up and into the truck, which had an extended cab, one of those jobs with a bed in the back. He sat behind the wheel for a few minutes, and Mitch wondered if he'd fire up the engine and pull out, but then he disappeared into the back.

Mitch waited, studied the other rigs to make sure no other truckers were watching, then shut off the Explorer's engine. He held tight another five minutes, during which time a couple exited the diner and, holding hands and laughing, made their way to their car. When all was clear, Mitch stepped out of the

Explorer and stole through the darkness to where the rigs were parked. The moon, darkened by a cloak of heavy cloud cover that had recently moved over the area, reflected little light, so the bulk of illumination came from the lot lamps. Mitch made sure to stay where the darkness was thickest and he was most concealed. He didn't need any do-gooder placing him at the scene of the crime at the time of death.

Where the rigs were parked, Mitch dashed to the rear of the trailers and crept from shadow to shadow. To his right were the trucks, seven in all; to his left was an open area of marshland and, beyond that, woods that covered the land for nearly a mile in each direction.

He came to Efforts's trailer and stopped. He'd have to get the trucker out of the rig somehow without causing too much of a disturbance. From his coat pocket he pulled a rolled-up ball cap and pulled it down tight on his head. Even if a neighboring trucker did hear people talking and look out a window, with the cap on and shadows between the trucks, it would be impossible to identify Mitch.

Mitch casually made his way along the length of the trailer to the rig, checked to make sure the knife was secure in his belt, and knocked on the door of the cab. Seconds later Efforts appeared. He was wearing jeans and a flannel shirt, no shoes.

"Yeah?" He did not look happy to see Mitch.

"Evening." Mitch kept his head low and pointed to his left. "There's something on the rear of your trailer you should see."

"What? What's this about?"

"I was driving by and noticed it; you have to see it for yourself."

"Can't it wait?"

"You really should see it now. You can't be on the road like this."

"Like what?"

"Your tires are unsafe."

"What's wrong with 'em?"

"You really should see for yourself."

Grumbling, Efforts slid to the back of the rig and a minute later reappeared with sneakers on. Climbing down from the cab, he said, "This better be good."

Mitch led the way to the rear of the trailer. Now they were out of view of any other driver or patron of the Wayside Diner. "Here." He bent low and pointed under the trailer to the inside rear tires. "See for yourself and tell me what you think."

Efforts pulled a flashlight from his shirt pocket and clicked it on. Bending at the waist, he pointed the light under the trailer. "What are you lookin' at? They're fine." He said it as though he thought Mitch to be an idiot, a blind idiot who didn't know the first thing about tires.

Reaching behind his back and feeling for the handle of the knife, Mitch said, "You don't see the inside tread?"

But before Efforts could answer, Mitch drove the knife just below the trucker's right shoulder blade, catching the lung and piercing it. With little more than a grunt Efforts jerked up in a spasmodic motion then collapsed to the asphalt. The flashlight dropped from his hand and rolled in an arc under the trailer. It came to rest with the beam on Efforts, a glowing solitary eye to witness the gruesome event.

Lying on his stomach, Efforts struggled for breath and tried to move. His body twitched and writhed. Mitch rolled the trucker over and stood over him. Efforts's mouth opened and closed like a fish taken from water and unable to pull air through its gills. His eyes were blazing and frantic. Mitch knelt beside him and put the knife to Efforts's throat. In the trucker's eyes he found what he had come for: respect. Satisfied that he'd accomplished his task, Mitch dragged the blade of the knife across the soft skin of Efforts's neck, taking what life was left.

With the temperature determined to dip over night, time of death would be difficult to predict.

Chapter 28

CHIEF DOUG MILLER sat at his kitchen table and sipped his coffee. He usually scanned the morning paper with his coffee, but this morning he had other things on his mind: little girls with no history and murdered bullies with too much history. His cell phone chimed, and he answered it on the second ring. It was Amber Steerwell, the department's morning dispatch officer.

"Morning, Chief."

"Amber, my morning is starting out on the fair end of okay, and I'm enjoying a very good cup of coffee. If this is gonna ruin that, I hope it can at least wait 'til I get in the office."

She hesitated. "It can't wait, sir."

Doug sighed and took another sip of coffee. "Okay, what'd'ya got?"

"Another murder."

He put the coffee mug down so hard some splashed out and over the edge, puddling around the base. The coffee didn't taste so good anymore. "Who?"

"Clint Efforts, truck driver from Savannah."

"Where?"

"Hailey's. Out on 81."

"I know where Hailey's is."

Doug closed his eyes and rubbed his temples. A dull ache had started behind his eyes.

"Sir?"

Keeping his eyes closed, he said, "What is it, Amber?"

"The coroner is en route and would like you to meet him there."

"Any officers on the scene?"

"Peevey, sir."

"Peevey. Yeah, okay. Tell 'em I'll be there in a few minutes."

"And sir?"

"Yes, Amber."

"Sorry to ruin your morning."

"And my coffee."

"Yes, sir."

He clicked off the phone and slipped it back into its belt holder. Another murder. Doug shook his head, picked up the mug, and drained the rest of the coffee in two swallows. It was lukewarm and bitter.

Grabbing his coat from the hook by the door, he left the house and climbed into his pickup. Hailey's was only fifteen minutes away, but first he'd stop at the gas station down the road and get a new coffee.

When he arrived at Hailey's, Frizetti was already there, talking to Peevey. A couple officers from the county's crime lab were there as well, snapping pictures and scanning the area for evidence. And Jackie Hale, the newspaper reporter, was there, hands in her pockets, standing by the police tape.

Frizetti met Doug at the truck, a coffee in one hand, a sandwich in the other.

"What'd'ya got, Jer?"

"Sausage and egg biscuit. Want a bite?"

Doug stared at him. "I mean with the body. Any connection to Cousins?"

"Follow me."

Hale stepped in front of Doug. "I'll have some questions for you when you're through, Chief."

"I have no doubt," Doug said, walking past her.

They went to where the body lay, behind the trailer of a big rig. It was a cold morning, and ribbons of steam rose from Doug's coffee. He sipped it slowly.

Frizetti wrapped his sandwich back in its paper and shoved the remains into his coat pocket. He squatted next to the body and lifted the shirt. "Look familiar?"

There, carved into the chest with the edge of a blade, was the letter *E*.

"Great," Doug said. "We got a wacko playing a game. Is this how he died?"

"Nope," Frizetti said, standing. "Stab wound in the back, just below the shoulder blade. I'm guessing it caught the lung. Then this." He tilted the chin upward, revealing a deep gash running from one angle of the jaw to the other.

"Time of death?"

Frizetti shrugged.

"Don't shrug, Jerry," Doug said. "It's your job to know."

Frizetti retrieved the sandwich from his pocket, unwrapped it, and took a bite. "I'm not a genie, Doug. It got cold last night, slows everything down."

"Give me your best guess. You can guess, can't you?"

Frizetti took another bite. He chewed thoughtfully, staring at the body of Clint Efforts. The gray, chalky skin of the trucker turned Doug's stomach. He'd seen his share of dead bodies over the past thirty years and never got used to it.

"Before midnight."

"And it was most likely after full dark. So what, between eight and midnight?"

Doug looked around and found Peevey by his patrol car, writing something on his steno pad. "Peevey."

Peevey looked up.

"Get over here."

Peevey jogged over. "Yeah, Chief."

"Who found the body?"

"Trucker from North Carolina, Art Spinotsky. Said he got up this morning and went around the back of his truck to check the tires, found Efforts there on the ground. I got his full statement and let him go. These truckers, you know, they run a tight—"

"I know. Did you talk to anyone else?"

"No. No one else here. They'd all pulled out before sunrise."

"Did this Spin-whatever guy know Efforts? Ever have a run-in with him?"

"No. Said he'd never even seen Efforts before."

Doug doubted that. These truckers knew each other, ran the same route every day or every other day and made the same stops. Hailey's was a popular rest spot.

"Okay. Get the surveillance footage, credit card receipts, talk to whoever was working last night. Find out who was here, how long they stayed, who ate what, how much they spent, who used the john, all of it. Then start questioning. Somebody had to see something. And see if anyone saw Fabry around here. I want a close eye on him."

Peevey nodded. "Yes, sir."

"And Peevey?"

"Chief?"

"Don't cut any corners, all right? I want this done by the book."

"Yes, sir."

Doug turned to Frizetti. "There's gonna be more."

"I guess we can hope he's spelling *red*."

"That's not funny, Jerry." He sipped at his coffee. "I hate this, you know?"

"The coffee? Where'd you get it?"

"No, this." Doug ran his finger in a circle above his head. "He's out there somewhere laughing at us. A couple of jerk small-town cops in way over their heads."

"You're the cop," Frizetti said. "I'm just a coroner."

"You used to be a cop."

"That was a long time ago. Why don't you go back to the office, see what you can do there, and I'll finish up here."

"Good enough. See ya 'round." He turned to leave.

"Let's hope not."

"Yeah," Doug said over his shoulder.

Jackie Hale was still at the tape, notepad and pen in hand. "Who is it?"

Doug crossed the police line and took a swig of coffee. "Clint Efforts, a trucker. Out-of-towner."

"Where's he from?"

"Georgia."

"Any connection with the Cousins murder?"

Doug looked at her and frowned. "I can't comment on that."

"That's not a denial."

"No comment."

"Was it another stabbing?"

Doug walked to his car, Jackie following. "Jackie, I don't want to cause any hysteria around here, you know what I mean?"

"I'm not out to cause hysteria, you know that. I'm out to just report the news."

At his truck Doug downed another sip of coffee and tossed the rest on the grass by the parking lot. He made a complete turn, taking in the parking lot, the diner, the gas station, the woods on either side and across 81. "Yes, a stabbing."

"Any distinguishing features?"

He opened the truck door. "No comment."

"Are you gonna do a press conference?"

One leg in the truck, Doug paused. "Now why would I want to do that when I have you to talk to?"

Hale smiled.

Doug sat in the truck and before shutting the door said, "You be good, Jackie. Handle this one with care."

He pulled the door closed and started the engine. The killer was out there, close, and yes, he was laughing at them. And Doug hated being laughed at.

Chapter 29

D ESPITE LOUISA'S BEST efforts to persuade him to make waffles and ice cream again, Jim made himself and Louisa a healthier breakfast of eggs and toast, even a sliced banana on the side. Louisa didn't complain but instead ate the meal like she hadn't filled her belly in days. When her plate was cleared and all the chocolate milk had been drained from her glass, she sat back, satisfied, and wiped her mouth with a napkin.

"Boy," Jim said, lifting his fork. "I'd never take you for an eggs and toast type. You came across more as a doughnuts and ice cream type."

"I love eggs, Mr. Jim," she said, still slightly out of breath from gulping the chocolate milk so quickly.

"You remember that?"

"I think so. Yes. Scrambled eggs are my favorite, with lots of cheese."

"Just the way I made them."

"I know. They were delicious. Thank you."

"You're very welcome. Did it bring back any other memories, anything else you like or don't like?" Jim hoped the trigger of one memory might start a chain reaction of recall. Maybe the memory of liking eggs would lead to the memory of who made those eggs for her or where they were eaten or even the store they were bought in.

"Well." Louisa glanced at the empty glass. "I really liked the chocolate milk too but can't remember if I've always liked it or just like it now."

Jim smiled. "Most kids like chocolate milk. Most grown-ups

too." He stood and set his plate in the sink. "Hey, Louisa, you wanna bring your plate over here and put it in the sink?"

She scooted from the seat and crossed the kitchen. "Mr. Jim, why doesn't Miss Amy ever eat breakfast with us?"

Jim leaned against the counter and crossed his arms. "You remember what I told you about our baby?"

Louisa looked up at him with those glistening blue eyes, and for a moment Jim felt like she was his daughter, that their baby had survived, and their daughter, their sweet, precious daughter, had grown up and was now standing before him. But as quickly as it came, the feeling waned.

"That she died," Louisa said.

A great sadness washed over Jim then, sadness for Amy and her pain of never being able to hold her child, cuddle her and feel the smoothness of her cheeks, smell her sweet breath; sadness for himself that he hadn't been able to meet his wife's deep needs; and sadness for Louisa, a girl lost, adrift in a great void with no direction, no past, and no future.

Tears pushed behind his eyes and tightened his throat. "Yes. She died." Jim swallowed hard and sniffed. "Well, ever since then Miss Amy hasn't quite been herself. She sleeps more and doesn't really like being around other people too much."

"But she can have another baby."

"Not according to the doctors, sweetie. She'll never have another baby, and even if she could, a new baby couldn't replace the one we lost."

Louisa seemed to mull that over for a few moments. Finally she said, "Miss Amy's like a broken doll, isn't she?"

The lump was there again in Jim's throat. "That's exactly right."

"But broken dolls can be fixed."

"Sometimes."

She tilted her head and looked him right in the eyes. "All the time if you believe."

Jim put his hand on Louisa's head and was about to speak when he was interrupted by a knock on the front door. He arched his eyebrows. "Wonder who that could be?"

Louisa shrugged. "Maybe the chief or Mr. Tucker again."

"Maybe."

Jim crossed the living room and opened the door. On the other side stood a middle-aged couple and a young girl about Louisa's size. Jim recognized her immediately as Audrey Murphy.

Audrey's father, a big man, with broad shoulders, a deep chest, and a full beard, stuck out his hand. "Jim Spencer?"

Jim took his hand and shook it. "Yes. You're the Murphys."

"I'm Jeff, and this is my wife, Shawna."

"And we know Audrey."

Louisa came to Jim's side.

Audrey's face lit up like fireworks, and she almost squealed. "That's her, Mom. That's Louisa."

Immediately Shawna Murphy began to cry and dropped to one knee, taking Louisa's hands in hers. She was a big woman, and her movements were anything but graceful. "We can't thank you enough, you sweet, precious child."

Not wanting to cause a scene, Jim stepped aside. "Would you folks like to come inside?"

Jeff Murphy helped his wife to her feet as she wiped tears and smeared makeup across her face. Jim shut the door behind them.

"We just wanted to stop by and say thank you," Jeff said. He smiled at Louisa. "You gave our daughter a whole new life."

Shawna Murphy was back on her knees, holding Louisa's hands. The tears flowed again, dragging mascara down her cheeks. "What did you do, dear? How did you do it?"

Jeff put a hand on his wife's shoulder. "Dear, please, don't interrogate the child."

"I'm not interrogating." She sniffed. "I just want to know, was it a miracle? Did you perform a miracle?"

Louisa glanced at Jim, obviously uncomfortable with the big woman's behavior and questioning.

Jeff must have noticed it too, because he reached for his wife's hand and pulled her to her feet. "Dear, please." He turned his head to Audrey. "Honey, get your mother a tissue, please."

While Audrey dug through her mother's purse, Shawna sniffed again and said, "Will it last? Will she be…whole the rest of her life?"

Louisa glanced at Jim again then shrugged. "I don't know."

Tears flowed from Shawna's eyes more heavily now. Audrey handed her a tissue. "You don't know? Well, what did you do?"

"I just prayed for Audrey."

"You just prayed for her? That's it?"

Jeff wrapped an arm around Shawna's shoulders and rubbed her arm. "Easy, dear."

"Jeff," she said, "we've been praying for years and nothing has happened."

"I know, but it's happened now."

"Folks," Jim said. He saw the need to change the subject, steer the conversation in a new direction. "We're all thrilled about Audrey's healing, but Chief Miller asked me to keep this quiet for a while…for obvious reasons."

"He spoke to us, and we agreed to do the same," Jeff said. He frowned and glanced at his wife. "But he was too late."

"Well, it's a miracle, Jeffrey," Shawna said, dabbing at her eyes with the tissue. "My little girl can walk and run. How do you expect me to keep that quiet? What was I supposed to tell our family, our neighbors, the people at church?"

Jeff patted his wife's arm. "We should get going, dear. Leave these folk alone now." Then to Jim, "We'll do our best to not bring any more attention to it."

"Thanks," Jim said.

Audrey stepped forward and hugged Louisa. "Thank you for praying for me."

Louisa smiled and touched the girl's face. "You're welcome, Audrey."

The Murphys left, and Jim closed the door behind them and leaned against it, shut his eyes.

"What's wrong, Mr. Jim?" Louisa said.

Jim opened his eyes. "Nothing." But even as he said the word, he couldn't help but feel as though a low-hanging line of black thunderclouds hovered just over the horizon, promising to bring trouble.

Chapter 30

ALICIA SIMPSON PUNCHED out at the Food Lion and headed for her car. Outside, the sky was gray and furrowed clouds threatened rain, and not just a steady, soaking rain either, but thunderstorms, violent and forceful. The town of Virginia Mills would soon be under attack by some of nature's most vicious weaponry. In the distance, miles away, thunder growled and rumbled across the heavens. A flash of silent lightning stuttered through the western sky. Seconds later more thunder barked, this time louder and closer.

Alicia hurried to her car and got in as the first raindrop landed on the windshield, leaving a quarter-sized splash of water. Then another hit, and another, and within moments the car was under a barrage of marble-sized raindrops.

Alicia started the car and pulled out of the parking lot. Her mind was not on getting home for dinner; it was on Derek and her need to get out of the relationship. No longer did she feel as though she needed him, as though she wasn't good enough for any other man. No longer did she loathe herself for who she was or what she had to offer. Instead she hated that she'd stayed with him for so long, endured his verbal insults and violence.

On the drive home, while the wipers pushed bucketfuls of water from the windshield and the car endured a constant shelling from above, she thought of how she would tell him, how she would confront him. Or did she need to confront him at all? He hadn't been home in a few days. She could just pack her things and leave, not tell him or anyone else where she'd gone.

But where would she go that he couldn't find her? She had no one but her mother, and she was too far away and too preoccupied with her new boyfriend. Without Derek she was alone, an island in the middle of a vast ocean. Derek was her only connection to the world and, despite his abuse and faults, the only one who cared about her. Her life minus Derek would be safer and less painful, yes, but it would be as empty as a used beer can, drained and tossed to the side without thought.

Alicia stopped at a red traffic signal and massaged the steering wheel. Rain beat on the windshield with such fury the wipers could barely keep up. Droplets, the size of grapes now, pelted the roof and hood of the car like the thick, stubby fingers of giants drumming out a death beat.

For Alicia it seemed there was a choice to make: endure the physical pain of Derek's temper, or live with the emotional pain of having no one to share life with.

But what was it that girl had said? Her image and voice had been in Alicia's thoughts since their encounter in the diner. She'd touched Alicia's hand, such a soft, tender touch too, so honest and simple, so sincere.

"You're never alone. He's with you."

She was speaking of God. Alicia hadn't thought of God, but for some reason she believed the girl, believed her so thoroughly and so genuinely that at that moment she would have given her own life for the truth of the girl's words.

Alicia had run the conversation through her mind a thousand times since it happened just two days ago. She'd said that God didn't know about her pain. She didn't believe the words, not really, but said them to convince herself of their truth. Because if God knew of her pain, why did He let her endure it? Why did He leave her in this nightmare with no method of escape?

"He does know, and He hurts with you. He loves you more than you could ever love Him back."

The traffic signal turned green, and Alicia pressed the

accelerator. The tires slipped a little on the wet asphalt then found purchase.

Alicia believed the girl's words; she had no reason not to. But still the questions were there. If God loved her so much, why didn't He intervene? Why didn't He stop Derek from hurting her?

"You're so full of light. You shine goodness and kindness. God wants to use you. He will use you. His love will heal your sores and give you new life and purpose. But you need to let Him ... because if you don't ... "

And that's when the girl's countenance had changed, when the confusion had clouded her eyes. And Alicia had had a vision, a horrible, grisly image, so quick she could hardly tell what it was, but she knew Derek was there, and blood, lots of blood, and a murderer. She still wasn't sure if the vision was a revelation or just her brain playing tricks, conjuring images from various points in her life and, under stress, splicing them together. But she was sure the girl had seen the same thing and that's what darkened her face and pierced her eyes with such astonishment. How it was possible, Alicia had no idea, but evidently the girl had seen what Alicia saw.

Lightning jumped and streaked from the clouds above in a brilliant flash, followed immediately by a crack of thunder as loud as a mortar shell.

Alicia made the final turn into the apartment complex's parking lot and found a space near the front door.

Once inside the foyer area she shook the excess water from her jacket and hair and headed upstairs to the apartment. She still didn't know what she'd do or where she'd go, but she was sure she had to do something.

At the door the key slipped into the lock and turned without resistance. It was already unlocked. Derek was home. Alicia turned the knob and pushed open the door, her muscles involuntarily tensing.

Derek was on the sofa, feet propped on the coffee table, a bowl of popcorn on his lap and a book in his hands. He looked at her, chewed, swallowed. "Hey, I was waiting for you to come home."

He put the bowl and book on the table, stood, and crossed the room. Alicia tensed even more, an involuntary response.

"What's the matter with you?" Derek said. "You act like you're not happy to see me."

Alicia made herself move and shut the door. The sound of the dead latch engaging the strike plate was like a gunshot in the silence of the apartment. "Where've you been?"

"What do you mean, where've I been? I've been working. We're short this week, and I've been pulling a double shift." He wrapped his arms around her and began kissing her cheek, her nose, her jawline.

She pushed away from him and took a step back, her heart thumping, fear suddenly blooming inside her.

Derek's eyes widened. "What's wrong with you? We haven't been together in days. We have catching up to do."

He came at her, but she put her hands up in a defensive position. "Derek, I don't want to." Her voice quivered, and she hated the way she sounded, so small and pathetic.

He stopped as if she'd struck him. "Don't want to? Why ever not? Didn't you miss me?"

When she didn't answer immediately, he clenched his fists and worked his jaw muscles. "Are you seeing someone else while I'm working?"

"No. It's nothing like that. It's just...it's—"

"It's what, Alicia? Geez, what, you picked up a stutter or something? Spit it out."

"You hear about that little girl, the one from the fire at Jake Tucker's?" She didn't know why she was telling him about her encounter with Louisa. Maybe she thought there was some humanity in him that would understand, some sense of decency that would actually listen to her, and maybe, just maybe, she could even tell him about her vision, warn him. How silly would that be?

"Yes, of course I know about her."

"I met her the other day at the Red Wing. She…she—" Alicia wrung her hands together nervously; sweat wet her chin and upper lip. "Well, she touched me, touched my hand, and, I don't know, I've changed. Somehow."

Derek scrunched up his face as if she'd spoken the whole thing in some little-known African tribal dialect. "What are you talking about? Have you been doing drugs? You better not be doing drugs."

"No. She's special. The girl is." Alicia's heart was in her mouth now. She knew she had to tell him, but she also knew he wouldn't want to hear it. She glanced at the door to make sure it was indeed unlocked. If he showed any aggression at all, she'd make a run for the door and bolt for the stairwell.

"What do you mean special? Like retarded?"

She shook her head. "No, not like that. She talked about God and—"

"Did you get religious on me? Is that it? Now you want to be pure and save yourself?" He smirked. "Too late for that, isn't it?"

Alicia took a deep breath and blurted out the words. "Derek, I want to leave, get my own place."

The silence between them was so profound and so deadening she swore Derek could hear her heart pounding behind its bony cage, knocking like an inmate intent on breaking free. And she also swore that she could hear his heart pumping, forcing blood through his veins, through that bulging one that ran down the middle of his forehead when he got angry.

Derek took a step forward then back. He opened his hands and splayed his fingers, shook his head. "I can't believe this. After all I've done, all I've contributed to this relationship, you're just going to walk away from it. Drop me like some bad habit you have to break now that you're all holy."

"It's not like that, Derek. You know you have a problem. I know you're working on it, but I can't stay here anymore. I don't feel safe."

Derek tilted his head to the side and studied her like she was an alien species discovered for the first time. "You don't feel safe around me? I'd give my life to protect you. You know that. How could you feel safer around anyone else?"

Alicia turned her face down, not wanting to make eye contact lest her body language be misinterpreted as a challenge. "Can you keep me safe from yourself?"

Derek blew out a breath. "Boy, that hit me right where it counts." He opened his arms, tilted his head to the side, and smiled. "Come here. I'm sorry."

Alicia hesitated. His mood swing was unsettling.

He took a step forward. "Come here, baby. We can work this out."

Still she hesitated and hated that she didn't know whether to trust him or not, this man she'd lived with for over two years, this man she'd given herself to in so many ways.

Finally she stepped forward.

Derek's hand moved so quick and hard she never saw it coming. But she felt it. His knuckles connected with her cheekbone and impacted with such force it spun her around and knocked her to her hands and knees. Dazed, confused, her mind spinning wildly, Alicia tried to scramble away, to move her arms and legs, but Derek was right there, grabbing a handful of hair.

He lifted her up as if she weighed no more than a bag of kitchen garbage and tossed her onto the sofa.

Alicia coiled into a ball, protecting her head and face with her arms. She felt Derek's presence near her, heard his slightly labored breathing.

He grabbed the back of her head with an open hand and shoved her face into a sofa pillow, held it there.

"You're just going to walk out on everything we've worked for? Huh?" Derek's voice was tight as if he spoke through clenched teeth. "We've come so far in our relationship. I was going to marry you."

Alicia tried to draw in a breath, but the pillow blocked both her nose and mouth. Panic clutched her. Derek was going to kill her, suffocate her right there on their sofa. She squirmed and fought against his pressure, but he leaned his weight against her and held her still. He was much too heavy and too strong for her to resist. Fear shot through her like multiple lightning strikes. She swung her hands behind her, hoping to land a blow anywhere on Derek's body, hoping to somehow, someway break his grip or at least snap him out of his rage.

But Derek only pressed her face harder into the pillow. His mouth was next to her ear now, his voice low and gravelly. "You really think you could make it on your own? You're nothing without me. You know that, don't you?"

Alicia's mind went foggy, like a morning mist had moved in and dulled any sliver of a coherent thought. Death was looming, and all she could think of was the girl's eyes, those blue eyes, and the feel of her tiny touch on Alicia's hand.

"You're never alone. He's with you."

Through the haze and instinctual panic, while she flailed her arms and reflexively struggled to breath, Alicia was able to conjure one thought, one plea consisting of only three words: *God, help me!*

Derek said something, but Alicia could no longer make out the words; they were nothing more than jumbled gibberish. Her brain was shutting down from lack of oxygen. She had no idea she could hold her breath for so long.

Suddenly the pillow came away from her face, and like a rush of cold water on the hottest of days air—precious air—flooded her nose and mouth. Her lungs heaved, respirations came fast and furious, and dizziness spun the room as oxygen-rich blood once again saturated her brain.

She sat back in the sofa, panting, sweat matting her hair to her face and forehead. Then she began to shake and cry.

"Oh, stop it," Derek said. "What? Did you think I was going to kill you?"

She didn't say anything. She couldn't. Exhaustion had rendered her useless, as limp as an understuffed doll. She could only sit on the sofa and pull air into her lungs and hope and pray that Derek's rage had been satisfied and his tirade was over.

Derek began to pace around the room. He now looked more like a man in thought, contemplating the solution to some complex problem, than a beast circling its prey before devouring it. Gone was the tension that had held his body rigid before. Gone was the crimson flush from his cheeks, the vein from his forehead.

Alicia relaxed just a little.

Outside, thunder boomed, but it was distant now. The storm was moving on, seeking fresh ground to pummel with lightning and rain.

Finally Derek stopped in front of her and wagged his finger. "I'm not going to take this. I don't deserve this. You know what? You don't have to leave. I'm leaving. You can have the place. Let's see you try to pay the rent with your lousy check from the store."

He approached her and jabbed his finger into her chest. "And don't you talk to anyone about our business. I can really mess you up; you know that. And no one will even know."

With that he grabbed his jacket and left the apartment. The concussion of the door slamming behind him was louder than a thunderclap and made Alicia jump. Silence ruled the apartment then, as heavy and dense as fog.

Alicia could hear the remnants of the storm moving out of town—a muted rumble of thunder, a smattering of raindrops.

But inside her the storm that had raged so fiercely earlier was gone, and she felt something she hadn't felt in years, maybe in her entire lifetime.

Peace.

Chapter 31

AMY SAT IN the middle of the nursery floor, an open cardboard box in front of her. Tears rolled down her cheeks, but she did nothing to swipe them away. She wanted to cry; she needed to. Following the miscarriage she'd cried for days, but then the tears had stopped flowing, just dried up like a shallow creek bed in the middle of summer's heat. The pain hadn't stopped, though, no, it had only gone underground, tunneling to such depths she thought she'd never find her way out. But then the girl showed up, Louisa, and touched her. Amy had no idea what that touch had done or what the strange little girl's intentions were, but a splinter of light was there now, piercing the darkness like a laser. It wasn't much, but it was a sliver of hope where before there was none.

Amy still didn't feel completely comfortable with Louisa in the house. The girl's behavior was odd and sometimes disconcerting, but there was something about her that Amy couldn't deny being attracted to. The whole thing with Audrey, for example, was both intriguing and confusing. When Jim told Amy what had happened, she'd almost started crying. On one level it was completely unbelievable; on another, given what she'd seen and felt from Louisa firsthand, it was totally plausible and didn't surprise her one bit. She still didn't know what to make of it, though. She didn't know whether she should be in awe of this girl in her house or in fear of her.

Amy was glad that Jim had spent most of the day with her, playing games, going to the library to pick up books, and making supper with her. Right now they were downstairs watching a DVD while the casserole they'd made baked in the oven. As for herself, Amy had spent the day as she usually did lately, taking naps, wandering the house, halfheartedly making attempts at various chores. Now some strange surge of energy or resignation had led her to this room, to tackle the worst job of all.

Amy tilted the box toward her and stared at the emptiness. She had to pack up the things in the room, it was time, but she couldn't bring herself to do it. She felt like she'd be closing the book on any memory or hope she had of her daughter, her precious little girl. The daughter she was going to rock to sleep and cuddle. The daughter whose poopy diapers she would change. The daughter she—

"What are you doing, hon?"

Jim stood in the doorway, leaning against the jamb, hands in his pockets.

Amy shrugged, sighed. She looked around the room. "I was going to start packing this stuff up, but..." She let her words trail off.

"But you can't bring yourself to do it."

"I guess."

Jim stepped into the room and leaned against the wall.

Lifting her face to him, Amy felt the sudden urge to stand and fall into his arms. Jim had been so patient with her, so loving and caring. He'd given her space, as much as she'd needed and probably more than she'd deserved.

She stayed on the floor and said, "Do you ever think about her?"

He was quiet a moment while he bowed his head and furrowed his brow. "I think about her all the time. Every day."

"What do you think about?"

He shrugged. "I don't know. All kinds of stuff. Who she would have looked more like—"

"She would have had your high cheekbones; it's a dominant characteristic in your family."

"Maybe. What her laugh would have sounded like—"

"Goodness. I hope she would have had your laugh and not my guffaw."

He smiled. "I like your laugh. I used to love to make you laugh just so I could hear it."

"Really? I haven't laughed in such a long time."

"You'll laugh. It takes time to find it again."

"What else?"

"I wonder if she would have been athletic or not—"

"Like you. I'm all left feet."

"Naturally gifted in anything—"

"Gifted with words, like you."

"If she would have had a good sense of humor—"

"Like you. You have a great sense of humor."

Jim stopped and tilted his head at her. "Wait a minute. I'm seeing a pattern here. She would have been like you in so many ways. She'd have your smile, your blue eyes. Your quick wit and gentle touch. Your way with people. My word, you can wrap anyone around your finger in a matter of minutes."

"It worked with you."

"Well, with me it took days, not minutes."

Amy almost laughed, and it felt liberating. For the first time she felt an ember of joy.

She reached for a stuffed rabbit on a shelf of the bookcase, stroked its soft fur and ran her fingers over its ear. "I miss her."

"I know."

She looked around the room and let her eyes fall on the rocker with the cushions decorated with colorful farm animals. "I used to rock in that chair and rub my belly while I talked to her."

"What did you talk about?"

"Anything and everything. I told her about you and me and how we met, that crazy amusement park with the haunted house."

"You were so claustrophobic."

"I've always been claustrophobic, but I did it because I didn't want you to think I was afraid…and I wanted to spend the time with you."

"What else?"

"I'd tell her all about your books and our house and the things we'd do together."

Amy paused and swallowed hard. "I miss her so much. I miss that time I had with her."

"I know." Jim's voice cracked. Amy looked at him and saw tears puddling in his eyes.

"You do too."

He nodded as his Adam's apple bobbed slowly.

"I feel so robbed, so cheated. I've been so angry with God." Tears began to flow again. "How could He give us a baby, give us such hope and the promise of such a bright and happy future, then just rip it all away? What kind of a God does that?"

Despite her attempts to shore up her own faith and quell the anger, it was still there, simmering just below the surface, occasionally bubbling up and materializing as questions, like arrows, aimed heavenward.

Tears pushed out of Jim's eyes and tracked down his cheeks. He lifted a hand and wiped them away, sniffed. Amy wanted him to say something, anything, to give her a reason for her pain. But Jim was asking questions too; she knew he was.

"I don't know," he said. "I just don't know. But I do know we can get through this. We can still have a life, still have children. There are other ways."

Amy reached for Jim's hand and placed it on her lap. "You really want to be a daddy, don't you?"

"More than anything."

She smiled at him through her own tears. "Well, we better put it on the fast track; you're gonna be forty in a couple months, old man."

Amy was suddenly startled by a figure appearing in the

doorway. Louisa stood there, arms at her side, eyes wide and confused as she looked around the room. Finally her eyes landed on the empty box in the middle of the floor.

"Miss Amy," she said. "What are you doing?"

Amy ran her hand over her cheeks and did her best to compose herself. "I was just going to put some of this stuff away. I think it's time."

Louisa entered the room and turned in a slow circle, taking in every piece of furniture, every stuffed animal, every baby toy, every article of clothing. "But it's perfect just the way it is."

Then she walked to Jim and took his hand. She reached out and touched his cheek with her finger. "Mr. Jim, you've been crying. Why?"

"This room has a lot of memories, Louisa. It's hard to put it all away."

She shrugged. "Then don't." Then, looking at Amy with sad eyes, she said, "And Miss Amy, don't be angry at God for taking your little girl. She was His to start with. I'm sure He's taking great care of her."

Unbidden, the tears came again. Louisa leaned into Jim, and Amy couldn't push away the thought that entered her mind: *father and daughter.*

Chapter 32

THERE WERE A few things that Mitch Albright hated. One, of course, was disrespect. It was to him as noxious as the putrid odor of rotting flesh or as irritating as his body covered with a blistered, oozing poison ivy rash. Another was hunger. The feeling of an empty stomach, the growling, the rumbling, he loathed it. That is why he never ate whole meals. Instead he grazed throughout the day. A sandwich at eleven, a handful of potato chips at twelve, some pasta salad here, a bowl of ice cream there. And last, Mitch hated the smell of body odor. It reeked of filth and poor hygiene, burned in his nostrils as if someone had shoved a blowtorch up his nose.

For reason of these three things Mitch paid careful attention to keep the Appletons well fed and gave them ample opportunity to shower, toilet, and properly groom themselves. He even supplied them with clean clothes and underwear each day.

At seven in the evening he descended the basement steps carrying a tray of food. He would once again eat dinner with his captives. He would have liked to call them guests, but since it was their home and they were unable to freely move about, *guests* didn't seem appropriate. As he approached their room, both Bob and Clare stood. At first neither offered a greeting, which bothered him slightly, but when he set the tray carrying three plates of food on the table, Clare said, "Did you make that?"

Mitch stared at the plates. On two of them sat Salisbury steak, green beans, and a heaping pile of mashed potatoes. On the other, his plate, was only the steak. He'd have the potatoes and beans later. "I wish I could say I did, but I'm not much of a cook myself. These were frozen, and all I had to do was pop them in the microwave."

Clare smiled politely. "Oh. Well, I'm sure it'll be delicious."

Mitch wasn't sure if he noted disappointment or disdain in her voice or not. He had the momentary urge to take the food back upstairs and let the Appletons go hungry for the night but decided against it. The thought of their stomachs complaining made his twist and tighten.

After arranging three place settings at the small table, he unlocked the door to the makeshift room and let the Appletons out. They sat at the table without saying a word.

Mitch took his chair and lifted his fork but stopped when Clare cleared her throat. She smiled again and said, "Would you mind terribly if Bob said grace before we ate?"

The request was odd as Mitch had never said grace before, had never even recognized that there was a God let alone one that took enough interest in the earth's peons to provide them with food. But he admired Clare Appleton for her faith, so he agreed.

She nodded at Bob, and they both bowed their heads.

"Father," Bob said, "thank You for Your presence even here in this basement. Thank You for the food before us and for the hands that prepared it." He paused briefly, long enough, though, that it caused Mitch to wonder about the old farmer's sincerity. Bob continued, "And Father, meet Mitch where he is and show him Your love. Amen."

Both Bob and Clare picked up their forks and began eating. Mitch, however, hesitated. Bob's prayer had affected him in a way he never foresaw happening. He wasn't sure what to think or feel. Should he be offended? Irritated? Or impressed? Those words "show him Your love" rumbled around in his head like a marble in a bucket. He'd never heard them before and wasn't sure even what they meant.

"Mitch." Clare's voice pulled Mitch out of his thoughts.

He looked at her blankly, forgetting about the plate in front of him, the hastily constructed room in the basement, his mission.

"Aren't you going to eat?" she asked. "It's very good." He noticed she had nearly finished her portion already.

Mitch shook his head. "Uh, yes. Yes, I am." He lifted the fork and cut off a piece of steak.

"Do you mind me asking where you're from originally?" Clare said.

Mitch chewed and swallowed. "North Carolina."

"Whereabouts?" Bob said.

He almost told them then decided against it. As much as he disliked thinking about it, Mitch knew when all this was done, he'd have to take care of the Appletons, but still he didn't like the idea of them knowing too many details. "Nowhere special."

Clare set her fork on the plate and blotted her mouth with the napkin. "Did you enjoy your childhood?"

"No." The answer came so quickly it surprised even him.

"No?" Bob's eyes were wide, as if he expected more of an answer. "Why not?"

Mitch pushed the plate away and sat back in the chair. He didn't want to sulk in front of the Appletons, but talk of his childhood always brought on the storm clouds. "My father was...harsh."

"Harsh as in strict?" Clare said. "Or harsh as in violent?"

"He..." Mitch stopped. He didn't want to go back to that time. If and when he did, it would be on his terms, not at the prompting of someone else. Those were memories he'd filed away in a special place in his brain, a place under lock and key, only to be retrieved when he needed to stoke the fires of his hatred.

Abruptly Mitch stood, knocking the chair over behind him. "I think that's all for tonight."

"I'm sorry," Clare said.

"Don't be. I think our dinner is over." He waited for them to stand. "In your room now."

Clare apologized again, but Mitch brushed her off. When he had secured both of them in the room and locked the door, he lowered his eyes to the floor. "I'll be back later to allow you time in the bathroom." Then he turned and left. At the top of the steps he rested his forehead on the door and grabbed the knob. His hand trembled. Memories of his childhood had stirred that familiar yet toxic blend of fear and rage within him.

He looked at his watch. A few more hours and he'd lock another piece in his puzzle. And take another step toward freedom.

Chapter 33

JIM STARTLED AWAKE and rolled onto his back. He'd thought he heard the front door click open. Or was it part of a dream he'd already forgotten? He was in that muddled state between sleep and reality where he couldn't tell what had happened in the tangible world and what had merely been part of his dream. Mercurial thoughts ran through his head, coming and going like quicksilver on a pane of glass. He stared at the ceiling, waiting a few seconds for his head to clear and his thoughts to congeal. Moonlight sneaked around the edges of the blinds, dusting the room in a bluish glow.

There, another click, this one definitely the sound of a door's latch engaging the strike plate. Spider legs tingled up and down Jim's limbs, crawled up the back of his neck, and tightened his scalp.

Jim sat up and rubbed his face, combed his fingers through his hair. Beside him, Amy slept. The digital clock read 11:48. He'd only been asleep for half an hour. He held his breath and listened. The house was as quiet as a ghost ship afloat in the middle of a watery graveyard. But that didn't mean someone wasn't in the house. The living room carpet would surely muffle the sound of footsteps.

Pushing back the covers, he slid his legs off the bed and stood, careful not to disturb Amy. Jim didn't own a gun, but now he wished he did. Instead he kept a golf club by his bed, a five iron. He picked it up and gripped it with both hands, holding it like a baseball bat over his shoulder.

Opening the bedroom door, he stopped to listen again, straining to hear even the slightest moan from the floorboards or the steady whisper of breathing. He'd made no noise himself crossing the bedroom and pulling open the door, so he was confident he still held the advantage of surprise.

Once in the hallway Jim stayed close to the wall. He knew where the creaky floorboards were and that they were all located in the center of the hallway. Near the wall, where the boards were more securely fastened, they were as solid as the day they were nailed into place.

From outside he heard a man's voice, then a woman's. Their tone was more urgent than conversational but muffled enough that Jim couldn't make out what they were saying. He took more steps down the hallway, rounded a short corner, and ducked into his office. Louisa's cot was empty, the covers pushed down to the foot of the mattress. Over by the wall and the window overlooking the front yard sat his desk, a solid oak antique partners piece Amy had bought him when they made the decision he should write full-time. The venetian blinds were turned slightly down so the moonlight filtering through cast long stripes of gray-blue light over the desk.

The voices were there again. A woman sounded like she was pleading.

Quickly, still holding the club over his shoulder, Jim crossed the room and rounded the desk. Reaching the window, he pushed the blinds aside. Four people stood on the front lawn, two adults and two children. Moonlight cast long shadows from their feet but hid their faces in a shroud of darkness. From his vantage point on the second floor the whole scene had an eerie other-worldly look to it, as if this was still part of his dream and he was hovering above some alien landscape watching the inhabit-ants below interact.

One of the children was a girl; he could see that much. Smallish, with blonde hair. It was Louisa; there was no doubt about it. The click of the door must have been her leaving the house. The other three were a man, a woman, and a young boy. As Jim watched, gripping the club, the man, a tall, thin guy, reached out for Louisa's hand.

"No," Jim whispered. His muscles tensed, heart beat faster.

The man took Louisa's hand in hers, and all four of them turned for an SUV parked in the driveway.

Jim let the blinds fall back into place and made a dash for the hallway. His mind raced, heart pounded like the hooves of a thoroughbred coming down the home stretch. Thoughts, disjointed and jumbled, clamored through his head.

Who were the people who had arrived at his home at such a late hour?

What business did they have being here?

Why had Louisa so willingly gone with them?

Were they her parents? Her lost family? Come to finally take her home?

Jim bounded down the steps two at a time. He didn't care now how much noise he made now.

If it was Louisa's family, why had she not hugged them? Fallen into her father's arms?

Why would she leave without saying good-bye?

In the living room he made a straight line for the front door and threw it open.

There was only one explanation that made any kind of sense: They were here to kidnap Louisa. The miracle kid was now a wanted commodity.

Jim stepped out onto the front concrete landing just as the foursome reached the SUV.

He raised the five iron off his shoulder, cocked like a homerun leader ready to swing for the fence, and made steps toward the driveway. "Hey, stop." The idea of a physical confrontation had pushed adrenaline into his bloodstream at such a rate that it tied his tongue in a knot and twisted his throat.

The man halted dead in his tracks and turned around, surprise widening his eyes. Jim couldn't tell if it was surprise at his sudden appearance or at the threat of a golf club wielded by a mad man with wild hair and clenched teeth. Whatever the reason, the man took a step toward the car while at the same time wrapping his arm around the woman and the other child, a boy about the same age as Louisa.

Jim reached them quicker than he thought he could and stopped in front of them, ready to helicopter the club in a wide arc if needed.

Louisa looked at him with calm eyes and lifted a hand as if to stop him with some unseen force. "Wait, Mr. Jim. Wait."

The man had stepped in front of the woman and child and now crouched in a defensive position.

Louisa took a step forward. "It's okay, Mr. Jim. They came for help."

Confused, Jim lowered the club to his shoulder. He noticed he was panting and must have looked a sight, barging out of the house in his pajamas cocking a five iron like it was a battle-ax. The look on Louisa's face and the fear in the man's and woman's eyes told him they meant no ill intent.

"I'm sorry," Jim said, his voice trembling. "Sorry." He turned to the man. "Who are you?"

The man relaxed and stood to his full height. One hand remained on his wife's arm. "I'm Ed Swanson, and this is my wife, Rosa…" Rosa was short and slight and appeared to be of Hispanic ethnicity. "And this is our son Eddie, and—" He opened the back passenger side door of the SUV. "—our son Armand."

"We call him Army," Eddie said.

Army slumped in a car seat. He looked to be about four or five but was as frail as a leafless branch. His pale skin stretched taut over every angle of his face. He looked at Jim with hollow eyes, forced a smile, and gave a weak wave.

Ed reached his hand into the vehicle and held his son's hand.

"Armand developed a brain tumor when he was just a year old. Every doctor we've been to has said it's inoperable. He's had so much treatment already, but the tumor is still there. They say he shouldn't be alive. But he's a fighter."

Eddie piped up again. "That's why we call him Army."

Rosa glanced at Louisa. "We hear from Eddie what this child did for the Murphy girl."

"And you want her to heal your son." Jim got it now.

"Yes," Rosa said. "We come at night so no one sees, and maybe the girl can pray for Armand. She come here to us before we even knock."

Jim's heart ached for the Swansons, for their life of living every day not knowing if it would be their last with the son they'd nursed for five years. But Louisa wasn't some circus sideshow, doing tricks and performing miracles under the cover of darkness. "Folks, I don't know if this—"

Louisa put her hand on Jim's arm. Her touch was so light and soft he barely noticed it. "Mr. Jim, I want to. I want to pray for Army."

Jim shifted his eyes between Louisa and the Swansons. Chief Miller said to lie low. The last thing he needed was a mob on his lawn at midnight, all of them clamoring for a touch from the miracle girl. Finally he knelt before Louisa. "You don't have to do this, you know."

"I know. But I want to. God can help Army."

"Well, okay then." Jim still wasn't sold on the idea, but it wasn't his place to stop the girl. He had no right to demand she not pray for a sick and dying boy.

Louisa stepped close to the SUV and rested her hand on Armand's leg. The boy placed his skeletal hand on top of hers and smiled again. Then Louisa closed her eyes and moved her lips in silent petition. The Swansons each bowed their heads. Rosa began crying. Ed pulled her close and kissed the top of her head.

When she was finished, Louisa removed her hand from Armand's leg and sighed.

Rosa cupped the girl's face in her olive hands and kissed her forehead repeatedly while rambling something in Spanish.

After they said their thank-yous and multiple apologies for coming at that time of night, the Swansons piled back into their SUV and pulled away.

Jim put his hand on Louisa's shoulder. "And all you did was pray?"

She nodded. "Army needs a lot of prayers."

"Yeah, I suppose he does. You ready to go back inside?" He slid his hand off her shoulder and turned for the house.

"Wait. Mr. Jim?"

"Yes?"

"There's something I have to tell you."

"Out here? It's kind of cold. Can we go inside?"

"I remembered something else."

Intrigued, Jim faced Louisa and bent at the waist. "You remembered something?"

"Uh-huh."

"Are you gonna keep me in suspense?"

"I have a brother."

Chapter 34

ITCH ALBRIGHT SAT in his car outside the home of Buck Petrosky. It was a humble home, an aging trailer situated on three acres of cleared and wooded land, tucked between two fields on Swamp Road. The trailer sat a good hundred yards off the road, concealed by a stand of mature oaks and maples. If one wasn't looking for the property, one would blow right by it without knowing it was even inhabited.

And that's the way Buck liked it.

Mitch knew more about Buck than he should have. He knew he had a criminal record, that he'd been busted for battery and disorderly conduct all on the same night. He knew Buck lived alone, that he worked for a tree service company and had a mouth as big and ignorant as a battering ram. Buck Petrosky was the kind of guy who drove a pickup with oversized knobby tires and flew the Confederate flag with pride. He was never seen in public without his greasy and stained ball cap, the camouflage one with the rebel crossbars on it. He was usually unkempt, unshaven, and smelled like body odor and stale nicotine. In Mitch's estimation Buck was as barrel-chested as a grizzly and ugly as a moose.

It was time to teach him some respect.

When the sun had properly set and the only light for miles was the tiny glowing windows of Buck's trailer, Mitch grabbed his flashlight, slipped out of the Explorer, and walked down the gravel lane to the trailer. Buck's truck was parked beside the trailer, dark and quiet. The light in one of the windows flickered erratically. The big man was watching television.

Above, the sky was cloudless and the moon almost full. Its light filtered down through the trees and cast the whole clearing in a dusty light. Shadows were irregular and fuzzy as if they were some undiscovered variety of mold growing along the ground, creeping closer to the trailer.

As silently as a ghost hovers above the ground, Mitch moved to the back door. A set of five wooden steps ascended to a small landing outside the door, and at the bottom of the steps, on a square of laid brick, were two metal trash cans, their lids held tight with bungee cord. Slowly, so as not to make a sound, Mitch unhooked one of the cords. He reached behind him and retrieved his knife, held it in his right hand, then kicked one of the cans over. Quickly he ducked behind the landing and crouched low to the ground, concealed by the moldy shadow of the trailer.

The trailer creaked and seemed to shift. Heavy footsteps thumped along the plywood flooring. Then the back light flicked on, one of those yellow bulbs that dispelled the light of the moon and colored the area with a mustardy glow, and the door opened. All was quiet for a moment except for Buck's labored breathing. Eventually Buck cursed and shut the door again. For a moment Mitch thought he'd lost his opportunity and would have to try another approach, but then, just seconds later, the door opened again and Buck stepped out onto the landing, mumbling something about shooting the raccoons. His heavy boots clunked down the steps, and with a grunt, he bent at the waist to pick up the can and the garbage that had spilled out of it.

When he stood erect again, pulling the can upright with him, Mitch moved. As quickly and quietly as a stealth striker, he approached Buck from behind and thrust the knife into the big man's lower back, in the area of the right kidney.

Buck grunted and arched his back, stumbled forward, knocked the trash can over again, but caught himself on the trailer's siding. Mitch had the knife in his hand, its blade red with smeared blood.

He followed Buck and, without a word, lunged at him. Buck

turned just as Mitch made his move and windmilled his arm, catching Mitch's and nearly knocking the knife out of his hand.

Buck's eyes widened to the size of eggs and his lips pulled back in a primal snarl. He growled like a bear whose wounds were not fatal and only managed to anger him.

For a few long seconds the two men faced each other, neither saying a word, crouched and ready to strike. Mitch knew the longer the standoff went on, the more advantage he had. Buck's wound had to be bleeding, weakening the beast of a man by the second. Besides, the internal damage alone would put him down eventually. But Mitch didn't want to have to wait. He wanted to end this quickly and teach Buck Petrosky what it was like to respect someone who held your life in his hands.

Mitch took a quick step left, and Buck flinched and stepped right, wincing with pain. His movements were slow and clumsy.

In the light of the yellow bulb, dewy sweat glistened on Buck's face. He wiped it from his eyes and pumped his fists like he was pounding on an imaginary tabletop. "Well, c'mon," he yelled. "Do it."

But Mitch didn't. He faked left again, and again Buck countered, winced, and faltered. Mitch knew if he attacked head-on he'd have to deal with Buck's tree-limb arms, but there was no other way. He'd lost the element of surprise. He also knew Buck's reactions were slow; he'd seen that by the way the big man responded to his fakes. That might be all the advantage he needed. In one quick motion, as if he'd practiced it a thousand times, Mitch faked left; Buck hesitated then dodged right, winced, grunted, cursed. Mitch moved right with him, throwing his prey off balance; Buck swung his arms, but the movement was clumsy and slow. Mitch ducked, lunged, and found the fat around Buck's abdomen with the blade of the knife. He pushed until the blade would go no farther.

Buck's breath escaped his mouth with a forced squeal. He

doubled over, the bulk of his weight now on Mitch's upper back and shoulders.

Mitch removed the knife and stepped back, following his move quickly with another lunge, another stab, another squeal from Buck. But this time Mitch didn't pull the knife out immediately. Instead he threw his weight against Buck and pushed him backward. Buck's foot caught on a brick, sending him to the ground. He landed with a wet grunt that sounded like the snort of a bull right after being shot between the eyes. The smell of body odor was all around Mitch, and he thought he'd retch at any moment. His stomach tightened and throbbed. He needed to finish this fast.

Wasting no time, Mitch pounced on Buck and stabbed him again. And again. But the big man wasn't dying. With each thrust of the knife he would grunt and curse and writhe weakly beneath Mitch's weight, but that final blow had yet to come.

Eventually, after three or four more stabs (Mitch wasn't counting) Buck stopped moving. He looked at Mitch with tired eyes and cleared his throat. Then, before Mitch could move, Buck spit a wad of phlegm that hit Mitch along the side of the neck. A second later Buck's eyes went blank and stared at the starry sky as if expecting one of them to fall and take some cosmic revenge on his murderer.

Slowly, panting heavily, blood sticking the knife's hilt to his palm, Mitch stood and stretched his back. His muscles ached, and his legs suddenly felt weak enough to give out on him. He sat on a nearby picnic table and shut his eyes, drew in air slowly, and swallowed the bile at the back of his throat. His gut reaction was to just leave, to chalk this up as a miss and get out of there. Buck had shown no respect; he hadn't learned a thing about power and the ability to control life and death. Mitch sought respect, and even in the throes of death with the gates wide open, he hadn't found it here. But in the end, after a few moments to clear his mind and catch his breath, he decided he had to use Buck. It would be disrespectful to his mission not to.

The thought of approaching Buck again gagged Mitch, but he had to keep going, get it over with. Things had deteriorated enough, and the longer he spent here, the greater his chance of doing something the crime scene guys would find.

Chapter 35

ALICIA WAS BUSY washing the few dishes she'd dirtied the previous night when a knock at the door startled her. She wasn't expecting company this early on a Thursday morning. Who would she expect? She had no friends and no family in the area, at least none who would bother to visit her.

Walking to the door, she had the feeling that it was Derek come to finish what he'd started yesterday. Maybe finish her for good.

He wouldn't go that far, of course. She knew he wouldn't. It would ruin his life forever. It was one thing to beat on your girlfriend, knock her around a bit and later apologize; it was a whole different animal to murder someone. Derek didn't have that in him. He had a short fuse and his engine often ran high when provoked, but it had a governor. There were limits to his temper. Still, the idea of Derek visiting her to settle any score put her nerves on alert and got her heart beating faster.

The knock came again, this time more persistent. Alicia peered through the peephole. Her intuition was correct. Derek stood in the hall, looking side to side.

He leaned in close to the door, glanced at the peephole. "Alicia." His voice was not strained, and there wasn't a hint of irritation in it. "Ali, baby, open up. I know you're home."

Alicia said nothing.

"I know you're there." He put his eye to the peephole. "You see me, don't you." He looked right, then left. "Look, I'm sorry, okay. I lost it. I can't believe I did that again."

It was the same story every time. He couldn't control himself. He's so sorry; he doesn't know why he does that kind of stuff.

He's working on it, just give him one more chance, just one more. He loves her so much and hates himself when he hurts her.

Still Alicia watched but said nothing.

"Look," Derek said. "I understand, okay. I get where you are. You hate me, heck, you loathe me and don't want anything to do with me. I get it. But let me at least say my piece face-to-face. Please?"

Finally she said, "Say it now. I can see you."

"But I can't see you. I'll stay out here. I promise. I won't come inside. Just open the door. C'mon, Ali."

"Don't call me Ali anymore." It was a term of endearment only he called her, and she no longer wanted that name associated with him.

"Fine. Alicia. Please?"

Alicia didn't know why, but for some reason she felt she had to open the door to him. She wanted nothing to do with Derek and would be perfectly happy if she never saw him again, but there was still a part of her that cared for him, maybe felt sorry for him. That vision was still bothering her too, the one with the murderer, and she felt on some deep level, deeper than her mere emotions, that it was her duty to warn him, whether he took her seriously or not.

Slowly, and as carefully as she would put thread through a poison-tipped needle, she slid the chain from the groove and let it hang by the door.

She put her hand on the knob. "Derek, I swear, if you take one step over this threshold, I'll scream like I'm dying and the neighbors will hear. Someone will pick up the phone. You know they will."

"Okay, okay. I promise I won't. Just open the door."

Alicia turned the knob and listened for the latch to disengage. She had one foot blocking the door in case Derek tried to shove his way in. It angered her that she didn't trust him, that she felt so threatened by him.

Inch by inch she moved her foot and opened the door against it. When it was open about eight inches, she peeked around the edge and said, "Back up a few feet."

"Oh, c'mon, Ali—Alicia—I'm not doing anything but standing here."

"Back up or I'm closing the door again."

He took one step back. "There. Okay?"

Alicia opened the door a little more but kept her foot firmly against it. "That's it. I'm not opening it anymore."

"Fine," Derek said. He reached for something on the floor, something out of Alicia's line of sight, and she almost slammed the door shut in a panic. But what he lifted was no weapon; it was a bouquet of the most gorgeous red roses, twelve of them. "Here. These are for you." He handed them to her.

As much as she loved roses, and as much as she appreciated his effort, Alicia shook her head. "I don't want them." She couldn't believe she was turning them down.

"Alicia, don't be like that. It's nothing but a peace offering."

"No. I don't want them."

Derek tossed the flowers on the floor by the door. "Fine. There they are if you change your mind." His jaw muscles flexed rhythmically. She could tell her refusal had stung, and his inner demon was awakening.

"You should leave now," she said.

Derek shook his head emphatically. "No, there's something I have to say to you." He drew in a deep breath. "I love you, Alicia. I know I don't act like it all the time. I know I have my faults that I'm working on. I was going to ask you to marry me, you know. I was." He shook his head and dropped his mouth at the corners. "I won't beg you, though. No way. If you can't love me back, well, then…there it is."

And there it was. The declaration Alicia had wanted to hear

from Derek for going on two years. And now it meant nothing to her. My, how drastically she'd changed in just a couple days.

"Derek, listen to me. I had a vision—"

"A what?"

"A vision, you know, like a daydream or something. You were in it, and you...you were in danger."

"Okay."

"Serious danger."

"Okay."

"Someone was killing you."

"Okay. And what should I do with this information?"

"Do with it whatever you want. I had to tell you."

"You didn't have to."

She looked at the floor, uncomfortable with where she knew he'd take the conversation. "No, I didn't. I just thought you should know."

"Did you see the guy killing me?" His tone implied he was mocking her.

"No. It was dark, and his face was hidden."

"Ah, the old hidden face thing. Clever. And this vision, it wouldn't have anything to do with this new religious side of you, would it?"

"No." She hesitated. Did it? "Maybe. Yes, it probably does."

Derek snorted. "I think I can take care of myself."

"I know you can. Just be careful."

"I'm always careful." He turned and walked away, down the hall until Alicia could hear his footsteps no more.

She closed the door, locked it, and leaned her back against it. Only then, when she was safely behind the locked door, did she begin to shake. She shut her eyes only to find the vision there again. The man holding the gun was still shadowed, but a beam of light now stretched across his abdomen and chest. He wore a flannel shirt and an old field jacket. His arms were raised as if holding a rifle. He pointed the gun at Derek, who had his back to Alicia, but she could tell it was clearly him. The gun discharged, muzzle flashed, and the concussion brought Alicia out of the dark. Her eyes flipped open and hands groped at the door. She was dizzy and disoriented. Suddenly nauseous.

Above everything else that had happened the past few days, everything with the girl, with Derek, with those cursed roses on the other side of the door and his sad declaration of twisted love, Alicia was sure of one thing: Derek was going to die.

Chapter 36

JIM WAS OUTSIDE edging the grass in the front yard when Doug Miller's patrol car pulled into the driveway. The engine cut off, and Miller exited the car, adjusted his utility belt, and removed his sunglasses. He crossed the yard with even, determined steps.

Jim stopped the motor of the edger and leaned on the handle. "Morning, Chief."

Miller didn't smile, nor did he return Jim's greeting. "I thought we agreed the two of you would lie low for a while."

Jim knew what he was talking about. Army Swanson. He had no expectation the Swansons would keep their lips buttoned, even if Army wasn't healed. Sooner or later word would get out, and then it would get to Miller, and then Miller would pay a visit. And here he was.

"We did agree."

"Then why is it that I was just at Judd's to fill up the cruiser and he told me about the miracle that happened to the Swanson boy?"

"Miracle?"

"Yeah, miracle. They had him at the doctor's first thing this morning. Had an MRI done, and guess what?"

Jim held his breath and shrugged.

"No tumor. It's gone. The boy is fine, walking around, laughing with his brother, eating like a horse."

"Wow."

"Wow? That's it? You know anything about this?"

Jim nodded. "Yeah. I mean, yes, I do. The Swansons were here last night, late. I was in bed and heard them out here talking to Louisa. I came out and the boy was in the car, looked terrible,

175

poor kid. They wanted Louisa to pray for him, like she had the Murphy girl. That's it. How could I tell her no?"

Miller brushed his hand over his mustache. "Well, half of Virginia Mills knows now. People are talking. I can feel trouble coming."

"Chief," Jim said, "how could I tell her not to pray for a sick kid, a kid that looked like he was hanging on by a thread? And all she did was pray for him. That's it. No theatrics. And look at the boy, healed, really *alive*, like he was born again."

Miller nodded slowly. "Yeah. Born again. I'd sure like to find out where this girl came from and how she got here."

"She remembered something else."

"And when were you gonna tell me?"

Jim glanced at the house. Louisa was inside watching a movie. "She asked me not to."

"Why?"

"She wouldn't say. I think she feels safe here, you know? I'm not so sure she wants to be found."

Again Miller stroked his mustache. "Well, let's have it."

"She has a brother."

His eyebrows arched, pushing his forehead into a washboard of lines. "Older, younger?"

"Nope. Just that. She has a brother."

Rubbing his chin thoughtfully, Miller said, "Well, it's not much, but it's something. Now we're looking for a family of at least four."

"I'm hoping this memory will trigger others." But it wasn't what he was hoping at all, not really. Louisa was turning out to be the daughter Jim had expected, the daughter that was so suddenly taken from him. Whatever void was there after the miscarriage was now being filled by this mystery girl and her odd but powerful gift.

The radio attached to Miller's shoulder beeped and a woman's voice came on. "Chief, we have another 10-55. 437 Swamp Road."

Miller closed his eyes, hesitated, then depressed the talk button. "Okay, Brenda. Hang on a sec."

"10-4."

Miller pointed his finger at Jim as he backpedaled. "You tell me if she remembers anything else, okay?"

"I will."

"And call me if you wind up with a lawn full of sick people lookin' for holy medicine."

Jim nodded and waved him off.

Miller turned and hurried back to the car. He sat behind the closed door for only a minute, jotting notes and talking into his radio, then brought the cruiser's engine to life and didn't waste any time getting out of the driveway.

Chapter 37

AMY SPENCER NEEDED to get out of the house. She'd spent the last two months sheltering herself from the world, afraid of the stares, the pitiful eyes, the empty condolences. She didn't want people's sympathy. She didn't want their empty smiles and limp hugs. She wanted to be left alone.

Her days had been passed by puttering around the house, watching television, starting one book after another but never finishing any of them, and spending way too much time in bed. Nights passed slowly as sleep avoided her like she was a deadly contagion. And the days moved even slower.

But now Amy felt like she had to get out of the house; she had to be around the daily activity of humanity. She had to see people, and not just by observing the movement of human forms, but really *see* them. And she needed to clear her head and think through what was happening in her home.

This girl, Louisa, had done it again—healed someone. It was surreal, like something Amy had read in a book or seen in some made-for-TV movie. She didn't know what to make of the girl anymore. Jim seemed to buy everything she was doing. He was amazed by her. But Amy was just bewildered. She had nothing against people getting healed, goodness no, especially children, but the way it was happening, it was just bizarre. But every day, and with every interaction, Amy found herself growing fonder of Louisa. It was evident the girl had a kind heart and meant no one harm. And if she was completely honest with herself, Amy would have to admit that Louisa was everything she'd wanted in a daughter. In fact, she couldn't get the child out of her mind.

Amy steered the car into a parking space in front of the Food

Lion and shut off the engine. Suddenly her heart began to hammer in her chest and her breathing went shallow. Maybe she wasn't ready for this. There was no guarantee she'd even see anyone she knew, but if she did, there would be that moment of awkwardness while the other person determined what etiquette called for. It had been several months; do they mention the miscarriage, how they haven't seen her around, or do they ignore the whole tragedy and act like the last few months never happened?

Pulling the key from the ignition and dropping it in her purse, Amy drew in a deep breath and exhaled a short prayer.

It shouldn't have, but that prayer stopped her breath and brought tears to her eyes. She used to pray all the time, just short sentence prayers peppered throughout her day, keeping her in constant contact with God. But since the miscarriage she hadn't prayed at all. God seemed distant and disinterested, as if there was suddenly a great gulf between Him and her and neither of them bothered to do anything about it. There were times when she'd inch up to the precipice of that chasm and peer over the edge, measure the distance between the two sides, but that was as far as it ever went. But thinking about praying is not the same as doing it.

She said her prayer again—*God, help me do this*—and noticed the way it made her feel: like returning home to a loving family and a house full of memories after being away in a dark and vile land for way too long.

Still feeling a bit uneasy, but not nearly as much as she had just a few seconds ago, Amy exited the car and entered the store. Strangely, surprising even her, emotions washed over her like a wave striking an unsuspecting beachcomber. Again her eyes flooded with tears. She had to duck into the medicine aisle and compose herself.

She'd been away for so long, tucked away in her own sorrow and shame, that she'd forgotten what it was like to live, to drive a car, to shop, to interact with people. To do the everyday things she'd done for so many years and had taken for granted.

Jim, poor Jim, had done the duties for both of them. He'd been the one gathering the groceries and cleaning the house. He'd made most of the meals, washed and folded the laundry, taken care of the yard. And never once had he complained or pointed a vindictive finger at her. Never once had he scolded her or turned away in disappointment. He'd loved her just the same as he always had, maybe more so.

From down the aisle Amy heard a woman say her name. Rachel Rucci pushed a cart toward her. Latched onto the cart was a baby carrier covered by a pink and white knitted blanket.

Amy tensed. She didn't know if she was ready to see Rachel's baby yet. She and Rachel attended the same church and had been pregnant at the same time. Amy had been due next January and Rachel in August. Jim had told Amy that Rachel had a girl, named her Sabrina, but Amy couldn't force herself to visit her after the birth. The joy and excitement they'd once shared over their pregnancies was gone.

Rachel pulled her cart up alongside Amy's. "Hi, Amy. Wow, it's nice to see you out and about."

Amy smiled. "Yeah, I thought it was time to come out of the cave and see what the world looked like again."

Rachel touched Amy's shoulder. Her eyes softened with deep concern. "How are you?"

Shrugging, Amy said, "Better. I'm out of the house, a huge step."

"Been a rough time for you and Jim, hasn't it?"

"Yeah, but we're getting through it."

"I tried calling you. I wanted to visit."

And she had. Amy received the messages Rachel had left on their machine but never called back. She didn't feel like talking to acquaintances, didn't feel like having to act like she was interested in their condolences.

"I know." Amy's eyes dropped to the floor. "Sorry about that."

Rachel patted Amy's hand. "Hey, I understand. It's great to see you now."

"And this is Sabrina?" Amy said, motioning toward the baby carrier.

Rachel's face lit up. "Yes." She pulled back the blanket. The baby was asleep, tucked into the carrier with a blanket and her pacifier. She clearly had her mother's black hair and olive complexion and her father's button nose and wide mouth. "Sabrina Avery."

"She's beautiful," Amy said. She reached in and stroked the baby's soft cheek with her finger. "Really beautiful. How is she doing for you?"

"Oh, it's been a struggle, colicky every night until after midnight. She screams like there is no tomorrow for four, five hours straight." She stopped abruptly, as if realizing whom she was talking to. "But I shouldn't complain," she said hastily, awkwardly.

Tears pushed on the back of Amy's eyes. She would have given everything to hear a baby cry in her home, to hold her and nurse her and cuddle her to sleep.

"We miss you at church," Rachel said. "I hope you will feel up to coming back soon."

A week ago, even a couple days ago, Amy would have winced at the idea. Jim would have told her she needed to get out, talk to people, and she would have refused and hidden in her home. But now she heard herself say, "Maybe this Sunday."

Rachel smiled and gave Amy a hug. "Wonderful. I can't wait." She pulled back but kept her hands on Amy's shoulders. In her eyes was a look of concern and care. "Are you sure you're okay? What you went through—"

"I'm fine," Amy said quickly. "At least, I'm improving. Getting better. Every day a little better."

"I've thought about you every day and have been praying for

you. The whole church has." She glanced at her watch. "Oh, I gotta run. I hope to see you Sunday, okay?"

"Okay."

Amy watched Rachel hurry away, pushing the cart that carried her precious Sabrina. She pulled the blanket over the carrier, adjusting it several times as if the baby beneath it was made of the finest wax and would melt if touched by a single molecule of light.

A knot formed in Amy's throat then, because for the first time in eight weeks she realized she was not jealous of another mother given a privilege she would never enjoy. How could that be? It seemed...unnatural.

A chill fell over her, dampening her mood. If she wasn't depressed and she wasn't jealous, then what was she? Who was she?

And the future scrolled out before her, as blank of direction or answers as Louisa's.

Chapter 38

DOUG MILLER STEERED his patrol car down the path leading to the trailer home of Buck Petrosky. Gravel popped under the tires and kicked up against the undercarriage of the Crown Vic. He knew Buck, big guy, rough around the edges, had a few run-ins with various locals over the last several years. Real loner type, liked to be left alone. It was when he wasn't left alone that Buck got irritated, and when he got irritated, his attitude ramped up, and before long his mouth started running, then his fists started flying.

Buck was arrested not long ago, spent a few nights in the county jail. A slap on the wrist for someone like Petrosky. Doug was sure the big guy had made plenty of enemies over the years, but right now there was only one he was interested in.

He pulled around the back of the trailer, next to Frizetti's Expedition, Officer Radcliffe's cruiser, and the county's CSU van. Frizetti met him at his car, coffee in hand. He sipped at it slowly and looked around at the woods surrounding the clearing. Tall, straight oaks, maples, and sycamores rose from the ground and formed a leafy canopy overhead. At ground level the woods was thick and deep, a myriad of trunks and underbrush until it all just faded into a collage of greens and browns and grays.

"You ever get the feeling you're being watched at one of these scenes?" Frizetti said.

Doug shut the car door and pulled on his latex gloves. "Haven't been at too many of these scenes until now."

"Third vic in as many days. Fits with the other two."

"How is it you keep beating me to them? What, are you just sitting around waiting for the phone to ring?"

"Something like that. Tough job."

Doug nodded at the Expedition. "You driving your wife's car today?"

"Mine's in the shop. Engine's been ticking like it has Tourette's."

Officer Radcliffe emerged from the other side of the trailer and approached Doug.

"Talk to me, Radcliffe. What gives?"

"Neighbor from down the road, Guy Sellers, said he came here to buy a chain saw off Petrosky. Said they'd agreed on it last week, Petrosky needed to clean it up, put a new chain on it. When he got here, he found Petrosky, called us."

"Where's Sellers now?"

"Sent him home after I questioned him," Radcliffe said.

The three men walked to where Buck's body lay by a couple overturned metal trash cans.

"Multiple stab wounds," Frizetti said. "One to the back, four to the abdomen."

"Big Buck wasn't going without a fight, huh?"

Radcliffe pointed to the disturbed ground, a broken clay planter, blood streaked on the trailer's siding. "Everything says there was a struggle."

"I wouldn't expect anything less from Buck," Doug said. To one of the crime scene officers he said, "You guys find anything interesting yet?"

The officer, Price, shook her head. "Nope. A few boot marks over by the picnic bench and here in the garden, but they're only partials, not enough to go anywhere with."

"You find anything, I want to know about it yesterday."

"Yes, sir."

Frizetti drew a long, slow sip of his coffee. "There's another letter too."

"I'm guessing it doesn't spell red."

"Take a look."

Doug squatted next to the body and lifted the shirt. The letter S was carved into Buck's chest. With the other two victims the letters were carved with such precision and delicacy it looked to be the work of a surgeon, but with Buck the work was anything but exact. The wound went deep and ran off course on the curves. This was done in haste and with a fair amount of aggression.

Standing and pulling off the gloves, Doug said, "Did you know Buck?"

Frizetti regarded the clearing again. "No, and I don't think Buck wanted to be known."

Buck's eyes were still open, staring blankly at the sky as if watching for a rare and reclusive bird to fly overhead and not wanting to blink in case he missed it. Frizetti should be disgusted by the sight of a corpse, especially one that had laid out all night in the elements and had turned a pale shade of gray/green clay. But he wasn't.

To Radcliffe he said, "Call Peevey and tell him he's gonna need to come in early. I want him on this. You too. Talk to the neighbors, find out if they saw or heard anything out of the ordinary last night. And have Peevey pay Jude Fabry a visit."

Peevey reported yesterday that Fabry had indeed been at Hailey's two nights ago when Clint Efforts was killed. Deb Hailey said the two men sat near each other but didn't talk, at least not that she'd noticed. Peevey paid Fabry a visit but got nothing out of him. Yes, he was at Hailey's, he likes their burgers, but he never talked to Efforts, never even met him. But still, that's two murders and at both Fabry was present.

"Jude Fabry?" Radcliffe said.

"Write it down."

Radcliffe slipped a pen from his shirt pocket and scribbled on the palm of his hand.

"What're you doing?" Doug asked.

"Writing it down. Jude Fabry. F-a-b-r-y?"

"Yes. You can't afford paper?"

Radcliffe motioned toward his squad car. "Left my pad in the Vic, don't want to forget this."

"And you can't remember a name from here to there?"

"You said to write it down."

Doug shook his head and walked away. He needed to call Amber and have her pull Tangier and Little from first shift and move them to second. Three murders in three nights meant there was a good chance this maniac would hit again tonight. He wanted as much manpower available as possible.

As he left the property, Jackie Hale got out of car and stood in front of Doug's truck. He stopped and rolled down his window.

"Nice of you to stop," she said, coming around to the driver's side.

"Here's your info, Jackie. Buck Petrosky. Yes, stabbed again. Can't comment on anything else."

"Why not?"

"Ongoing investigation. You know the game."

She frowned and lowered her notepad. "And you always play by the rules?"

"Not always." He winked and rolled his window back up.

Chapter 39

MITCH SAT IN a wingback chair in the Appletons' living room, sipping from a can of Red Bull. He didn't dislike coffee, but when he needed a jolt, he turned to energy drinks. Red Bull was his drink of choice. Lightning in a can.

The Appletons had a simple yet elegant style. The house was furnished with antique pieces in every room, most likely items that had been passed down from generation to generation, kept in the family to preserve the memories that had attached themselves to each chair and sofa and table. Good memories too, unlike Mitch's.

The house was not over-cluttered, which Mitch appreciated. He disliked clutter very much, so hard on the eyes. No, the Appletons seemed to know how to evoke a feeling of peace and rest and security in the way they decorated. The sparseness of wall hangings and knick-knacks, the placement of furniture, the conservative use of color, it all served to calm and soothe, to lower the heart rate and ease the tension.

And Mitch needed all the help he could recruit. The ordeal at Petrosky's had left a cloud over him, dark and looming. It wasn't satisfying, not like the others. The beast had put up such a fight; his will to survive was incredible. The look in those eyes right before they blanked was not one of respect; they were full of spite and hatred, even pig-headed defiance. And though he'd showered two times since then, Mitch could still feel the wad of phlegm along the side of his neck as it oozed down to his collarbone, and he could still smell the stench of the brute on him.

Concentrating on work last night had been tough, knowing what he knew, doing what he'd done. Several times his supervisor had asked him if he was feeling all right, and every time Mitch had responded that he was fine, just dealing with some personal issues. He'd be fine, though. Then he couldn't sleep when he got home. Usually he read for an hour or so then slept for a good four hours. That's all he needed. He'd been blessed with a race-horse metabolism, the only good thing his father ever gave him.

Taking another sip of his drink, Mitch stood and crossed the room to where a framed photo of Secretariat hung on the wall above a lamp with a carved gooseneck base. He ran his fingers over the horse's neck, the withers, to the shoulder tracing the outline of the bulky muscles. "To run with no restraint," he said to the picture, "and gain the respect of the world. What was it like?"

His mood darkened further, those gray and furrowed clouds looming closer. They had to be respecting him by now—three murders in three nights—so why didn't he feel any satisfaction?

He didn't want to face the Appletons; they would sense his dreary mood. Their respect had not been easy to earn, they were people of high quality and standing, but he'd managed to do it. He could tell by the way they looked at him, spoke to him, con-ducted themselves in his presence. And that's why he'd keep them alive as long as he could.

But now he needed to feed them. It was earlier than usual, but there was something he had to do that required a change in his daily schedule. He was tempted to forgo their evening meal, avoid their watchful and knowing eyes, but the thought of them going hungry, of their stomachs growling in emptiness, turned his own stomach and itched his nerves. No, he had to feed them something. During an earlier inspection of the refriger-ator and freezer he'd noticed three frozen pizzas. In the kitchen he removed one and stuck it in the oven. It wasn't much, but it would have to do.

The pizza was hot and smelled delicious when Mitch opened the door to the Appletons' room and handed it to Bob on a pottery platter. He gave Clare two napkins and two cans of Coke he'd found in the refrigerator. He'd precut the pizza into eight symmetrical pieces.

The Appletons politely thanked him, but when he turned to leave, Clare said, "Won't you be joining us?"

Mitch stopped but didn't turn around. He knew if he did those eyes of hers would pierce his skin and see directly into his heart. She'd see the wounds there, and the pride, and the evil. She'd see his desperate need for respect. His demand for it. Because he deserved it. His childhood had been a living hell, and he'd not only survived it but also went on to make something of himself, really be something. Still no one gave him the respect he'd earned and now was entitled to.

"I'll be eating upstairs today. Alone."

"Whatever for?" she said. "A man who eats alone is missing out on the best part of the meal."

The philosopher had emerged in her again.

Mitch hesitated, looked at his feet. "I'm not much in the mood for company today."

"You're upset." It wasn't a question. She'd made a declaration based on the obvious. "Oh, dear. I hope we haven't done anything to upset you."

He could hear the uncertainty in her voice, the fear even. She was a brave woman, braver than any he'd known, but she wasn't fearless.

Slowly, as if he were a disfigured man revealing for the first time his true identity to a woman who had given him her love without ever seeing his face, Mitch turned and faced Clare. He felt exposed to her, naked, vulnerable. It was an uncomfortable feeling and one he hadn't felt in years, not since he left his father and their horror-filled home when he was seventeen.

She stared at him, and he knew instinctively that she was studying him, dissecting his soul and finding the layers upon layers of scar tissue there.

"You've done nothing," he finally said.

Her head tilted to one side as she gazed at him with sad eyes. "You've been deeply wounded, haven't you?"

Bob stood in the background, still holding the pizza, swaying slowly from side to side as if he'd topple over at any moment. His eyes bounced between his wife and his captor.

"Wounds are overrated," Mitch said. "A crutch for the weak and useless."

"But they're still real. You can't deny that."

Of course he couldn't.

When he didn't reply, she said, "What happened to you? It must have been as a child."

It was as a child, and as a teen, and as an adult. Mitch clenched his fists and pressed his molars together. He didn't want to tell her, didn't want to tell anyone. But something about Clare Appleton said it was okay to say it, all right to shine a little light on his demons. She was very motherly, though Mitch had no pleasant memories of his own mother. He only knew what a loving mother should be, never what one was.

Shoving his hands in his pockets, Mitch shuffled his feet and swallowed. "My mother, she was an angry person. That's really all I remember about her. She never called me by my name. It was always just Dummy."

"Where was your father?"

"Oh, he was there, when he wasn't anywhere else. When he was home, all they did was argue. My mother had a very short temper. She never hit me, though, I'll give her that." He paused, glanced at Clare then Bob. Bob had stepped closer and had his arms crossed over his chest, one hand on his chin. Clare leaned against the doorway, both hands covering her mouth. "No, that was my dad's job."

Memories rushed in, like stagnant and dirty waters, dammed for decades, finally breaking loose. And with the memories came a gust of emotion. Mostly anger but some pride too. To think what he'd come through, what he'd survived, and then where he'd ended up. He deserved the respect of the world. Stories like his showed up on the morning talk shows, the evening news, in magazines, books. He was a living, walking, breathing example of how not to let a hellish past ruin your life.

"Your mother never stopped him?"

Mitch laughed, not because there was any humor in her question but because if she had known his mother, she would realize to even ask the question was absurd. "She'd stand there like a warden and watch." He remembered the first time his father really let loose on him, as if it had just happened earlier in the day. He was four and he'd spilled his milk for the second time that evening. His mother made him get on his hands and knees and lap up the spilled milk like a dog; then she brought his father in. The beating wasn't nearly as bad as the image of his mother standing over him, arms crossed, sneering with narrowed eyes and cold, almost inhuman indifference to her son's abuse.

"When I was seven," Mitch said, "she finally had enough and left us. I came home from school and she was gone. That was it. I was left alone with my father." Those old feelings of abandonment surfaced and tightened his skin.

"And how did your father react to that?"

There were tears in Clare's eyes. She was getting it, seeing him for the warrior he really was. And in those eyes he found not only the respect he craved and deserved but also admiration as well. Mitch didn't want to tell any more, the rest was too painful, too horrific, but someone needed to know the truth. And the Apple-tons were as good as anyone.

"He reacted by ignoring me for a week straight. Didn't talk to me, didn't put me to bed or make sure I took a bath. Didn't get me up and ready for school in the morning. Didn't make me meals. Didn't do any of the things parents do for a seven-year-old. I was on my own. He never wanted to be a father and fully blamed me for my mother's leaving."

And the outside world never knew. Even at seven Mitch got himself up every morning, packed his lunch, and walked to school. He didn't want anyone to know what a messed-up family he had. He was too ashamed and embarrassed. No one knew his mother had left until a full year later.

Clare shook her head. "You poor boy."

"Nope," Mitch said. "Not yet. That was the easy part. At least he wasn't torturing me. That stuff came later."

His watch said it was time for him to go. Without another word he closed and locked the door to the Appletons' room. The creak of the wooden steps leading to the first floor conjured a memory that had lain dormant for almost two decades. He was eight, and his father was drunk and out of work and bored. And there was nothing a boy his size could do when his father came at him with a length of rope and malevolent mischief in his eyes.

In the Appletons' living room Mitch dropped himself on the sofa and ran his hands over his head. He grieved for that boy tied in the basement, forced to stand for a full day. Finally, when eve-ning had come and he was filthy from his own urine and feces, he heard his father descending the steps and that familiar creak of the wood under his weight. Mitch thought he was coming to untie him, to finally let him loose and send him to bed, but instead he showed up carrying a six pack of Busch and a box of matches.

Chapter 40

R ONALD HARMAN III thought he owned the world. At least that was the way he acted around Mitch the few times they'd interacted. It seemed being the CEO and president of Rockingham County's only Fortune 500 company had somehow vaulted him to the top of the food chain. He thought he was untouchable, unapproachable, above the established law of the land. Anyone challenging him was dismissed as easily as one waves off a fly.

Harman's father had started the food processing plant seventy years ago to service the town and the surrounding area. Before his death he had grown it into a national supplier and made it a publicly traded corporation. But it wasn't until his son, Ronald III, took control that the company really grew. Harman was known as a hard-nosed businessman who would step on anyone to achieve the success and power he craved. Nothing was sacred; nothing was off-limits. He obeyed no one and disregarded any sense of decency or ethical responsibility. Ronald Harman respected no one but himself.

But that would soon change.

The Harmans lived ten miles outside Virginia Mills in a mansion they'd built after tearing down the old family home. The property covered fifty acres of rolling hills carpeted with manicured weedless lawn and dotted with landscaped oases of weeping willows and ornamental grasses. Each area provided a bench on which to sit in the shade and enjoy the spectacular view of the home and gently undulating hills from varying angles around the property. The home, a fifteen-thousand-square-foot Tudor-style behemoth, sat atop the tallest rise overlooking the entire area.

Spreading out in any direction was Rockingham County, a servant bowing to its lord.

Branching off Crestlawn Lane, an asphalt driveway lined with cherry trees wove and wound over hills and around shaded groves until it reached the Harman residence. There was a security gate, but the stone wall on either side only extended forty feet then yielded to a line of Japanese yews that ran the perimeter of the property. The Harmans believed themselves so beloved by the people that they saw no need for further protection. And in spite of his devilish ethics and heartless decisions, Ronald Harman and his wife Betsy were respected by not only the citizens of Rockingham County but also by all Virginians for their hefty donations to local hospitals and charities.

Mitch sat in the Explorer at the entrance of the driveway and kneaded the steering wheel. Why was it that those least deserving of respect were the ones most receiving of it while those most deserving starved? Tonight Mitch saw himself not only as a vindicator of the poor saps in Harman's shadow but also as a bringer of justice. Tonight a small corner of the universe would be brought into balance. The respected would be humbled, and the scorned would earn his most-deserving reverence.

He glanced at his watch. Time was short tonight.

He pulled the Explorer ahead another hundred feet and steered off the road, behind a stand of dense pines so the vehicle would not be visible from the road in the dark. There he shut off the engine and exited. After carefully passing through the yew hedge, he stole through the darkness on foot covering the two hundred yards to the house like a lunar shadow following the arc of the moon as it crosses the night sky.

On the front porch he stopped and collected himself. He knew it would only be Harman and his wife home. They had two sons, but they were both grown and had families of their own. One was Daddy's vice president and lived on the other side of town;

the other had abandoned the family business for a career in medicine. He was a successful thoracic surgeon in Cincinnati. Mitch
would have to work quickly. He didn't want to give Ronald or
Betsy time to scream or fight back. That ordeal with Buck was
too sloppy and took much too long.

Mitch pushed the button to ring the door chime and followed
it with three heavy knocks on the solid wood door. Seconds later
he heard footsteps inside the house. The porch light flipped on and
the door opened. Ronald Harman stood there in brown leather
loafers, pleated khakis, and a pin-striped dress shirt stretched
tight over his protruding abdomen. Reading glasses perched on
the tip of his nose.

Harman narrowed his eyes. "What are you doing here?"

"Mr. Harman, is your wife home?"

Harman removed his glasses and frowned. "What's this about?"

"Is the missus home?"

From another room Mitch heard Betsy's voice. "Who is it, Ron?"

Turning away from the door, Harman said, "No one, hon. I'll
take care of it."

Mitch wanted to make his move, but the time wasn't right.
He'd get only one chance at this and needed it to be swift and
stunning. "Please, can I speak with both of you?"

"You can talk to—"

Harman was interrupted by Betsy entering the foyer. "Who is
it, dear?"

She came into view and stopped when she saw Mitch. A short,
plump woman, Betsy Harman had an attractive face and warm
smile. But her smile was deceiving, for she was just as arrogant
and condescending and cunning as her husband.

"What's he doing here?" She said it like Mitch was a foul creature that had no right to intrude upon their evening and contam-
inate it with his petty concerns.

They both looked at Mitch as if expecting him to humbly

apologize and crawl back into the hole he'd emerged from. "It's about your son," he said in the calmest voice he could muster.

Betsy's hand went to her mouth, and she took a step closer to her husband.

"Which one?" Harman demanded.

Mitch said nothing but shifted his eyes between husband and wife, letting the suspense linger, letting them feel what helplessness was.

Harman put his arm around Betsy's waist. "Well, out with it, man. Which one?"

Anger burrowed into Mitch's chest, and heat radiated up his neck and into his face and head. "Frederick."

Harman glanced at his wife, confusion twisting his face.

Without warning Mitch stepped over the threshold and brought his hand up and into Harman's nose. Something cracked, and Harman let out a weak grunt and stumbled back into his wife. Before she could scream, Mitch jammed his elbow into her face. She dropped like her legs had been cut out from under her. Harman moaned and rolled over on the floor. He opened his eyes, and in them Mitch found what he'd come for: respect. Harman knew who was in control, who had the power of life and death in his hands. Quickly Mitch removed the knife from his belt and went to work.

Before he took Betsy's life, he roused her from her daze. She turned her head lazily to the side and found her deceased husband beside her. Mitch grabbed her chin and made her look at him, made her respect him. No longer would she look down from her throne and despise the common man.

When Mitch was finished, he stood and wiped the blood from the knife's blade. From the formal living room to his right footsteps on the hardwood flooring startled him. Then, "Dad? Who is it?"

Without hesitation Mitch moved toward the voice. At the

doorway between the living room and the foyer Frederick Harman met him.

Tall and lean, Frederick was imposing only in a gaunt, lanky kind of way. He'd be tough to wrestle because you'd never control those spidery limbs. He scowled at Mitch and looked him up and down. "Who are you?" His eyes went from Mitch to his dead parents on the foyer floor then back to Mitch.

Right before Mitch stuck the knife in Frederick's abdomen, the younger Harman's eyes widened, his mouth formed an O, and his face went as white as paper.

Chapter 41

AT EXACTLY MIDNIGHT Jim awoke with a start. The bedroom door was open, and Louisa stood in the doorway, her thin frame outlined by the light of the hallway.

"Louisa, what's the matter?"

Next to him Amy stirred and mumbled incoherently. She'd slept better the past few nights, deeper and more peacefully, than she had the previous months.

Louisa entered the room and rounded the bed. She said not a word, and at first Jim thought she must be sleepwalking. But when she stood next to the bed and faced him and the light from the hall fell on her face, he saw the clarity in her eyes.

Jim nudged Amy. "Babe, wake up."

She stirred, mumbled, stretched her arms above her head. "What is it?"

Jim turned the question to the girl. "What is it, Louisa?" he asked.

The girl put her hands over her face and began to cry.

Amy sat up and pushed off her covers. "Oh, sweetie, come here."

Louisa approached as Amy swung her legs over the edge of the bed and wrapped her arms around the girl's shoulders. She pulled her close into a motherly hug and stroked her hair. "What's the matter?"

Jim put his hand on Amy's back and rubbed in slow circles.

Through her tears Louisa said, "I had a bad dream." She pulled her face away and rubbed her eyes and cheeks with her hands. "There was a fire, and it was really hot. I was in my room calling for help, but no one could hear me. I heard my mommy screaming my name, but I don't think she could find me." She sniffed and wiped more tears away.

Amy pulled her close again. "Oh, baby girl. I'm so sorry, but it was just a dream. You know that, right?"

Louisa nodded then said, "I miss my mommy."

Jim leaned over and put his hand on her head. She'd never shown any emotion about her mother before. "Sweetie, do you remember your mommy?"

Louisa looked at him. "I think so. I saw her in my dream. She was in my room. She told me everything would be okay. But then she was gone again, and fire was still there."

"Could you tell us what she looks like?"

Louisa shrugged. "I don't know. I think so."

"What color hair does she have?"

"Blonde, I think."

"Like yours?"

She nodded. "But a little darker. And cut to about here." She measured her hand just below her shoulders.

"Anything else about the way she looked?"

The girl was quiet for a moment, thoughtful. Then, "She had blue eyes, real blue."

"Like yours."

"Yes. And a nice smile, like Miss Amy's. And..." She hesitated, glanced at Amy. "And she had a little dimple in her chin."

Like Amy. A chill spread over Jim's arms. If he didn't know better, he would have said Louisa was describing Amy. Of course, maybe she was. Maybe her subconscious was messing around with her memory and imprinting an image of Amy where the girl's mother should be.

"Do you remember her name?"

The girl shook her head.

Amy held up a hand. "Not tonight, Jim. That can wait until

morning." To Louisa, "Honey, do you want to get in our bed and sleep with us?"

The girl nodded again and climbed up into the bed. Amy moved over closer to Jim to make room, and Louisa laid her head on Amy's arm. "Hon," Amy said to Jim, "would you mind closing the door?"

As Jim got up to get the door, Amy began to hum a tune and stroke Louisa's hair. It was the same lullaby she used to sing their baby while she rocked in the nursery and rubbed her belly. Amy had been better the last few days, eerily so. Was Louisa starting to take the place of their lost daughter? And if so, what would happen to Amy when they found Louisa's real mother?

Just then he heard the muted sound of car doors slamming and then the unmistakable sound of voices. He strode across the room and peered out the window. "Oh, for goodness' sake."

"It's midnight," Amy groaned from the bed. "This can't keep happening."

"Stay there. I'll take care of this." Jim slid his feet into his slippers and padded across the room. At the door he turned to Amy. "Be ready with the phone."

"Whatever for?"

He had an uneasy feeling about visitors showing up at his house in the middle of the night demanding a healing. If he refused them... "Just in case."

He stepped out into the hallway, but Amy called to him. "Jim, wait."

"I'll be careful."

"What are you going to tell them?"

"That the grill is closed and we stopped serving alcohol an hour ago."

"Seriously."

"Probably not what they want to hear."

Still shielding Louisa, she reached for her cell phone on the nightstand. "Be careful."

Jim headed down the stairs. Outside, Jim could hear what sounded like a small crowd of people gathered on the porch. He walked to the front window and pulled the curtains aside with one finger. There looked to be about six or seven people out there, talking amongst themselves. He couldn't make out what they were saying, but their voices sounded urgent, almost angry.

Jim turned and found Amy and Louisa standing at the bottom of the stairs, arms around each other. Jim went to Louisa and knelt. "How do you feel about this?"

She frowned. "I don't have a good feeling about it."

"Yeah, me neither."

Amy brandished the phone. "Shall I call the police? I don't like this."

He shook his head. The last thing he needed was a bunch of angry neighbors and townsfolk because Jim Spencer overreacted and caused a lot of embarrassment. "No need for that yet. It'll be fine. Just keep the phone nearby."

Jim went to the door and flipped the dead bolt, turned the knob. There were seven people there altogether, but Jim only recognized two of them, Charlie Bucher and his wife, Adele. Charlie was friends with Jake Tucker. Ever since Jim had known him, Charlie walked with a double limp. His legs were so bowed you could fit a basketball between his knees when he stood with his heels touching. Charlie said both knees were bone on bone and that the only cure was two new knees, but because of his chronic heart condition no surgeon would touch him. He lived with pain every day.

Behind the Buchers were a middle-aged couple and teenage son who looked to have Down syndrome. Beside them was another middle-aged man and woman.

"Hey, Charlie." Jim nodded.

Charlie leaned to the side and tried to look around Jim and into the house. "Is she here?"

"Who?"

"You know who. The girl."

"Yes. She's here."

When Charlie spoke again, his impatience was evident. "Well, let's see her." He glanced at the other folk. "We all need some of whatever it is she does."

"Charlie, I don't think she's comfortable with this. And I'm not sure I am either." Jim knew his response wouldn't be popular.

Charlie furrowed his brow. "Why don't you let her decide that?"

"Folks," Jim said, "I'll ask you to kindly leave our porch and let us go back to bed. It's late."

"Oh, c'mon, Jim. You know us. We're all neighbors here." Charlie turned to the couple with the son. "These are the Bakers and their son, Timothy. Look at him, poor boy." He put his hand on the arm of the other woman. "And this is Reed and Jessi Teal. Jessi just found out last month she has multiple sclerosis. You gonna turn these good folk down?"

"It's not about turning anyone down, Charlie—"

"That's exactly what it's about." He pointed to inside the house. "That girl in there, she has the power to cure all these people, to heal my knees. You know how bad they are."

"I'm sorry, really—" He looked around at each person on the stoop. "—but I'll ask you again to go home."

Reed Teal put his arm around his wife's shoulders and pulled her close. "You can't do this, Spencer. It ain't your call who she heals and who she don't."

Mr. Baker jumped in. "She healed that Mexican boy. Why isn't my son good enough?"

Charlie took a step closer to the open door and narrowed his eyes. His voice was low and serious when he spoke. "Jim, you got no right to do this. She ain't your daughter. She was given to this town, not just you."

With the door open as it was, Jim was the only person between the small crowd on the porch and Louisa inside. He adjusted his feet so he could shut the door quickly if needed. "Folks, I'm going to ask you one more time, and then I'll call the police. Please, go home."

Charlie shook his head. "You can't do this, Jim. You don't have the authority. She belongs to this town."

Reed's face twisted into an angry scowl. "It ain't right, Spencer. It ain't right."

Jim stepped back. "I'm going to close the door, and if you're not off my property in ten minutes, I'm calling the police." Then he pushed the door closed.

Outside he could hear Reed going on. "It ain't right, Spencer. You can't do this to us. We'll be back. I ain't lettin' this go."

Jim turned and leaned against the door. Only then did he notice two things. One, he was shaking and his heart was beating like a rabbit's. And two, Louisa was on the sofa, nestled into Amy's side, crying softly.

"Should I have called the police?" Amy said.

"No. I don't think they meant any harm. They're just frustrated, is all."

Jim went to Louisa and knelt by the sofa. "Louisa, I'm sorry you had to be here for that."

She sniffed. "They don't understand, Mr. Jim."

"Understand what?"

"It doesn't come from me, and it's not magic. They're going to come back, and I won't be able to help them."

Amy rubbed Louisa's arm, and Jim reached for her golden hair and stroked it. And for a long time before returning to bed they simply huddled together, wordlessly sharing grief and fear and comfort.

Chapter 42

ALICIA AWOKE EARLIER than usual, went for a jog, showered, and arrived at the Food Lion a full ten minutes before her shift started. Her dismissal of Derek yesterday had given her renewed energy, as if a backpack full of bricks had been removed from her shoulders. Her head seemed clear, her thoughts pure and positive. Her outlook on life had taken a 180-degree turn from where it was just a few days ago.

The only thing that still bothered her was the vision she'd had again. The shooter. Derek. She still had a gnawing in her gut that Derek was in trouble. But she'd tried to warn him, and he didn't want to hear of it. So she tried to write the visions off as nothing more than her mind playing games with her, conjuring morbid thoughts to deal with some deep-seated guilt she felt about staying with Derek as long as she had. Or maybe a subconscious anger and resentment that she'd repressed for far too long were finally bubbling to the surface and manifesting itself in these visions of hers.

With ten minutes to pass before she needed to punch in and get to her register on the front line, Alicia headed for the break room to down a coffee. Rosie Jonquin was there, as well as Mary Beth Anderson, both seated at the small dinette table.

Rosie nodded at Alicia. "Well, look at you—" She glanced at the clock on the wall. "—strolling in ten minutes early. I ain't never seen this before. You're usually bustin' your tail to get to the front before Eysler can pounce on you."

Rosie was a middle-aged woman, a perfect pear shape, who kept her thick brown locks rolled tight beneath a hair net. She worked in the bakery and often boasted that she ate more than she sold.

"I got up early this morning," Alicia said. "Even went for a run."

"Whoa, now ain't that a start to the day. You must be mighty proud of yourself." Rosie winked at Mary Beth, an elderly woman with a lisp whose sole responsibility was to keep the doughnuts rotated and box up the day-olds for the discount rack. "You lookin' to impress someone?"

"Nope. Just felt like running."

"Since when does anyone just feel like runnin'?"

"My son runs," Mary Beth said, nodding. "Every day. Miles he runs. Did I ever tell you—"

"About the time he did that Iron Man thingy in Hawaii? Yeah, about forty times."

"Well, did I tell you how hot it was? That it—"

"Could melt the soles right off a pair of sneakers? Goin' on thirty times."

Alicia smiled and got a Styrofoam cup from the cupboard.

"You be careful runnin' out there," Rosie said. "You hear about the murders been happenin'?"

"It's awful," Mary Beth said.

Alicia turned and leaned against the counter, crossed her arms. "I am. I take my cell phone."

Mary Beth leaned back in her chair and laced her fingers. "So far they've taken place at night. And to men."

"But you never know when one of these wackos will change his MO," Rosie said, shaking a spoon at her coworker. "You keep a close eye out when you run, girl."

"Thanks for the concern, Rosie," Alicia said, "but I think I'll be fine as long as I run in town."

"Hey," Rosie said, "you hear what happened at the Spencer place last night?"

Alicia was used to Rosie's gossip. She was the type of woman who knew everything about everyone in Virginia Mills. There was no telling how she found out most of what she knew, but she

liked to talk, and when she got a hold of a juicy morsel, it wouldn't
be long before half the town knew. And they'd tell the other half.

"Nope."

"You know they're keepin' that girl, right? The one from old
Jake Tucker's fire."

"Yes. Louisa." Alicia dumped sugar in her coffee and stirred it
with a plastic spoon.

Rosie widened her eyes and dipped the corners of her mouth.
"Oh, look at you, first-name basis with the girl and everything."

Mary Beth laughed and leaned in. "Well, what happened,
Rosie? What happened?"

Rosie's eyes twinkled. "Well, I heard old Charlie Bucher and
his wife went there with the Bakers, you know, the ones with the
son who's, watcha call it, mentally dismembered? And the Teals.
Do you know Reed and Jessi?"

Alicia shook her head, and Mary Beth said, "No, but go on any-
ways."

"Well, Jessi has this disease, can't think of what it's called now,
but it ain't gonna get no better, and they went there for that girl
to heal them, like she done that little girl and the Mexican boy."

"And what happened?" Mary Beth's eyes were as wide as quar-
ters. "Did she do it?"

Rosie sat back in her chair. "No, she did not. What I heard is
that Jim Spencer wouldn't let her. Told 'em all to get off his property or he was callin' the cops."

Mary Beth gasped dramatically. "He had no right, no right at
all. Why shouldn't they get a healing too?" She rubbed her right
shoulder. "And here I was hoping she'd take this rotary cup away
from me."

"Fat chance of that happenin' now," Rosie said. She rolled her
eyes. "I'll tell ya both what, though. Reed Teal ain't happy, not at all.
He did not appreciate bein' driven away and threatened like that,
not with his Jessi how she is. He's not goin' to take this sittin' down."

Alicia sipped her coffee. "Maybe Jim just doesn't want the girl used as some circus side show. Maybe she was uncomfortable with it. You don't know how it really happened."

"Let me tell you something, little miss," Rosie shook her finger at Alicia, "and I'll tell anyone this. That girl's got a gift, somethin' special, and she should be sharin' it with the world. She could take a whole lot of hurtin' from people. Ain't right to keep her hid away in the Spencers' house. It just ain't right. And word is gettin' 'round town about it too."

After drinking the rest of her coffee, Alicia looked at her watch. It was time to go. "Well, I agree, she is special, but I think people should just leave her alone. She's lost without her family. Poor kid. Think about it."

"What if she ain't got no family?" Rosie stood and tossed her soda can in the trash. "What if she's an angel sent from God to cure the world's hurts?"

Mary Beth stood as well. "You think she might be?"

"No tellin'," Rosie said. She lowered her voice. "But I hear there's a lot of murmuring 'round town about the whole thing. That Jim Spencer better be careful."

Chapter 43

Doug Miller's head throbbed from the same head-ache he'd had since yesterday morning. He leaned over his desk, over the open mug of steaming coffee, and rubbed his temples. There'd been three more murders last night, this time at the Harman estate. More victims, more letters carved into flesh. *P-E-C*. The bodies had been laid out in the foyer, side by side, so when the housecleaner arrived for her morning duties, she'd be the first to find them. It was obvious now what the killer was spelling: *respect*. It didn't take a professional profiler to see what he was after, what he lacked in life and craved more than any-thing.

And still there were no leads, no solid ones anyway. The CSU was coming up with nothing at every scene. No fingerprints, no hairs, no skin under the nails of the victims. A couple partial boot prints and tire tracks and grainy, black-and-white security footage from the Harman residence was all they'd been given so far. The footage showed a man, medium build, dressed in dark clothes, approaching the house. His face was obscured. He walked with an odd hitching gait, like he was walking on a bed of hot coals. The stride was obviously faked, which meant the killer knew he was being videoed and also knew there was a good chance he'd be recognized by his gait. Was it a local then? That would sure fit with what his gut was telling him.

The only person of any interest thus far was Jude Fabry. He was at the bar the night Billy Cousins died, at the diner when Clint Efforts was killed, he'd bought a weed whacker off Buck Petrosky just three days before murder number three, and he did some deck repair work on the side for the Harmans. Fabry was the only common thread. And he was local.

And then there were the reporters. Apparently word of the murders had gotten around and piqued the interest of the larger media. At the Harmans, Jackie had been accompanied by at least five other reporters and a television crew. Doug hadn't taken the time to count as he drove past them on his way off the property. His headache had been so intense he didn't want to talk to anyone. Then, just a few minutes ago, he'd foolishly agreed to do a press conference. He'd hold them off until tomorrow, Saturday, and hope his head would settle down by then.

Doug took a sip of his coffee and rubbed his temples again. If the killer was spelling *respect*, there would be one more victim. Would it happen tonight? And would the killer then stop? And then what? Just fade off into history as the Virginia Mills Murderer? Doug doubted it. Crazies like this were never satisfied; one lust led to another, and their hunger was never quenched. It only grew and grew and became bolder, more demanding, until eventually they made a mistake and got caught. But how many more lives would it take for this lunatic to get caught?

In the middle of another sip of coffee, Cindy Cummins, the officer on clerk duty, knocked on the door to Doug's office, opened it, and stuck her head in. "Chief, Jim Spencer is here to see you."

Spencer. Yes, the whole ordeal with the girl and her lost parents. Doug's headache only worsened. He closed his eyes and stroked his mustache. "Send him in."

She started to shut the door.

"Wait. Cindy?"

"Yes, Chief?"

"Get Officer Peevey in here."

"He's off his shift, sir."

"I don't care if he's out to breakfast with the queen of England. I need him here."

"Yes, sir."

She shut the door.

Doug was going to have Peevey bring Fabry in for questioning. Hopefully they could hold him at least overnight. If there was no murder tonight, it would only strengthen their case against him, and if the questioning went his way, they might have enough probable evidence to place an arrest.

Another knock sounded on the door. It opened and Jim Spencer entered.

He nodded but looked uneasy, nervous about something. "Chief, how are you?"

"I've been better, Spencer. Have a seat."

Spencer sat and crossed his legs. "Chief, we had an incident at our house last night. Nothing too serious, but I want you to know about it in case it turns into something serious."

"Go on."

"Some folks—locals—showed up on my porch around midnight demanding Louisa come out and heal them."

"How many?"

"Seven in all."

Doug cocked his head and tented his hands. He had a feeling it was going to come to this. "And did she?"

"No. I think the whole thing made her uneasy. It was all I could do to get them to leave. If they come back—"

"You'll call us. Don't do anything stupid."

"Of course not."

Doug picked up a pen. "Who were they?"

Jim smiled sheepishly. "Well, I'd rather not say, Chief. They all left eventually, and I don't want to get anyone in trouble. If they come back tonight, I'll be sure to call you. I just wanted you to know what was going on. Any headway on finding Louisa's parents?"

Doug spun the pen between his fingers. "Nothing yet. We've been kind of busy around here."

"With the murders. I read about them in the paper. And the Harman murders were on the news this morning. People in town are talking; they're scared. Tension is high, which I think is partly the cause of our visitors last night. Do you have any leads?"

Doug frowned by way of answer.

"Well, for what it's worth, we're doing fine with Louisa. Don't worry about her a bit."

"How's Amy?"

"She's really taken a liking to the girl."

"I'm glad to hear it."

Jim uncrossed his legs and leaned forward. "Chief, last night Louisa came into our bedroom; she had had a nightmare and it rattled her. She was in her house, and there was a fire."

"Not uncommon for what she's been through, with Tucker's fire."

"No, what's remarkable is that she said she saw her mother in her dream. And she remembered what she looked like."

Doug inched his chair closer to the desk and rested his elbows on the top. "Go on."

"Well, the thing is, she swears the person she's describing is her mother, said it was her mother in the dream, no doubt about it, but the person she described down to the eye color, hair color, build, height, everything…is Amy."

Chapter 44

AFTER HIS VISIT with Doug Miller, Jim stopped at the Food Lion for a few necessities: milk, bread, iced tea, frozen waffles, and Neapolitan ice cream—the staples of a well-balanced diet. Business was slow for a Friday morning. As he gathered his items, he saw only three other shoppers in the whole store. They eyed him suspiciously, and two of them, an elderly couple, murmured back and forth as he passed and nodded a hello.

At the register there was no one in line. The clerk, a young woman, smiled at him politely and said good morning but did her job quickly and bagged his items. She tore the receipt from the register and hesitated.

"Mr. Spencer?"

Jim lifted one of the bags. "Yes?"

"Um, you don't know me—"

"You're the girl from the Red Wing. The one Louisa talked to."

Her eyes flitted side to side as if she were scanning the area for prying eyes and eavesdropping ears. "I am." She handed him the receipt. "I'm Alicia."

"Hi, Alicia."

She smiled but it was forced, to hide her apparent uneasiness. "Where is she?"

"Louisa?"

"Yes."

"She's home with my wife."

After glancing around the store again, Alicia leaned forward and almost touched Jim with her hand. "There's talk around here, Mr. Spencer."

"What kind of talk?"

Alicia lowered her voice even more. "When I saw Louisa in the diner, she touched me. Just placed her hand on my arm." She rolled her eyes. "This sounds crazy, but there was something to that touch. It changed me somehow."

Jim remained quiet and let her talk. What she'd experienced was what so many others now wanted.

Alicia looked around again and put her hands to her mouth, as if she were afraid some secret informant trained in the art of reading lips was hiding in the canned foods aisle, watching their conversation from a safe distance. "I heard what happened last night. At your house. I also heard people around here aren't too happy about it. They're planning to go back."

"When?" Jim suspected they'd return sooner or later, but he hoped his hunch was wrong and that the people of Virginia Mills would have enough sense to let it go, to let a little girl be a child and either find her parents or get settled into her new home without a bunch of drama.

She shrugged. "I don't know. Now. Later. Tonight. Tomorrow night. It seems everyone is talking about it. They're getting pretty stirred up too. These murders have everyone acting weird."

"I know."

"Be careful, please. Louisa, she's a special girl."

At once Jim's skin began to tingle as if his nerves had been plucked like guitar strings. He lifted the other bags and nodded at Alicia. "Thanks for the warning. I better get going."

A feeling of panic rose up suddenly, beat at the inside of his chest like a caged bird in hysterics. And suddenly a thought was there, a warning maybe, all neon lights and blinking in the dark. He needed to get home. Now. Amy and Louisa were in danger. He never should have left them alone, not after what happened last night. He'd put too much faith in the citizens of Virginia Mills, too much faith in mankind.

Reaching his car quickly, he threw the bags in the backseat, slid in behind the wheel, and cranked the engine to life. Not even bothering to look for oncoming traffic, Jim hit the gas and left the parking lot, the tires complaining with a high-pitched squeal.

Their house was only fifteen minutes from the store on a good day. But now fifteen minutes seemed like ten hours, and he didn't have that kind of time. As he pressed the accelerator between traffic lights, the engine whined and the speedometer needle climbed.

And as each minute passed the sense of fear in him, the warning light, the blinking, blinking, intensified. He couldn't go fast enough, couldn't get home quick enough. They could be there right now, knocking on the door, kicking it in, busting the windows.

Drawing in a deep breath, Jim told himself to settle down; he was overreacting. No one would be stupid enough to be so bold in broad daylight. But people did crazy things when they had no sane alternatives left, and desperation had made a fool—and a violent fool—out of more than one man.

Finally he turned onto his street. The accelerator went to the floor, and half a mile later he was hitting the brakes and turning into his driveway. There were no other cars there. The windows were all intact and closed. The front door was in one piece and also closed.

Jim shut off the engine and exited the car, leaving the groceries for later. He looked around, wiped sweat from his brow and chin. They lived on a semi-remote road where the homes were spaced far apart. Behind and to the left of their home was farmland, ripe with soy beans, and to the right was the home of the Murrays, a retired couple who mostly kept to themselves. But the Murrays' home was a good hundred yards away and blocked from view by a row of tall spirea.

He scanned the area again, checking the shrubs around the house, the trees, the roofline. Above the roof the sky was darkening. He didn't think they were calling for rain today. But the area was clear, not a soul around. And that's what bothered him.

At the door Jim checked the knob and found it unlocked. The tingling was there again, covering his arms and neck and upper chest like sand being poured over his skin. He turned the knob and pushed open the door, listening for the unfamiliar sound of scurrying feet or the click of a handgun's hammer. But he was met with silence, as still as any cave buried deep beneath a mountain.

Entering the house, Jim left the front door cracked. He and his family might need to make a quick escape out of it, and he wanted to be prepared. In the living room he looked around for anything that might appear out of place, but there was nothing. All was as it should be in the Spencer home. The kitchen was no different. The back door was also unlocked. It led to a brick patio that overlooked the yard, which led to a harvested field and abutted the woods.

Jim thought of the murders that had been reported. Six so far. He checked the first-floor bathroom and found it also empty and undisturbed. At the bottom of the staircase he stopped and rested his hand on the railing. He really should take a weapon with him. What if the murderer was here in his house? What if the murders were somehow tied to the sudden arrival of Louisa and the two parallel strands finally merged? Back in the kitchen he grabbed a wood-handled chef's knife.

Jim took the steps to the second floor one at a time, careful to avoid the loose boards and invoke a squeak that would alert any intruder to his presence. In the hallway he stood still and listened.

First he checked the bathroom, then the nursery. The bathroom was undisturbed, but the nursery had been messed with. Two boxes sat open on the floor. The walls had been stripped of all pictures, and near the crib lay a framed photo of a pregnant Amy, the glass broken out of it and lying in pieces across the carpeted floor.

Jim's heart began to race faster, beating so forcefully that he feared it would be heard from another room. He left the nursery and turned to his office. The desk hadn't been moved; the book-shelves appeared untouched. Everything was as it should be.

Lastly the bedroom. The door was closed, and Jim had to force himself to open it. Holding the knife high, pushing images of a bloodied bed from his mind, Jim leaned his shoulder against the door as he pushed it open. It swung on silent hinges. His heart was in his mouth, and his palms sweated. At any moment he expected to be charged by a crouching invader. But the room was quiet, the shades turned down, the bed covers intact and unmarred.

They were gone. Abducted? Murdered? Jim's mind raced for an explanation, one that didn't include death. Even as tears pooled in his eyes and his hands began to shake, he scolded himself for jumping to conclusions. Just because they weren't home didn't mean they'd been forced to leave, or worse.

He stepped out of the bedroom and said, "Amy?" His voice seemed to echo throughout the house and bounce off the walls as it would in a great subterranean cavern.

No answer came. Again, "Amy." This time louder. "Louisa."

It was clear the house was empty, the doors unlocked, the nursery left a mess. Something was wrong. Descending the stairs in a hurry, digging in his pocket for his cell phone, he was startled by the front door opening.

Amy and Louisa entered, smiling. But their smiles disappeared when they saw him.

"What's the matter?" Amy said. His fear and concern must have been obvious. "You look like you just saw a ghost."

"Where've you been?" He put his phone back in his pocket.

"We went for a walk. What is it? What happened?"

"Nothing. I came home and you weren't here. The doors were unlocked. I thought...what happened in the nursery?"

"Oh, that. The picture." Amy glanced at Louisa and smiled. "Louisa and I were doing some packing and that picture fell, hit the crib, and shattered. We both needed some fresh air, so I thought we'd go for a walk then clean it up when we got back. You didn't cut yourself, did you?"

"No, nothing like that." Jim went to them and wrapped his arms around both of them. "I'm just glad you're both okay."

"Why wouldn't we be, Mr. Jim?" Louisa said.

"Oh, I don't know. No reason." And while his heart had settled, Jim still felt a vague and weighty foreboding. It was as if a storm were coming, a great tempest with churning black clouds and rumbles of thunder, and he needed to do something to prepare but lacked the knowledge to complete the task.

Jim kissed Louisa on the head and Amy on the lips. "I'm just glad you're both home and okay, that's all."

Chapter 45

THE BASEMENT SEEMED cooler than usual, damper too. With the approaching storm inching closer, bringing an armada of dark, chiseled clouds, the air outside had grown damp and thick with the smell of ozone. Mitch stood at the top of the stairs, holding another frozen pizza he'd tossed in the oven, and shivered. He didn't want to face the Appletons, didn't want to talk to them. Their encounter yesterday had left him shaken and irritable. He didn't like talking about his past and stirring up all those memories and feelings he'd so carefully and diligently packed away.

And then there was the issue with the Harmans. Mitch wasn't expecting Frederick to be there. Taking a family like that had left him feeling uneasy. It was too personal, too intimate. The look on Betsy's face when the knife found her husband's abdomen would stay with Mitch for a very long time, maybe forever. But she had respected him, hadn't she? My, how she'd respected him. At the moment he stuck her and she squealed so softly he felt like God. He held her life in his hands, and she knew it. That was a feeling he could get used to. It was respect he deserved.

Descending the steps slowly, balancing the pizza in one hand, a pitcher of water in the other, Mitch held his breath and counted off the steps. Fifteen in all. The steps creaked beneath his weight. At the bottom of the staircase a musty odor met him, and he almost turned and went back upstairs.

Clare was first to speak as Mitch approached the room.

"Hello, Mitch," she said. She looked worn and older than she had yesterday. Her hair was uncombed and her clothes wrinkled and stained. Had they looked like that all along? He couldn't remember. If they did, he hadn't noticed, or maybe he hadn't wanted to notice.

Mitch opened the door and handed Clare the pizza, Bob the pitcher of water.

"Are you okay?" Clare tilted her head to the side.

Mitch said nothing. He turned to retreat, leaving the door open, but stopped when she spoke again. "What did your father do?"

With his back to the Appletons, Mitch closed his eyes as the memory burst in like a backdraft. Sweat beaded on his forehead, and he bit his lower lip.

"Mitch? Turn around." Clare was using her motherly tone with him.

He didn't, but neither did he move for the steps. He was stuck to the floor, unable to advance, to get away from the memory, from Clare's voice, from his story that needed—begged—to be told. He'd been such a wounded child, scarred in so many ways.

"Mitch." Clare again. "Please, turn around."

For some reason he was unaware of, he felt compelled to turn, to face her and her lovely eyes and warm smile. She was not your average farmer's wife. Slowly he turned, still biting his lip, almost drawing blood from it.

"Tell us, Mitch." Her voice was soft and comforting, a mother's voice caressing the wounded spirit of her child. Mitch never heard that voice in his own mother. From her there was never anything but sarcasm and cynicism and scorn. *Dummy.* Never any love, never any kindness or encouragement. *Dummy.* She was not like Clare Appleton at all. *DUMMY!*

"He set me on fire." He'd put the match to Mitch's pant leg and waited for his son to scream before extinguishing it. Then he moved to the other pant leg. Over and over he repeated the act, and over and over fear so clutched Mitch that he nearly passed out. All the while his father laughed and taunted him while waving the box of matches in the air. "But that wasn't the only thing he did, and it certainly wasn't the worst." Mitch drilled Clare with an icy stare, daring her to react or cower away in disgust.

Instead a tear formed in Clare's eye and spilled down her cheek. "You poor boy." To her left Bob bowed his head.

"Don't feel sorry for me. It only made me stronger, more determined." And it had. He'd risen above his disadvantaged circumstances, clawed his way out of the hell he'd been born into, and actually made something of himself. Which is why he deserved the respect he'd not been freely given until now.

"But the wounds, the weight you carry." She dashed the tears from her cheek.

"It's made me stronger," he repeated.

Bob looked up. "But at what cost?"

Mitch said nothing. The cost had been great, he knew that, and the price continued to rise. But to him it was a price worth paying.

"Look what you've become," Bob said. "Look what your hatred has done to you."

Mitch clenched his jaw. He didn't like Bob the farmer judging him, casting a condescending look down his nose. He stepped forward. "My hatred has fueled my drive, made me who I am today. You don't know how hard I fought to put that behind me."

Clare took a step out of the room. Bob placed a hand on her arm, but she cast him a look that said everything was okay, she knew what she was doing. "But it's not behind you, is it?"

It wasn't. She was right, and Mitch hated that fact. The memories haunted him almost constantly. Hatred and anger still boiled inside him. His rage was sometimes uncontrollable.

"Is it?" She was pushing him now, challenging him, and it made Mitch angry.

"You don't know what you're talking about," he said.

Clare took another step forward, her hands clasped at her chest. Tears leaked from her eyes now, and she sniffed rhythmically.

"Your heart is so hard, so full of need and vengeance. You're miserable, aren't you?"

"I don't need this," Mitch said.

Bob put a hand on the doorjamb. "Clare—"

But she ignored him. "You need to forgive your father. You need to let this go and move on."

"Forgive him?" Mitch's anger was now in its full, thorny bloom. He stepped closer to Clare, tightening his fists. His muscles were taut, bringing out more of a sweat on his forehead and neck. The musty odor of the basement mingled with the smell of the pizza and turned his stomach. His eye twitched uncontrollably. "You think I just need to forgive that monster and get over it? Like it's that easy?"

Clare stood her ground. If she feared him, she did not show it. For her part, though, she showed him no disrespect. "Forgiveness is never easy. But it's necessary."

Mitch huffed. "Necessary. There's only one thing that's necessary for me now." Getting the respect he so well deserved.

She eyed him without blinking. "Forgiveness is the only way to find freedom, Mitch."

"Oh, I can think of a hundred ways to find freedom."

"And every one of them will be wrong."

Before he realized what he'd done, Mitch's hand had left his side and contacted Clare's face along her cheekbone and temple area. She let out a weak grunt and tipped to the side, stumbling into the furnace first then the wall. Bob rushed to her side and steadied her.

Mitch pointed at the open door to the room. "Get back in there, both of you."

Bob helped Clare into the room. She held the side of her face and winced. At the door she turned and faced Mitch. He didn't want her to; he couldn't look her in the eyes. His temper had flashed in a burst of flames. The violence had come on so suddenly he hadn't time to extinguish it.

"Get in," he said, his voice quivering with the aftershocks of his outburst.

"Mitch…" She reached out her hand for his.

He pulled away.

"I forgive you."

"Get in." He didn't want to hear that, didn't want to hear anything she had to say. Forgiveness was an escape for the weak, for those too timid to face their demons and take them head-on.

Bob and Clare finally obeyed, and Mitch closed and locked the door behind them. He'd return later, after he calmed himself, to give them their visit to the bathroom.

Still shaking, Mitch headed upstairs, where he proceeded to take out the remaining portion of his anger on the furniture in the study. His rage was so hot, so fueled by frustration and disgust and hatred, that he scarcely knew what he was doing. Glass shattered, wood splintered, books soared through the air and collided with lamps and wall hangings. His vision blurred, and sweat poured down his back and chest.

Finally, exhausted and spent, Mitch collapsed in the middle of the floor and turned his mind loose. He'd known joy once. When he was sixteen, his father kicked him out of the house, told him to pack his duffel bag and get out of his sight. Mitch went to live with his grandparents on their farm. There, for the first time in his life, he experienced love. They were good people, kind, giving, compassionate. His grandfather taught him how to find his way through a toolbox, how to work with pride, how to be a man. His grandmother was the only real mother he ever knew. But it had only lasted a year. Right after Mitch turned seventeen, they were both killed in a car accident and he became a ward of the state and placed in a foster home where he was once again neglected and ignored.

Mitch slumped and rested his wrists on his knees. His heart still pumped out a rapid rhythm. Around him lay almost the entire library, books splayed with pages torn like so many broken-winged birds, grounded and dead. The coffee table lay on its side, two legs busted clean off. A wingback chair was pushed over, its feet in the air like sun-swollen roadkill. One picture remained on the walls, a painting of Secretariat, and it hung precariously from one corner. Below him, in the basement, he could hear Clare crying.

At that moment Mitch Albright hated himself.

Chapter 46

SUNSET CAME EARLY, quickened by the rutted ceiling of swollen thunderheads that had moved in and hovered over the town of Virginia Mills like an alien craft waiting for the opportune time to set lasers to annihilate. Jim stood on his front porch, arms crossed, and looked up at the clouds. Lightning flashed horizontally through them, illuminating the angles of their underbelly, but did not break from their atmospheric home and descend to earth. Thunder rumbled like the growl of mighty turbines. Soon enough the clouds would open, and the world around this small, unassuming town would be drenched by an autumn deluge.

Inside, Amy and Louisa played a game of Uno at the kitchen table. All three of them felt the impending storm, and it was so much more than the clouds above them. Earlier in the afternoon Louisa had asked him if he was afraid.

"Of what?" he said.

"Of them," she replied. "People will do crazy things when they think they deserve something."

She was right. Trouble was coming, and people would no doubt do some pretty crazy things. Jim could only hope the promise of rain and lots of it would ward off any troublemakers. Doug Miller told him not to hesitate to call for help if he even felt like trouble was brewing. "Better to call and be safe than not to and be sorry," he'd said.

At exactly nine o'clock the first wave of cars arrived and parked along the road at the edge of Jim's property. The Buchers, Bakers, and Teals were there, along with a couple other families Jim didn't recognize. Jim rose from his chair as if to greet guests he'd been waiting on and positioned himself at the top of the porch's stairs.

The small crowd crossed his yard and huddled near the sidewalk. Charlie Bucher and Reed Teal broke away and approached the porch.

"Charlie," Jim said, "what are you all doing here?"

"You know why we're here," Charlie said. He walked up to the steps as if he were going to shake Jim's hand but crossed his arms instead. "There's more comin', you know. We all got somethin' wrong with us, somethin' that needs a-healin'."

"I wish you wouldn't do this."

"They're comin'," Charlie said. "Ain't nothin' gonna stop 'em now, 'cept that girl in there." He pointed toward the open door.

Jim crossed the porch, opened the storm door, and pulled closed the heavy front door. His action would be interpreted as an act of defiance, and that was exactly what he wanted. These people needed to know he stood between them and his wife and Louisa.

Charlie pointed a finger at Jim and shook it. "You got no right, Spencer."

"No right at all," Reed said. He was a big guy with thick arms and a deep chest. Jim hoped that if things went bad, Reed stayed out of it.

At the road two more cars pulled up, parked, and shut off their lights. Overhead the storm clouds continued to flash and rumble. Inside the house the living room lights switched off. Amy wasn't taking any chances.

"Bring her out so we can all get our healin'," Charlie hollered. "Don't make us come in there and get her."

Jim put both his hands in front of him. "Settle down, Charlie. You don't want to do anything like that and have the police here making a bunch of arrests."

Two other families joined the group on Jim's front lawn and murmured amongst themselves.

A truck arrived in a hurry and pulled into Jim's driveway. Jim recognized it as Jake Tucker's pickup. Jake climbed out and hustled to the porch. "What's going on here?"

"You stay out of this, Jake," Charlie said.

"Charlie, what are you doin'? What's gotten into you?"

Charlie turned on Jake and shook a finger at his old friend. In his eyes was the daze of desperation and lunacy. "I said stay out of this. You got your miracle; why shouldn't the rest of us get ours? Huh?"

"Is that what this's come to?" Jake said. "Treating this girl like she's handin' out free soda pops? Go home, Charlie." Then he turned to the assembly on the lawn. "All of you, just go on home. Leave this family be."

"You go home, Tucker," someone hollered.

And then it started. The crowd crawled closer, moving as a many-eyed, thousand-legged organism, hollering and shouting. As they approached, three more cars arrived, and more townsfolk looking for a healing poured out and onto Jim's lawn.

Jake stepped up onto the porch with Jim and waved his arms like he was flagging down an aircraft. "Folks. Folks," he hollered. Finally they quieted down enough that he could speak. "People, I know you're hurting, all of you, but this ain't the way. Not at all. Look at yourselves. You—"

"No!" A woman's voice rang out from the back of the crowd. Voices hushed and heads turned. "No." Ruth Stitely, the daughter of Bishop Stitely, pastor of the Shekinah Tabernacle outside of town, made her way through the throng of people who had gathered. Back straight as if someone nailed a board to it, chin high, hands clasped in front of her at the waist, she strode right up to Jim as if she owned the very porch on which he stood. Her hair was gathered behind her head in a tight bun, and she wore a plain gray dress that went all the way to her ankles. No more than twenty-five, Ruth had been touted as a prophetess by her father since she was seven. Most of the townspeople made light of his claims but secretly feared her.

She turned and faced the crowd. "Dear ones, that child is a gift to our town, a blessing from God. She is the bringer of healing and salvation. God loves us and wants us to have this blessing. We have gathered here tonight to claim her as our own." She turned to Jim and lifted her chin high. "Bring her out."

"No. No way."

"Bring out the child."

"Go home, all of you," Jake hollered.

"Bring her out." Ruth raised her voice and stomped her foot. She wasn't used to being defied. "I speak the will of God!"

"If you all don't leave now," Jim said, "I'll call the police." He should have earlier, as soon as the group entered his yard.

Ruth swiveled around and faced the crowd again. "If they won't bring her out, then we must get her. No man shall stand in the way of God's will. Today is the day of salvation."

The crowd cheered and rumbled and inched closer.

Two things happened then that stopped their progress. One, the sky opened and the water came. Great drops fell from above, exploding like water bombs. And two, the wail of a siren sounded in the distance, and soon after, the flash of blue and red and white lights appeared against the surrounding trees. Amy must have made the call. The crowd, now half-drenched, turned toward the street. A police cruiser pulled up, lights still strobing. The siren died with a whine. An officer stepped out and crossed the lawn, heading right up to the front porch. He nodded at Jim then Jake. "I'm Officer Peevey. Looks like you could use some help."

"Thanks for coming," Jim said.

"Why don't you go inside and let me take care of this."

The crowd on the lawn, now over fifty strong, huddled closer and throbbed with pent-up frustration.

"You cannot thwart the will of God, young man," Ruth said, her voice muffled by the rain. Her hair was plastered to her head and her dress clung to her body. Water dripped off her long, thin nose and chin and ran into her eyes.

Peevey put a hand on Jim's chest. "Go inside. I got this. Backup is on the way."

Jim and Jake opened the door and slipped inside. Amy and Louisa were in the kitchen. Jim went to a window and pulled back the blinds. The crowd had moved closer again, feeling bolder with the numbers they possessed. Someone cried out, "Give us the girl."

Peevey reached to his side and rested his hand on his canister of pepper spray. Rain continued to fall in great sheets, blurring Jim's view of the entire lawn. He couldn't see beyond the light of the lamppost.

"Back up and go home, folks," Peevey said. "More officers are en route, and we won't hesitate to make arrests."

"You can't arrest us all," Reed Teal hollered. "There's too many of us."

And then everything broke lose. A flash of lightning struck somewhere nearby, followed immediately by a clap of thunder so jarring it seemed to shake the house from the very foundation to the roof joists. The window Jim was standing near exploded in a spray of glass, and a brick landed on the living room carpet. Stunned, Jim stared at it. He couldn't believe what had just happened. His mind told him lightning had struck the house and knocked a brick loose, tossing it like a baseball. But even as his mind tried to accept that, he knew it was untrue. The lightning was close but not that close. Someone had thrown a brick through his window.

Something hard landed on the porch and thudded against the outside wall of the house. Peevey hollered something unintelligible.

More sirens sounded in the distance, growing louder. The crowd screamed and cursed.

Jake grabbed Jim by the arm and pulled him away from the window just as another brick broke through and took what little glass was left with it. Outside, the sirens continued for a moment then stopped. Voices, strong and decisive, rose above the hum of the throng. And then there was a sickening thud, right outside the door, and an awful thump against the side of the house.

The crowd went quiet, and all that was heard was the thrum of rain on the porch roof.

A man's voice finally broke the silence. "Officer down!"

Chapter 47

J IM THREW THE door open and found Officer Peevey on his back on the porch, a puddle of bright red growing around his head. The left side was already swelling, and his hair was matted thick with blood. A few feet away lay a brick.

Two other officers bent over him; one hollered details into his radio. Peevey's eyes were open but glazed, one appeared slightly off center as if it had suddenly gotten bored and decided to focus on something other than the porch ceiling.

The crowd retreated, like high tide pulling back into the ocean. A few of them talked in hushed tones and wagged their heads. Others kept to themselves and made a line to their cars. Within seconds the lawn was clear and the last of the cars was pulling away.

One of the officers, a middle-aged man whose nameplate read Lorenzo, felt Peevey's neck for a pulse. "He's got one," he said. "Barely. We're losing him."

Louisa appeared beside Jim, leaned against his side, and took his hand.

The other officer, a young guy, early twenties, paced the porch. "Where are they?" He spoke into his radio again. "Is the bus en route?"

The dispatcher said it was.

Officer Lorenzo groped Peevey's neck. "We lost him, Evans. He's gone."

In a hurry he clasped his hands together and began compressing the fallen officer's chest.

Lightning crackled across the sky and thunder boomed, a long, moaning rumble.

Evans put the radio to his mouth. "We lost his pulse. Get that bus here now!"

While Lorenzo performed CPR, Louisa released Jim's hand and left his side. She knelt beside Peevey and placed her hand on his forehead.

Lorenzo kept up with his compressions. "Stay away, kid." He glanced at Jim.

Jake came through the doorway and put a hand on Lorenzo's shoulder. "Let her be. She's the only one who can help him now."

The rain continued to fall in waves, pummeling the ground with great droplets. The clouds blinked bright again and thunder rolled through them.

Hesitantly Lorenzo slowed his compressions then stopped altogether. He was breathing heavy, and his hands trembled when he lifted them.

Louisa placed her other hand on Peevey's chest and closed her eyes. Her lips moved slowly with an inaudible conversation.

She began to shake. Quickly, as if Peevey's body had suddenly turned scalding hot, she pulled her hands away. Her eyes went wide and mouth dropped open. She fell back and pushed herself to Jim's feet.

A second ticked by and nothing happened. Then two.

Louisa climbed to her feet and dashed inside the house.

Another second passed, and another. In the far-off distance a siren sounded, like the wail of a woman who'd just lost her only child. Lorenzo locked his hands together and was about to resume his compressions when Peevey's eyes focused and he gasped for breath.

Peevey sat up and lifted his hand to his head. The bleeding had stopped, and the swelling was already visibly decreasing. He pulled his hand away, blotched with clotting blood. His eyes found the brick on the porch. "I never saw it coming."

Lorenzo turned Peevey's head and inspected where the gash had been. "You okay, Peeve? You feel okay?"

Peevey nodded. "Yeah. I think so. Who threw it?"

Another lightning flash lit up the sky, the yard, the cruisers jutting into Jim's lawn, lights still dancing.

"Beats me," Evans said. "Came out of nowhere. Several of 'em did."

"Lucky hit," Peevey said. "Help me up."

Lorenzo grasped Peevey's hand and hoisted him to his feet. "Lucky is right. We lost you, you know."

Peevey studied the blood on his hand and touched the side of his head again. "Am I still bleeding?"

"Nope," Lorenzo said.

"Lost me how?"

"You coded on us, pulse was gone."

An ambulance arrived and pulled into the driveway, behind Jake's truck. Two paramedics jumped out and ran to the porch.

"Who brought me back?" Peevey said.

Evans motioned toward the doorway. "The girl did."

One of the paramedics, a short guy, thick around the middle, jumped up onto the porch. "What happened, Peevey?"

"Mears, why are you here? I'm fine. I don't need a bus."

Mears looked to Lorenzo, then Evans. "I thought you said he kicked it."

"He did," Lorenzo said.

The paramedic looked Peevey up and down. "He don't look dead."

"He don't?" Lorenzo said. "Maybe it's because he isn't."

"So what happened?"

"We're not really sure, okay? He was a goner one second, then the girl comes out, puts her hands on him, and he's alive, talking like he was just taking a snooze or something."

"Yeah," Evans said. "I think the whole thing spooked her as much as it did us. You shoulda seen the look on her face, like she'd seen the devil."

Peevey glanced around the porch and wiped his hands on his pants. "Hey, guys, I have to go."

"What?" Mears said. "You're not goin' anywhere. We gotta take you in so the docs can check you out, make sure you got all your parts in place. You might feel fine now, but that's the adrenaline. Once that wears off, you're gonna be feelin' like a truck ran over you then backed up again."

"No. I have to go."

Mears grabbed Peevey's arm. "At least let us check you here."

But Peevey was having none of it. He looked back at Jim in the doorway, then past him and into the house. There was fear in his eyes, real fear. He pulled away from Mears. "Not tonight. I'm okay. I'm leaving."

"C'mon, Peevey, you ain't in any shape—"

"Mears, I said not today. I'm leaving. I'm refusing your care, okay? Write that down." He shoved his way past Lorenzo and the other paramedic. They all watched as he crossed the lawn, got in his car, and tore off in a spray of grass and dirt.

"He's nuts," Mears said. "He's gonna get himself killed."

Chapter 48

T HE DEPARTMENT WAS quiet this late at night. Chief Doug
Miller sat at his desk and rubbed his temples. He still had
a nagging headache, and the pills he'd taken an hour ago weren't
even touching it. The lights were off in his office; the only illumination came from the computer monitor and the small desk
lamp. Behind him and beyond the light of the lamp the darkness
seemed to encroach like a horde of malevolent spirits intent on
perpetrating some hideous crime under the cover of lightlessness.

Outside, rain tapped on the window, the drum of fingers
counting off a disjointed beat. Occasionally a volley of thunder
would ripple through the night, but it was distant now. The fury
of the storm had passed, leaving behind a steady rain to soak the
earth.

After the meltdown at the Spencer place Peevey had returned
to the office to clean up and change his uniform. Doug checked
him over and found nothing that would keep the young officer off
his beat. The gash had stopped bleeding, his skull was in one piece,
and cognitively he seemed as lucid as ever, albeit a bit irritated,
which was to be expected after what he'd been through. Doug
suggested he go to the hospital just as a precaution, get checked
for a concussion or internal bleeding, but Peevey insisted he was
okay to get behind the wheel of his cruiser. In fact, he'd even vol-
unteered to go and sit in front of the Spencer place, keep an eye
on it for the night in case any of the rowdies returned looking to
chuck more bricks. But Doug denied his request and insisted he
at least take the rest of the shift off.

Now Doug sat in his office with the door closed and sifted
through what little evidence they'd collected on the six murders

thus far. Earlier he'd interrogated Jude Fabry and placed him in a holding cell. Fabry didn't offer anything new to the investigation but was cooperative, even agreeing to stay the night, just to clear his name. Now the real test awaited: with Fabry behind bars for the night, would there be a seventh murder?

For the third time this evening Doug scrolled through the cases, one at a time, scanning the reports to see if anything had been missed, any other connecting factor overlooked. The first three victims were similar but didn't fit any obvious pattern. What did a mill worker have in common with a truck driver or a tree trimmer? Blue-collar workers. The county was full of white, male blue-collar types. Hardly a pattern. And that didn't fit with the Harmans anyway. If Fabry turned out to be innocent, a victim of coincidence, then it seemed the deceased were chosen at random, picked out of a crowd or maybe the phone book.

Doug slapped the desk with an open palm, rattling his coffee mug and the penholder the department had given him for his sixtieth birthday.

He scrolled down a few pages in Buck Petrosky's chart, not really focusing on anything, just letting his eyes move over the words. He'd read over these so many—

Wait. What was this? He thought...

Doug brought up each chart then minimized it. One by one he scrolled through them until he found it. Every victim had come in contact with the same person, and it wasn't Jude Fabry.

Heat climbed up the back of his neck, and his hands began to tremble. It couldn't be, though. It was impossible. Why hadn't he noticed it before? He checked each chart again just to be certain. Surely it was a coincidence.

Doug picked up the phone. He had to call Lorenzo; there were more questions he needed answers to.

Alicia awoke in a cold sweat and sat straight up in bed. The sheet, soaked through, fell off her shoulders, and she shivered in the cool air of the bedroom. The clock said it was 11:22.

She panted like she'd just run a mile in work boots. Grabbing the sheet, she wiped the sweat from her face and chest. Her mouth was as dry as bone. She needed a drink of water.

Alicia pushed her legs over the edge of the bed and sat there in the darkness trying to collect her thoughts, the images that swirled in her brain as if tossed by a tempest at sea. The nightmare had included her vision of Derek and the shooter, but it was so much more than that. So much more gruesome and violent. How had her brain concocted such awful images? She hadn't watched a horror movie since she saw that exorcism flick as a kid. She'd slept with the bedroom lights on for weeks after that. But this was different, so much more real and vivid than any movie could be. Derek, stabbing victims. Slitting throats. Derek, doing disgusting things, vile acts of violence and murder.

The shadows in the room seemed to move and shift suddenly. Alicia froze, and the hair on her arms stood on end. Panic put a vise on her chest. Quickly she reached for the lamp on the bed table and switched it on. Light flooded the room but did not push back her fears.

Rising from the bed, Alicia made her way down the short hallway and into the living room. There she checked the locks on the front door, the chain lock and the dead bolt. Both were engaged and secure. She then headed into the kitchen, turned on the light, and retrieved a glass from the cupboard. She filled it with water, downed the entire thing, then filled it a second time. Her hand shook uncontrollably each time she put the glass to her mouth, and the edge rattled against her teeth. She had to call someone and tell them about her dream, warn them. They'd think she was nuts, but she had to try. She'd seen what Derek was capable of firsthand, the rage and violence, and if what she'd seen in her nightmare was a warning, he was capable of so much more.

Suddenly the full realization of what she'd seen in her dream hit her with the heart-stopping force of a battering ram to the chest. She'd lived two years with Derek, slept with him, ate meals with him, went to the movies with him. She'd fallen victim to his temper on multiple occasions. She knew him. But she never knew this side of him, that such a monster could reside in the soul of a man.

She wanted to tell herself that it wasn't true, couldn't be. That it was just a bad dream. Maybe something she'd eaten yesterday or the stress of the breakup and the miracle of the child Louisa colliding like two storm fronts in her brain. But as much as she tried, she couldn't convince herself. Somehow she knew the nightmare was true, that it had given her a glimpse into the soul of the man she once thought she loved and wanted to marry.

The phone call needed to be made. Others had to be warned. Alicia crossed the kitchen and grabbed her cell phone from the table. She took a deep breath and dialed the numbers.

Chapter 49

RAIN FELL LIKE tinsel sparkling in the light of the porch lamp. The lightning and thunder were only a distant memory now, echoing over the night sky like a journeyman whistling a tune of farewell as his ship sails into the endless ocean. At midnight Jim Spencer was still awake. As were Amy and Louisa. After the excitement of the evening none of them felt like sleeping, nor could they. After the police and paramedics had left, Jake Tucker hung around to help Jim tape a piece of thick plastic over the broken window to keep out the cool night air and any stray raindrops the wind might blow in across the porch. When the job was finished and the window was sealed, Jake left, and the Spencers found themselves alone in the silence of their home.

Ever since putting her hands on Officer Peevey and bringing him back, Louisa had been acting strangely, not saying more than three words and mostly keeping to herself. She kept going to the window, pulling back the blind, and checking the front yard. When she wasn't at the window, she stayed on the sofa, knees pulled up to her chest, casting furtive glances at the door. Something had disturbed her. Jim tried to get her to talk, as did Amy, but Louisa seemed lost in her own mind, a captive to whatever it was that had rattled her confidence. It was unlike her and made Jim worry. He presumed the source of her uneasiness must have either been the primal display the folks of Virginia Mills put on in their front yard or the sight of so much blood coming from Peevey's head, not to mention the distant, lifeless look in his eyes when he'd stopped breathing. He had to remind himself that despite her strange maturity and miraculous abilities, Louisa was only nine, just a child. The mayhem and violence she witnessed tonight would cripple any nine-year-old, especially one as sensitive and thoughtful as his Louisa.

His Louisa.

Jim watched her on the sofa, knees pulled up to her chin, eyes moving from the door to the window and back again, amazed at how quickly she'd worked her way into his heart. Just days ago he'd agreed to take her in on a temporary basis out of pity, or rather guilt. He had no intention of forming any kind of bond with her. He wasn't ready for that, wasn't equipped for it. But it had happened anyway. And now, well, now she was *his* Louisa.

When the crowd had moved closer and threatened to encroach upon the porch, and when the temperature within the throng had risen, Jim felt a sense of protection for Louisa he'd not felt for anyone except Amy. It was as if she were his daughter and he had been sworn by almighty God to protect her with his life. It was a fatherly instinct and now struck him as peculiar.

For the seventh time Louisa unfolded her legs, slipped from the sofa, and as lightly as if she were walking on a cushion of air, padded across the living room to the window that was still intact.

From her seat in the recliner Amy said, "Louisa, honey, you don't have to keep checking, you know."

"It's okay now," Jim said.

At the window Louisa said nothing as she pulled back the blind and scanned the night. The glistening light of the porch lamp illuminated the angles of her face and gave it a radiant quality, almost as if she were indeed an angel sent to seek out evil and ward it off.

Finally, after a minute of watchfulness, Louisa let the blind fall back into place and returned to her perch on the sofa.

"What do you keep looking for?" Jim said.

"Or *who*?" Amy added.

Louisa looked at Jim with wary, pitiful eyes, then at Amy, but said nothing. She pulled her knees closer to her chest and drew in a deep, hitched breath.

Jim leaned forward in his chair and rested his elbows on his knees. "You know, it's okay to tell us what frightened you."

Louisa shut her eyes for a moment. When she opened them, she lifted her head and said, "I'm not afraid. Just…someone's coming."

"Who?"

"Him."

"Him who?"

"He's coming."

Poor child, she was making no sense. Jim got up and went to the sofa to sit next to her. He put his arm around her and pulled her closer to his side. "Louisa, who is coming?"

But she was back to saying nothing, playing the role of the silent yet watchful angel.

Outside, through the steady pitter-patter of falling rain, Jim heard a car's engine shut off and a car door close quietly. Like a startled cat Louisa jumped up and rushed across the living room. She pulled back the blind an inch and peeked out. When she turned and faced Jim, there was such alertness in her wide eyes, such alarm in the shape of her mouth, that Jim stood and crossed the room to her.

"What is it, sweetie?"

Her lips tightened. "He's here."

"Who?" Jim slipped his finger around the edge of the blind and pushed it aside enough that he could see the porch and sidewalk and driveway. Officer Peevey walked up the walk, one hand resting on his utility belt. Oddly his cruiser was not in the driveway. Instead a dark gray Ford Explorer was parked there. Since when did a cop make a house call at midnight in his own car?

"It's only Officer Peevey," he said. Maybe Peevey was on his way home and wanted to stop by and make sure everyone was okay, or to thank Louisa for what she'd done.

But the look on Louisa's face told him the reason for this visit was none of the above, that it was not so cordial.

Amy stood and came to the window as well. She put her hand on Louisa's upper back. "Honey, what's the matter?"

When Louisa spoke, her words were hushed and rapid, jumbled together like a sentence with no spaces. "When I touched him, I saw something."

"What did you see?" Amy said.

Louisa glanced at the window. "Evil. He's done horrible things."

Jim didn't know what she meant, but he had no reason to doubt her. Until now, regardless of how unbelievable the things Louisa had done were, *she* was totally believable. She had not seemed easily rattled, nor had she seemed like a child prone to exaggerations and attention seeking.

Peevey's footsteps made it to the porch.

"We need to hide," Louisa said.

Jim met eyes with Amy. She nodded at him, her unspoken sign that she believed Louisa as well and they were both putting their lives in Jim's hands. He had to get all three of them out of there unscathed. He didn't know what the evil or horrible things were that Louisa spoke of, but he didn't want to stick around and find out either.

"To the basement," he said.

As they left the living room, a soft knock sounded on the front door.

Chapter 50

B Y THE TIME the knock came a second time, Jim, Amy, and Louisa were already in the basement. Seconds of silence followed. The only sound was that of the rain brushing on the metal outside doors that led to the basement. Louisa huddled close to Amy, wrapping her arms around Amy's hips and leaning her head in the curve of her waist. They'd kept the lights off for fear that Peevey would see the lights flick on through the small basement windows at ground level. Their only hope at this point was to wait him out and pray he left when there was no response to his knocking.

The seconds turned into minutes, and finally Amy whispered, "You think he left?"

"I don't know," Jim said. "I'll go check."

"What do you mean?"

"I mean I'll sneak upstairs and check. It's the only way."

Louisa grabbed Jim's hand and squeezed it with both of hers. "Mr. Jim, don't. He's still here; I know he is."

"How can you be so sure?" Jim said.

"He knows that I know."

Jim remembered the way Peevey looked at him on the porch earlier, the fear in his eyes, and the way he'd looked past Jim and into the house. He was looking for Louisa. "Know what?"

"The evil he's done."

Her whispered voice and simple proclamation put a tingle in Jim's flesh that coursed over his arms, leaving waves of gooseflesh in its wake.

"I need to check. To make sure. He may not be looking for trouble."

Jim pulled away from Louisa's grip and slowly climbed the stairs, careful not to bump into any of the household tools hanging on the wall or knock over any of the stacks of newspaper and old books piled on the steps. At the top he turned the knob without making a sound and opened the door a couple inches. There he waited and listened. The basement door was not visible from any of the windows on the first floor, so he didn't have to worry about Peevey seeing him from outside. No, his fear was that the officer was already in the house. They hadn't heard any doors open, but still the thought was there.

Opening the door wide enough for him to slip his body through, Jim entered the kitchen, sticking close to the wall. It was at times like these he wished he'd gone ahead and gotten that shotgun. But if he had a gun, he'd keep it in his bedroom, and what good would a gun in the bedroom do him while trapped in the kitchen? He held his breath and listened, but he heard nothing out of the ordinary over the sound of the rain outside.

When he exhaled he heard it, the soft clink and rattle of a key in the knob of the front door. Only it wasn't a key; it couldn't be. Peevey was using a professional's lock-picking tool or maybe a bump key. The lock disengaged and the knob turned. Quickly Jim retreated to the basement even as he heard the front door open. He pulled the basement door closed behind him without making a sound and tiptoed down the steps. Amy and Louisa met him at the bottom of the staircase.

"He's in the house," Jim whispered.

Amy moaned and pulled Louisa closer. In her hand she held a long screwdriver. "I won't let him get her." She held the screwdriver up as if it was a dagger she had just unsheathed. "I'll stick him in the eye before I give her up."

Jim leaned close to Amy's ear. "We need to get out of here, use the outside doors."

"And then what?"

Jim thought for a moment. "The car."

"What about your truck?"

"He has it blocked in." Jim had noticed earlier when he peered outside from behind the blinds that Peevey had pulled the SUV right up to the truck's bumper, blocking any escape. But they had a two-car garage attached to the house, and the other half, the half that housed Amy's Toyota, was unobstructed.

Above them they heard Peevey's footsteps moving about the first floor, going from living room to kitchen to dining room. Any reservation Jim held about Louisa's declaration of Peevey's intent for evil vanished. No upstanding, honest officer of the law would break into someone's home and sneak around like a common burglar unless they had a motive for malicious intent.

Jim took Amy by the arm and led her and Louisa across the basement to the steps that led up and outside.

"What about the keys?" Amy said.

The keys. Both sets were in the kitchen.

Peevey's footsteps faded. He must be climbing the stairs to the second floor.

"I'll get them," Jim said. "Take Louisa and go outside. Go around to the back door to the garage and I'll meet you in there."

He left them in the dark, crossed the basement, and hurried up the steps. At the top he again turned the knob without making a sound and opened the door. Crouched as if he were the burglar and this some unsuspecting family's home, he crossed the kitchen floor, listening but not hearing anything. He must still be creeping around upstairs. Quickly he pocketed his cell phone and lifted the keys from the key hook, careful not to let them jingle. He hoped Amy and Louisa were able to get out of the basement okay and that they'd make quick time getting to the garage.

The door from the garage to the kitchen always squeaked. Jim meant to oil the hinges, but it was one of those little jobs that kept getting put on the back burner and forgotten about. He turned

the knob and pulled the door open, slowly so the hinges only pro-
tested with a low moan. When the door was open no more than
a foot, he slid through the opening and into the garage.

Amy and Louisa were not there.

Amy pushed open the overhead metal basement door as raindrops
landed on her face and caused her to blink. The door opened on
dry, gritty hinges but did not make a sound. Outside, the air was
cool and thick, and rain fell straight down.

She pulled Louisa up the stairs by her hand and shut the door
behind them. Amy thought it strange that even in the midst
of such distress she was concerned about water getting in the
basement.

"Are we okay?" Louisa said, gripping Amy's hand tightly.

"Yes, but we have to move quickly."

The outside basement doors were located on the opposite side
of the house as the door leading to the garage. Rounding the
corner at a hurried jog, Amy suddenly lost her grip on Louisa's
hand. She spun around and found the girl belly down in the grass.
She hurried back and lifted Louisa to her feet.

"Hurry, honey," Amy said.

Off they went again, Amy being careful to keep her footing on
the wet grass. The rain had already drenched her head and nearly
soaked her clothes. Water ran into her eyes and over her nose and
mouth. On the patio they passed in front of the sliding glass doors
that opened to the kitchen, and a surge of panic rushed through
Amy at the thought of Peevey being inside watching them pass
by. She pulled Louisa along. The garage door was just feet away.
She put her hand on the knob and turned, but it didn't move. She
tried again with the same result. It was locked. They always kept
the door locked.

Amy glanced toward the glass doors, fully expecting Peevey

to come bursting through them, weapon drawn, hate and death in his eyes. Turning to the garage door again, she knocked softly. When Jim didn't come immediately, she feared he hadn't made it out of the house. Peevey must have heard him walking or picked up on the sound of tinkling keys or Jim's breathing. She pulled Louisa close to her and kissed the top of her head, a motherly gesture of protection for certain. Amy could no longer deny the affection—love?—she felt for the girl, this child who came to them from the fire.

She knocked again. "C'mon, Jim. Be there."

Jim circled the car, went to the back door. A knock came then, soft but urgent. Of course. They always kept the door locked. Quickly he pulled the door open, put a finger to his lips, and escorted a soaking Amy and Louisa to the Toyota. He opened the back car door, urged them both in, then whispered to Amy, "Don't slam the door till the garage door starts. Okay?"

"Got it," Amy said.

Jim got in the car and glanced in the rearview mirror at his wife and Louisa. They both looked terrified—hair matted to their heads, eyes wide, lips drawn. "Ready?"

They both nodded.

Jim hit the button on the garage door opener, the motor sprang to life, the chain began to pull, and the door lifted. Almost simultaneously they slammed the car doors shut, and he started the engine.

Using the rearview mirror, Jim kept his eye on the garage door opening behind him. Peevey had to have heard the car start. He had to be on his way.

The door seemed to move in half-speed, inch by inch.

"C'mon, c'mon," Jim said. "Let's go." He glanced from the overhead door to the kitchen door. If Peevey came through and found them sitting in the garage, they'd be dead. He'd pull out his handgun and squeeze off three rounds faster than Jim could step on the gas and bust through the door. They needed at least a couple seconds of head-start time to get going and build up some speed getting out of the driveway.

When the overhead door was nearly four feet off the ground, Jim put the car in gear.

"Hold on," he said. They couldn't wait any longer. Peevey would come through that door any second. He stepped on the accelerator, the tires chirped on the concrete garage floor, and the car lurched backward. The car's trunk cleared the door with plenty of room, but the bottom edge of the door dragged along the roof of the car with an awful scrape. In the backseat Amy screamed and ducked her head.

Once in the driveway Jim took his eyes off the mirror and glanced at the garage. The door was the whole way up now, and Peevey was racing for the SUV.

Jim pressed the accelerator to the floor. "Hang on."

The car bounced out of the driveway and onto Valley Road where Jim hit the brakes, shifted to drive, spun the wheel, and stomped the accelerator. Rain pelted the windshield while the wipers worked hard to keep the glass clear of water. Valley Road cut straight through a long stretch of fields then entered a winding section called The Narrows where it was flanked by a sharp embankment on one side and a fast-moving creek on the other. Along the way roads branched off at varying angles leading to every part of the county.

"Why aren't we going back to town?" Amy said, her voice tight and infused with fear.

Jim glanced at the mirror. Peevey hadn't gotten out of the driveway yet. Any second, though, the headlights of the SUV would appear. "And do what?"

"Go to the police!"

"He *is* the police, Amy." In the mirror the SUV bounced out of the driveway, and the headlights glowed like devil eyes in the rain-darkened night. "You think they're gonna believe us over him? He'll say it was all a big misunderstanding."

"Where are you going?"

Jim slowed enough to yank the steering wheel right and turn onto Crescent Road, a narrow secondary road that connected Valley to State Road 117. The wheels lost their traction on the wet asphalt, slid the tail end of the car to the left, but quickly regained traction and pushed the vehicle ahead. "Gonna try to lose him first."

"Then what?"

Jim tossed her the phone. "Call someone."

"Who?"

"Anyone!"

"The police?"

"No. Maybe Jake."

Behind them the SUV made the same turn. Peevey was gaining on them already. The Toyota was a good car, reliable and responsive, but its two-wheel drive was no match for the SUV's four on these rain-slick roads. And Peevey had been trained in the finer points of handling a vehicle at high speed. He would soon be upon them, and then Amy's question would be there again: Then what?

"No bars," Amy said.

"It's this valley."

Jim glanced in the mirror at Amy and Louisa. "Louisa, now's a good time for praying."

She said nothing, but the look on her face told him she was already sending petitions heavenward.

Crescent Road was not a route Jim normally took; in fact, it had been months since he'd last driven it. He wasn't familiar with all the turns and bends, and with the rain muting the light of the headlamps, visibility was very poor. He had to slow or risk driving right off the shoulder. On either side the road was lined with grassy meadows that extended a hundred feet or so then butted up against wooded hills. But even as he slowed, the road turned sharply to the left and caught him by surprise. He stepped on the brake and the tires locked, but the car didn't slow. The tail end drifted and caught the gravel on the road's shoulder. From there things deteriorated quickly. Jim tried to straighten the vehicle's front end by turning the wheel to the left, but the tires did not cooperate. Momentum pulled the car farther off the road and into the grass. The vehicle continued to spin and finally stopped facing the opposite direction, directly at the oncoming SUV.

Jim knew there was no getting back onto the road. The grass was knee high and wet, and the rain-soaked ground was soft. The tires would never gain traction

"Out! Out!" The SUV was closing the distance quickly. His only hope was to see Amy and Louisa off safely, and he'd stay and delay Peevey.

All three of them jumped out of the car.

"Head for the woods," Jim told Amy. "Take Louisa and find help. I'll stall him."

"He'll kill you," Amy said.

"Just go. Go!"

She took off running, pulling Louisa beside her, just as Peevey and the SUV skidded to a stop.

Peevey exited the SUV like a man with one thing on his mind and rounded the front.

Jim looked back at Amy and Louisa—they were halfway to the woods—then faced the oncoming Peevey.

"What are you doing, Peevey?" he hollered.

When Peevey was within ten feet, Jim charged him. Peevey drew from his hip and had something in his hand that looked like a gun. He fired, but there was no muzzle flash, no gunshot.

In an instant the world went black, and every muscle in Jim's body contracted, pulling him inward and tightening more and more, as if he'd been wrapped in a steel cord and drawn tight with a winch. And even as he tried fruitlessly to focus his mind, to make sense of what was happening, he lost all voluntary control and crumpled to the wet ground.

Chapter 51

SECONDS LATER—SECONDS that seemed to be hours, maybe days, where time stood still—the contraction stopped, and Jim's body went flaccid. He lay on his side in the grass, the rain pattering on his face, his mind reeling, unable to move. Thoughts circled through his head, the drive in the car, the thunderstorm that had passed, the darkness of the sky, but one that kept looping through, passing like a painted horse on a carousel, was Amy and Louisa on the run for the woods. He tried to focus on that thought, to jump on the carousel and grab that horse, but it was always just out of reach.

Jim blinked rapidly. He could feel saliva slipping out of his mouth. He wasn't sure if he'd lost control of his bladder or not. Peevey was close, he could sense him standing nearby, gloating.

Still uncertain what had happened, whether he'd been shot in the head or sprayed with some neurotoxin, Jim tried to move his arm and found he could. He lifted it to place his hand on the ground and discovered two thin wires attached to his shirt. And just when he realized what had happened, that he'd been Tasered, the jolt came again.

Thousands of volts ripped through his body, putting a firework display of lights and flashes in his head, drawing every muscle taut until he had no more control of his limbs and they curled inward like a squashed spider. Again the shock lasted only seconds, but the impact was profound. Jim's muscles twitched and ached, his eyelids fluttered and lips quivered. His mind was in a fog with only vague outlines of thoughts visible. Amy and Louisa were there again, but he didn't even know why. There was a great urgency, though, a needing. And he could do nothing about it. He would die here in the grass with the rain pelting him, soaking his clothes.

Before he could regain movement again, the hit came again and seized Jim in a paralyzing contracture. This time the pain was almost unbearable, and he could only think of death. Third time was the charm. He writhed in the grass until his muscles tightened to the point that they felt as though they'd rupture from their bony attachments. The jolt lasted longer this time, only a mere eternity, until it finally faded and left him limp and wasted. His brain stuttered on Amy's name, like a bad television reception tuned to the wrong channel. The world around him was shrouded in profound darkness—such darkness that the first cohesive thought he formed was that he'd died and this was the afterlife, or some holding room before being escorted to the final judgment.

It wasn't until he felt the rain again, cool on his skin, that he realized he was still alive and still on his side in the grass. Seconds passed, then what seemed like minutes, until he could move his eyes, his mouth, turn his head. Slowly, like the awakening of a butterfly from its cocoon-sleep, Jim regained motion and discovered his right wrist was handcuffed to his left ankle.

When Doug Miller steered his cruiser into the driveway of the Spencer home, the place looked quiet with sleeping occupants. Only one light was on in the front windows, one of them covered with thick plastic. The garage door was open and the garage empty, but Jim's truck was in the driveway. He'd talked to Peevey and read his report, talked to Lorenzo also; he knew what had transpired at the home just hours ago, the hopped-up crowd, the brick tossing, the girl, Peevey.

After shutting off the engine, he climbed out of the car and walked up to the front porch, not sure if he wanted to knock and disturb the Spencers or not. Stepping up onto the porch, he reached for the doorknob expecting it to be locked but instead found it turned easily. He cracked the door and listened. The house was quiet, what would be expected if everyone was asleep in their beds. But something wasn't right; he could sense it. Virginia Mills was a quaint town, and the Spencers lived in a fairly rural neighborhood outside of town, but no one left their garage door open and doors unlocked at night. Maybe thirty years ago they did, but not now. Of course, it could be that with all the excitement tonight they simply forgot about the door. But no matter how many excuses he gave himself, no matter how much he tried to talk himself out of this queer feeling, it remained, warning him, putting his police instinct on high alert. He'd been a cop long enough that he knew to trust that instinct, for it was right far more times than it wasn't.

With the door already open a good foot, Doug knocked on it and said, "Hello?"

When no reply came, he pushed open the door the rest of the way and entered the house, half expecting to see the Spencers and little Louisa dead on the floor with more of the alphabet carved into their chests. But the living room was empty. As were the kitchen and dining room. In fact, after a quick search of the second floor he found the entire house empty, even the basement and garage. Odd. He knew the Spencers had two cars, and only Jim's truck was in the driveway. Why would they go out at such a late hour? Even more odd was that there was no sign of forced entry, no sign of struggle. It was as if they'd gone out for a late-night snack and merely forgot to lock the front door.

Doug was about to conclude that his discovery at the office was just coincidence as he'd hoped, that the Spencers had possibly gone to sleep in a hotel for the night, not trusting the plastic on the front window to ward off any more visitors bent on stirring up trouble, and that his police instinct had been wrong, as unlikely (but possible) as that was, when his cell phone rang. He didn't recognize the caller's number.

Doug hit the talk button. "Chief Miller."

"Derek Peevey's in trouble." It was a female, but he didn't recognize her voice.

"Who is this?"

"He's going to do something terrible."

"How did you get this number?"

"The dispatcher gave it to me. It's Alicia."

"Who are you?"

"I'm...I was Derek's girlfriend."

Doug paused to collect his thoughts and make some sense of this conversation. "How do you know he's in trouble?"

"I can't tell you how I know, but I know. He's going to try to kill someone."

Goose bumps puckered the skin on Doug's arms as if a sudden arctic wind had blown through the house. At any other time he would have dismissed such a bizarre call as a revengeful ploy of a disgruntled girlfriend. But not this time. Everything made sense: The fact that Peevey had had contact with every victim, whether it was arresting Billy Cousins or Buck Petrosky for disorderly conduct or pulling over Clint Efforts or Ron Harman for traffic violations. Lorenzo's description of Peevey's odd behavior after the girl brought him back. His volunteering to watch the house. The missing Spencers and their missing car. Doug's instinct rang the high-alert bell.

"Okay," he said, but he barely heard himself voice the words. "Stay where you are, you hear?"

"I'm not going anywhere."

"Do you know anything else?"

The girl on the other end of the line hesitated; she seemed frightened, and why shouldn't she be? "He's a monster."

"Do you know where he may have gone?"

"No."

Then, as if he were putting together a complex puzzle and finally found the one piece he'd been missing, the answer found Doug. Of course. He should have seen it before, but there was no way he could have. Clenching his free fist, he said, "I do."

Chapter 52

THE RAIN HAD slowed but continued to fall and soak Jim's clothes through to the skin. Shivering now, he pulled himself over and onto his knees. Peevey's SUV was gone. The Toyota was still there, but with no way to drive it he was stranded. He looked around, peering through the falling rain and into the darkness for any sign of Amy and Louisa. Jim had no idea how long the Taser's multiple jolts had blanked his brain. It could have been minutes or even hours. He checked his wrist for the time, but he wasn't wearing his watch. He had no memory of taking it off, but his brain was still operating in fits and starts, jumping from one line of thought to another, skipping tracks as easily as a hobo hops trains.

But one thought he kept landing on was what had happened to his wife and Louisa. Had they escaped into the woods and Peevey grown tired of looking for them? Had he captured them and taken them away? Had he killed them, and their bodies were now lying somewhere in the meadow, concealed by darkness and wild grass? If anything happened to them…

In a panic Jim turned in a complete circle and said his wife's name. When no response came, he called it louder. There was no danger of Peevey hearing him. The evil cop with a fetish for Tasers was no doubt long gone. But still no reply came.

The more time that passed, the clearer Jim's head grew, and the clearer it became, the more he feared the worst. He remembered his phone he'd taken from the kitchen and tossed in the Toyota's center console cup holder. He could call for help. But who would he call? He didn't know if he could trust the police. Either they were just as malevolent as Peevey, or they wouldn't believe him anyway. Chief Miller seemed to be a good man, but Jim didn't know him that well. Cops were professionals when it came to appearances, making you see them the way they wanted you to see them.

In a manner as awkward as a two-legged turtle, Jim crawled to the car and opened the door. The phone was right where he thought it would be. Slumped in the driver's seat, he flipped it open—one bar, it had to be enough—and scrolled down through his contacts, dialed the number.

Three rings later: "Hello? Jake here."

"Jake." Jim choked out the name of his old friend. Tears of relief sprang to his eyes. At last something this evening had gone right. "They're gone. I can't find them."

"Whoa, slow down there. Is this Jim?"

"Yes. They're gone, Jake. I think he took them." The words tumbled out of his mouth like blocks.

"Who, Jim? Amy and the girl? Who took them?"

"Peevey." He almost shouted the name.

"Officer Peevey?"

"He's not...he's not who you think he is."

There was a brief pause on the other end, long enough to cause Jim to panic. "Don't hang up, Jake. Please."

"I ain't goin' anywhere. I'm just tryin' to figure out what you're goin' on about."

"Peevey, he Tasered me then took them. I'm handcuffed here." He strained at the cuffs, trying to slip his hand through it, but it was much too tight.

"But why, Jim? I ain't followin'."

"She knew. Oh, God, protect them."

"She knew what?"

"That he was the one, the killer."

"Jim, where are you?" Jake sounded exasperated.

"I'm..." He couldn't think where he was. There was a road just a few yards away, but his mind couldn't recall which road. He'd come down Valley Road, he remembered that much. "I'm...off Valley Road, on, uh...God, please. Crescent."

"Jim, you hold tight. I'm coming there. Okay? I know just where you are."

"Just hurry. He's got them."

Jim clicked off the phone and, leaning against the steering wheel of the car, slipped it into his pocket. How would they ever find where Peevey had taken them? They could be anywhere. He shut his eyes. A prayer came easily then, a cry from his heart, pleading for the life of his wife and the girl he'd come to love.

Five minutes later he saw headlights approaching from the direction of Valley Road, only they weren't the lights of Jake's truck.

He was lying there in the grass. Like he was dead. Amy had walked right by Jim, and he had been soaked, so pale and motion-less. She had no idea if Peevey had killed him or not. She and Louisa had almost made it to the edge of the woods when Peevey caught them. She tried to fight him, but he was much stronger and had threatened to shoot them. They didn't stand a chance. And as he dragged both her and Louisa back to his SUV, she'd asked several times if he'd killed Jim, but he gave no reply. Her only hope—and prayer—was that Jim had somehow survived his confrontation and was even now looking for help.

But despite her best intentions, she doubted it. Why would Peevey let him live? He had no use for Jim.

Peevey had shoved them both into the SUV, her in the driver's seat and Louisa in the back with him. He had held his handgun to Amy's head and said, "Drive where I tell you to and nowhere else, or I'll blow the kid's brains to kingdom come."

Now, after driving several miles, she broke the silence.

"Did you kill my husband?" she asked.

"Shut up and drive."

"Not 'til you tell me." Her boldness surprised even her.

Peevey grabbed a handful of Amy's hair and yanked her head back against the headrest. The cold steel of the gun's barrel pressed against her skull. "Keep driving or I'll blow your brains out, and then the girl will be all mine." He put his mouth to her ear. "I'd like that."

For the first time since fleeing the house, tears pushed behind Amy's eyes, and her throat constricted. She couldn't leave Louisa alone with this beast. She had to be strong. They both had to make it through this alive. She nodded and tightened her hands on the wheel.

Fifteen minutes later, the rain slowing to only a sprinkle, he directed her to pull onto a gravel lane and cut the headlights. The darkness was so thick, so shroud-like, she couldn't see a thing beyond the glass of the SUV's windows. And they'd taken so many turns getting here that she'd quickly become disoriented and had no idea where they were.

"I can't see the lane," she said.

"You can hear it, can't you?" he said. "Feel the gravel under the tires? It's a straight shot, just keep the wheel where it is."

They came upon a slight rise in the terrain, and when it leveled, she saw in the near distance, maybe a hundred yards off, the dimly lit windows of a house.

Chapter 53

THE HEADLIGHTS GREW closer, and when they stopped along the side of the road, Jim noticed they belonged to a police cruiser. The door opened and cab lights blinked on. It was Miller. Jim tensed and his heart began to race. He was so vulnerable sitting in the car, his wrist handcuffed to his ankle. There was no way to defend himself. He was totally at Miller's mercy.

Rain on the windshield blurred Jim's view of Miller as he made his way through the tall grass to the car and rounded the front of it. He stopped by the passenger side door and bent over to look through the window.

"What's going on, Spencer? You okay?"

Jim's first thought was to lock the doors and avoid Miller, but he knew that if Miller was in with Peevey and bent on murder, a single piece of glass wasn't going to stop him. So he opened the door.

Miller came around the door and squatted next to Jim. "What happened here, Spencer?"

Cautiously Jim said, "You don't know?"

"I have an idea."

"Peevey."

Miller cursed and produced the key for the handcuffs. After freeing Jim, he said, "C'mon, you have to come with me."

Jim hesitated. "Jake Tucker is coming." He was still unsure of Miller's motives and wanted him to know that someone else was aware of what happened and where he was. If anything happened to him, Tucker would know it.

"I know," Miller said. "He called me. C'mon, let's use my car."

Jim relaxed a little and rubbed his wrist. "I think Peevey took Amy and Louisa."

"And I think I know where he took them."

Under Peevey's coercion Amy steered the SUV right up to the front porch of the large farmhouse. The porch light was not on, but she could tell by the feeble light spilling out of the window that the place was well cared for, that the occupants took pride in the way they kept their home.

"Turn it off," Peevey said.

She obeyed and shut off the engine.

"Now get out slowly. You try to be a hero, and I swear I'll blow her head off."

Amy opened the door and stepped out of the vehicle. Peevey rounded the tail end holding Louisa by the arm, the barrel of the handgun pressed against the side of her head. Louisa's eyes met Amy's, and in them Amy did not find fear but rather sadness, a deep sorrow that brought the tears to Amy's eyes again.

Peevey released Louisa and nudged her forward. "Inside. Both of you."

Amy took Louisa's hand and crossed the porch, opened the door, and entered the living room of the home. If it once served as a place of rest and comfort, a room where weary muscles found respite after a long day of labor, there was no sign of it now. Furniture was toppled, books strewn across the floor. A lamp lay on its side, the shade bent and torn.

"This way," Peevey said, as he passed through and headed for the kitchen.

The kitchen showed none of the signs of the destruction so evident in the living room, other than dishes littering the sink area. Peevey opened a door that led to a staircase that descended to the basement of the house. He motioned with his gun. "Down."

Amy hesitated. With one step Peevey reached her and grabbed her arm. His grip was unbelievably strong, and she almost cried out in pain. He shoved her toward the steps, and if not for the railing to grab onto she would have toppled headlong down them. Amy stumbled down the steps, Louisa staying close behind her. At the bottom she turned and surveyed the large concrete-floored room. The walls were fieldstone and the ceiling open-beamed. In the far corner there was what looked to be a small room only half-completed. The bare studs were placed extremely close, a door was on one end, but no drywall yet and no electrical wiring.

Peevey nudged her toward the room. "That way."

As she got closer, Amy noticed something that made her squeeze Louisa's hand tighter and almost burst into tears. There were people in the room, an older man and woman, standing next to each other, caged like animals.

As Jim's head cleared more and the trauma from the Taser wore off, panic exploded in his chest. They needed to find Amy and Louisa soon. No, now! Time was not on their side.

Jake arrived five minutes after Miller had found Jim and pulled his truck up alongside the cruiser. "Where ya headed, Chief?"

"You know the Appletons' farm?"

"Sure do. Bob and I go back some ways. You think he took them there?"

"Got a hunch and can't ignore it."

Jake paused, looked straight ahead out the windshield, then back at Miller. "Why?"

"Just stay close. If I'm right, I'll explain later."

"You callin' in help?"

Miller massaged the steering wheel as if he was trying to work the tension out of it. "Not just yet. Let's wait 'til we get there and see what comes of it."

Jake shrugged. "Your call. I got my twelve gauge."

"You let me handle the guns if it comes to that."

He rolled the window up and shifted the car into gear. Once on the road Miller radioed in to the dispatcher informing her where they were headed and to be on standby for backup. If he needed it, he'd holler.

Jim said, "So who are the Appletons?"

"Couple who lives out on Pine Grove Road. They have a farm, nothing big, just small time, but it suits them."

"Why would Peevey go there?"

"Tuesday afternoon I got a call from some big shot with Enviro-Pride. Said one of his sales guys, Cody something, had gone missing, never checked in at the end of the day on Monday. He wondered if we'd gotten any calls. Apparently his family was pretty worried."

"What's that have to do with Peevey?"

"At the time of the call I didn't think anything of it. This Cody guy was young, just out of college, you never know with those types. He may have decided the sales gig wasn't for him and split. But I checked into it, asked for his schedule for the day. He had four farms to visit, and he only got to three. Guess which one he never got to?"

"The Appletons."

"Bingo."

Miller hit the turn signal, slowed, and turned left. Rain continued to fall, and the wipers continued to swoosh back and forth, clearing the windshield with each arc.

"Why didn't you check it out then?"

He shrugged. "I did try to call the Appletons a couple times, but there was no answer. Even drove out here Wednesday, but no one was home. I figured maybe they went away for a couple days. They do that from time to time. I guess…" He let the words fade as he made another turn.

"You know there was no way to put the two together," Jim said, trying to alleviate Miller's remorse even a little.

Miller shook his head and checked the rearview mirror. "Looking back on it now, I don't see how I could have missed it."

"You still don't know if there's any connection."

"No. I don't know, but I feel it. I didn't feel it yesterday. Should have, though."

They rode in silence as the darkness outside the cruiser loomed just beyond the blurred light of the headlamps. Who knew what lurked in such lightlessness, what evil, what malevolence. The panic was still here, clawing at Jim's chest, itching his nerves, screaming a warning that he was about to find out what true evil was.

Chapter 54

DEREK PEEVEY WAS in no mood to talk. He should have killed Spencer back there. Should have put a bullet in his head and been done with it. But for some reason he couldn't. Jim Spencer was a good man, respected the law, respected everyone. He didn't deserve to die like that. Derek thought the Taser would be enough to disorient him until they got out of there, and it didn't disappoint.

Derek held the handgun shoulder high and pointed it at Spencer's wife. She was a pretty thing, trying to appear brave, but he could tell she was ready to do it in her pants. He could always tell right before they dumped on themselves. It turned his stomach. The kid showed no fear, though. She looked at him with those tired, sad eyes and could see right through him; he knew she could. He hated the way she eyed him, exposed him like an X-ray, pitied him. He needed no one's pity.

"Quit looking at me," he said to the girl. He motioned to the wall with the gun. "Stand over there, both of you."

When he unlocked the door to the room he'd built for the Appletons and pulled the door open, Clare was right there. She shifted her eyes between him and the woman and girl. "Mitch, what have you done?" There was disappointment in her voice.

Derek motioned toward the room and said to Spencer's wife, "Get in, the kid too."

She leaned against the wall and gripped the stones with both hands. "No. I'm not doing anything until you tell me if my husband is still alive."

Derek didn't have time for this. He'd made a stupid mistake in letting Spencer live, and now he had to get out of there. Funny, how he'd never really come up with an escape plan. Maybe he wanted to be caught. Maybe he wanted the respect of a trial. All those lawyers, giving him the benefit of the doubt. Innocent till proven guilty. Respect.

He reached the woman in two steps and in one quick motion slapped her across the face. Her head snapped back and her knees buckled, but she didn't go down. The blow had so weakened her, though, that Derek was able to pull her from the wall and toss her into the room with no resistance. The girl followed without a word. Once they were in, he shut the door and locked it.

Clare guided Spencer's wife to the floor and put the woman's head in her lap. "You didn't have to do that," she said, scolding him like a child who'd just been caught tormenting the family cat.

Bob came to the wall and gripped the two-by-fours with both hands. "Why are you doing this?" He glanced at the kid who was on her knees next to Spencer's wife. "She's just a child." His lips quivered when he spoke, and there was a flash of contempt in his eyes.

Derek had lost their respect. He'd enjoyed the Appletons and let them live because they had respected him, genuinely, but now that respect was gone, and he had no use for them. And the girl had to go too. She'd seen too much. When she touched him back at the Spencer house, brought him back from that cliff where there was nothing but blackness below, she peered over the edge and saw into his soul, saw his dark side, his thoughts, his desires, his wounds, everything. It was as if his life was a picture book and she'd flipped through every page at once, saw every photo, every illustration, every gruesome image. He had no secrets with her. And the exposure scared him.

Derek turned his back to the room and headed for the staircase. An image was in his head then, the fire, his father. The fear.

At the bottom of the steps Derek had to grab the simple banister to steady himself.

From across the basement Clare said, "You don't have to do this, Mitch. You don't have to give in to those demons. Don't you see, even after all these years, your father is still controlling you."

She was right, of course. He was controlling him, that old sack, even from his grave where he belonged. But at the moment Derek didn't care. He had to be strong. He had to clean this up and get out of there. He'd find a nice secluded place and disappear, find a new life and start over. No one would find him, not even his father.

He rushed up the steps and out of the house. It was still raining, but it had slowed to only a mist now, not enough to thwart his plans. In the barn he felt for the light switch and flipped it. Inside it was dry and warm and smelled of hay and grease. In the far corner, under the workbench, he found what he'd come for: the red fourteen-gallon rolling gasoline container with a siphon handle.

Chapter 55

AMY CLUTCHED LOUISA to her chest and rocked back and forth, humming a tune her mother used to sing to her when she was a child and afraid in the night. The woman who had introduced herself as Clare sat in a chair, one arm wrapped around her chest, the other hand over her mouth. Tears spilled from her eyes and ran down her cheeks. Her husband, Bob, paced along the wall, both hands in his pockets.

Overhead, on the first floor of the house, Peevey's footsteps crisscrossed back and forth, thudding like he'd come through the boards. Whatever he was doing up there, he was in a hurry to get it done.

Another sound was there then, like water splashing. Clare looked up and found her husband's eyes. "What's that?" she said.

Bob stopped pacing and listened, his eyes following trails on the basement ceiling.

The splashing continued and seemed to follow Peevey's footsteps around the floor.

"Sounds like…"

But before Bob could finish, Amy smelled the unmistakable fumes and said, "Gasoline."

"Get up," Bob said to Clare.

She stood and he took the chair, lifted it above his shoulders, and rammed it into the studs that made up the makeshift prison. The collision made a solid thud, but the studs didn't budge.

"You tried that already," Clare said.

Bob lifted the chair again. "But this time I'm not going to stop until we're out."

He tried again and again, but each time the chair merely bounced off the studs.

Ever since his father put a match to his son's pants, Derek had dealt with an abnormal fear of fire. But it was a fear he had to overcome; he could no longer be its slave. He must be strong. For that reason he chose to destroy the house and everything (and everyone) in it in a blazing inferno. It would be his final statement, his stand against the fear that had gripped him so tightly and anyone who had disrespected him since his mother and father first did. No longer would they cast condescending looks his way. No longer would they show their indifference and disdain for him. He would be legendary. Yes, a roaring blaze was a fitting conclusion.

After dousing the interior of the house with gasoline, being ever so careful not to get any on his shoes or pants, Derek poured a line out of the house, across the front porch, and around the perimeter of the stone foundation. With the age of the house being well over a hundred years, it would burn hot and quick, like taking a match to the driest of kindling after soaking it with lighter fluid.

Standing in the gravel driveway, Derek retrieved the matchbox from his pocket, withdrew a match, and stepped up to where the trail of gasoline ended. His movements were quick and determined. He struck the match head against the striking surface and watched it ignite. The flame was insignificant compared to the chain reaction it would start, but the sight of the flame made him tremble. He must be strong.

Quickly Derek dropped it on the gasoline. It flared with a *whoosh* and took off from there, splitting in two directions, one following the perimeter of the house, the other racing through the front door. Within seconds the house was ablaze, the heat of it buffeting Derek like a torpedo heater.

Shielding his face, Derek backed up, turned to get in the Explorer, and saw headlights cresting the hill of the lane.

The arrhythmic glow just over the rise reminded Jim of the soft light that emanated from a jar full of fireflies. At first the source of the light was a mystery. But as the cruiser drew nearer and Miller's foot got heavier on the accelerator, the lights seemed to have a breath of their own, a familiar movement pattern that put a rock in the pit of Jim's stomach.

And when the cruiser crested the small rise and the source of the light was in full view, a guttural groan, involuntary and unbidden, escaped his throat.

Miller cursed and the cruiser lunged forward, spitting gravel from under its tires. The shocks creaked and moaned as they absorbed the impact from the uneven path.

Ahead, not even a hundred yards away, a farmhouse sat ablaze with a growing fire.

Grunting with each effort, Bob Appleton rammed the chair against the studs again, and this time one of them cracked and splintered. He stopped and looked at his wife and Amy. Sweat soaked his hair and wet his face, and he panted heavily. Amy was afraid he'd hurt himself. He had to be nearing seventy, and although he looked to be in good health, one never knew what lurked under the surface.

She could hear the fire crackling above them, and some smoke had begun to make its way through the floor joints and collect around the beams in the ceiling.

Again Bob shoved the chair at the stud, and again it cracked, this time bent like an elbow slightly flexed.

"One more," he said, and reared the chair back before thrusting it forward again. The two-by-four snapped and folded and broke in the middle. Bob lost his balance from the exertion and would have gone to the floor had it not been for Amy stepping forward quickly to steady him. He apologized and wiped sweat from his eyes.

"I can take it from here," she said.

"No, no," Bob said, shaking his head. "I'll do it. One more should be all it takes, and then…"

And then what? That was the question pounding in Amy's head. The first floor was an inferno; there was no hope of escaping that way. Their only chance would be the outside cellar doors, the same kind she and Louisa had exited back home when Peevey was the menace above them.

The smoke was beginning to thicken and roil along the ceiling, following the subtle drafts that made it through the old windows and seeped down through the joints in the flooring.

Bob heaved the chair one more time at the stud, and it finally broke loose and fell to the concrete floor.

"Out," he said, motioning toward the opening in the prison. "Quickly now."

Amy and Louisa went first, followed by Clare then Bob. He was still panting heavily, and his face was as red as raw meat.

"Are you sure you're okay?" Amy said.

Bob dragged his sleeve across his face, mopping up the sweat. "I'll be fine. Quickly now, the doors."

Amy ran ahead and tried the outside doors, but she found them sealed shut. They had a locking mechanism on the underside, but it was already disengaged. The doors were locked from the outside. She pushed up on them, and they gave a little but didn't open.

"They're locked," she said. "From the outside."

Bob came over and stood on the stairs so the back of his

shoulders were pushing up on the doors. He tried to straighten his knees and wedge the doors open, but they refused to cooperate.

"Go check the other door," he said.

Amy hurried across the basement, leaving Louisa with Clare, and ascended the steps. About halfway up she was met by a wall of black, sooty smoke. She held her breath and climbed the rest of the staircase. At the door she put her hand on the wood and immediately pulled it away. It was too hot to touch. The fire raged just on the other side. To open the door would be to feed the fire the cool oxygen-rich air from the basement and send her flying down the steps in a backdraft. Returning to the outside doors she screamed, "No use. Too much smoke, and the fire is right there."

"Then this is our only way," Bob said, moaning as he pushed up against the doors again.

In the far corner of the basement, near where the furnace stood, part of the floor gave way in a burst of sparks, and fire began crawling along the ceiling beams. Smoke poured in through the opening, surging and churning as if it were stirred by a deep ocean current.

Clare screamed and pulled Louisa close.

Again Bob pushed upward, straining with all his effort until the veins bulged in his forehead and neck and his muscles became as taut cords.

Fire continued to eat up the ceiling, moving to the electric circuit breaker box on the wall. When it reached it, the box exploded in a burst of sparks and the lights along the ceiling blinked out. Flickering firelight filled the basement now, reflecting off the smoke and casting the basement in an angry Halloween hue.

Bob, seeing the fire clawing closer, choking on the smoke that now lingered around the doors, gave another effort, groaned, pushed, and almost fell down the steps. He stumbled forward, clutching his chest, went to his knees. An orange tint colored his twisted face. His hands trembled, teeth gnashed. He tried to draw in a breath but only coughed and hacked. Teetering on his knees, he groped at his chest and fell to his side, eyes rolled back in his head, only the whites showing, like two golf balls in a jack-o'-lantern head.

Chapter 56

FIRE SPEWED FROM the home's windows as if from the mouth of a dragon, seeking oxygen, craving it, devouring it in huge gulps. When the cruiser skidded to a stop in front of the house, Jim threw the door open, but before he could leap out, Miller grabbed his arm.

"Wait, Spencer."

"For what? My wife may be in there. And Louisa."

"He's here."

Jim hadn't missed the SUV parked in front of the home. He knew Peevey was there and didn't care. If Amy and Louisa were inside that house, he had to get to them; there still might be time.

He pulled away from Miller's grip. "I don't care. I have to find them."

Outside the car the heat from the fire was almost unbearable. The front door had already been consumed and the windows blown out. The fire rumbled and snarled like a ravenous beast. There was no chance for entrance. Jake Tucker arrived at Jim's side and put his hand on Jim's shoulder. Miller rounded the front of the car, using his arm to shield his face from the heat.

Inside, wood cracked, popped, splintered, and a burst of flames shot into the night sky. Rain continued to fall in a light mist, but it did nothing to extinguish the fire. They'd have a better chance of putting it out if they stood in a circle and spit on it, Jim thought.

"It's no use," Miller shouted over the hiss of the fire.

As the last word passed over his lips, a crack sounded, loud and close, almost like the popping of a giant balloon. For an instant Jim thought it had come from inside the house, maybe one of the second-story support beams split or the gas stove had ignited and exploded. But when Miller went down, first to his knees, then flat on his face, he knew where the sound had come from and dove behind the cruiser.

Jake hollered, "You go find Amy and the girl. I'll take care of Peevey."

Jim peered out from around the car but didn't see anyone by the light of the fire. But beyond the light was thick darkness, and Peevey could be standing in the wide open and never be seen. He'd have to make a run for it. Dashing from the car to the corner of the house, he ducked around the far wall. The fire had only just reached this portion of the house but was overtaking it quickly. Jim ran around the side, looking for cover, and that's when he saw it.

Clare knelt next to Bob as Amy rushed for the doors leading to the outside. Louisa crouched and touched Bob's head, his chest, his neck.

Amy banged her fists against the doors, screamed for help. She tried pushing them, but they wouldn't budge. The smoke loomed close; like a living thing it writhed and coiled. Her lungs constricted, nerves itched. She felt as though her heart would burst from her chest. The claustrophobia was acting up. She pounded again. She'd rather take her chances with Peevey than suffocate to death by smoke inhalation, or worse, be burned to death by the encroaching fire.

All-out panic driving her, Amy shoved her body upward at the door several consecutive times until she finally collapsed on the steps, winded and choking on smoke.

Louisa was bent over Bob and rocked back and forth, her eyes closed. She almost seemed to glow in the murky air.

Fire cracked and popped around them; smoke stirred and boiled as if it were poured from a cauldron.

Maybe she is an angel, Amy thought. Maybe she'll save us all or usher us into heaven.

Amy slid down to the bottom of the stairs where the smoke had not yet taken over and drew in a lungful of hot, dry air. She returned to the doors and once again threw her fists at them.

Jim crossed quickly to the cellar doors. And suddenly he heard it: knocking, rapid and panicked, like a frenzy of tribal drums. A thick piece of wood was jammed into the handles, locking the doors from the outside. He kicked the wood away, bent down, and lifted the doors up and out. Smoke as thick and black as charcoal bubbled out, stung his eyes, and momentarily blinded him.

"Jim!" It was Amy's voice

She fell into his arms and nearly knocked him over. Louisa was there too.

When his eyes cleared, he could see his wife. Her skin was blackened with soot and dust, and tears streamed down her cheeks, leaving pink tracks in the dirt. Louisa clung to his waist. He stroked her grimy hair.

"Jim, they're still down there."

"Who?"

"Bob and Clare."

But before Jim could rush for the basement, another shot cut through the night. Jim flinched as Louisa was ripped from his side and tossed to the ground. She lay motionless. Amy dropped next to the girl, sobbing.

Jim searched the darkness and found him, Peevey, standing at the corner of the house, handgun held chest high and aimed. Behind him the fire grew and licked at the cool air, lapping up oxygen.

"This is it, Spencer," Peevey said. He stepped forward.

As he did, an explosion sounded from Jim's left, accompanied by a muzzle flash. Peevey's handgun discharged as well, but by then it was too late and the cop was already being pushed into the house, into the fire. He stumbled and was at once consumed by flames. His dying screams hung suspended in the air, then fell. Silence.

Jim spun around and fell to the ground next to Louisa. Jake arrived soon after that, shotgun in hand.

"The Appletons are in the basement still," Amy said to Jake.

Jake nodded and disappeared into the cellar. The open doors were now belching thick, acrid smoke into the night air.

Jim cradled Louisa's head in his arms. Her right hip area was misshapen and red. Tears pooled in Jim's eyes, but he did nothing to wipe them away.

Louisa's eyes fluttered opened, and her lips parted. Her eyes found Jim's. A single tear slipped out and ran over her temple, clearing a line in the soot.

"Tell me what I need to do," Jim said.

"Pray." Her voice was thin and weak, on the verge of cutting out.

"That can't be it." The tears came from his own eyes now and caught at the corners of his nose.

She opened her mouth again. "Believe."

"I can't," he said. It had been so long. He was so wounded, so far away from God.

Louisa's eyes fixed on him, and in them he saw the peace that transcended all she did. There was no doubting in her and no fear at all. Jim remembered a line in the Bible that used to pique his curiosity. He couldn't recall who had said it, but the words spoke to him now, and in his heart he repeated them: *God, I believe; help my unbelief.*

Louisa lifted a hand and touched Jim's face. "I remember, Mr. Jim," she said. "I remember so much now."

Chapter 57

THE HOSPITAL ROOM'S lights were dim. Just one illuminated lamp above Louisa's bed washed the corner in a soft radiance, as if a light from heaven fell on its wounded angel. Jim and Amy had spent the night in the surgical waiting room, each sleeping in a chair, and Jake Tucker had stayed too, passing the time reading magazines on a small sofa.

The surgery had taken nearly three hours, and afterward the lead surgeon filled the Spencers in on the extent of Louisa's injuries: fractured femoral head, fractured pelvis, torn colon. All was repaired, and he expected the hip joint to heal completely after a lengthy recovery period. She would need more surgeries, of course, as the bones grew and lengthened, but they would be minor compared to what had to be done to piece the bones back together after the bullet had ripped through them.

Now Louisa slept peacefully in her hospital bed, the sheets pulled up to her chest. Amy slept in a chair beside the bed. She'd cleaned up in the hospital bathroom, but remnants of soot still outlined her face and streaked her hair. Jim marveled at how peacefully she slept, despite the nightmare she and Louisa had been through. Amy had changed so much in the past week, come so far.

At nine o'clock Louisa's eyes blinked rapidly and opened. She looked around the room until she found Jim.

"Hey, kiddo," Jim said. "You're awake."

Her eyes closed slowly and opened again. She licked her lips.

"Are you thirsty?"

She nodded.

Jim touched her cheek. "I'll be right back with some ice chips."

He left to get the chips from the small kitchen area down the hall, and when he returned, Amy was awake as well, holding Louisa's hand and stroking her hair.

Jim slipped some ice chips into Louisa's mouth using a plastic spoon. "There you go. That'll wet your whistle a little anyway. Doctor said no water until they say you're ready."

Louisa let the ice melt in her mouth then swallowed. "Thank you, Mr. Jim."

"You're welcome, sweetie. No problem at all."

She looked at Amy then Jim again. "I mean, thank you for taking care of me. I...I remember what happened."

She'd said that last night before passing out, before he helped Jake drag Bob and Clare Appleton from the burning basement, before Jim got on the police radio.

"You don't have to talk about it now," Jim said.

"I want to. I might forget again."

Amy was still holding the girl's hand, and now Jim took the other one. "Okay, but only as much as you want to. Okay?"

"There was a fire," she said. "I woke up in my room, and it was filled with smoke. I couldn't see anything, but it was getting really hot. I could hear my mom calling my name and coughing. I tried calling back to her, but I don't think she could hear me. Then I heard my brother crying." She stopped and stared at the sheets. Tears pooled in her eyes. "I couldn't do anything. There was so much smoke I couldn't even find the door. Then I didn't hear anything except the fire right outside my room. I couldn't breathe, there was so much smoke." Tears slipped down her cheeks, and Amy wiped them away. "I laid on the floor. I thought I was gonna die, but I wasn't scared at all. And then..." She turned her face up and looked at Amy and Jim. "And then I was in Mr. Tucker's house, and I saw him there and knew I had to help him. I didn't remember anything about the fire or my mom or dad or brother. Not until the fire just now. Is Mr. Bob okay?"

Amy squeezed Louisa's hand and wiped another tear from the child's cheek. "Mr. Bob didn't make it, honey. He had a heart attack."

She was quiet for a moment, contemplative. "What about Miss Clare?"

"She had lots of smoke in her lungs, but the doctors fixed her up."

"I'm sad for her."

"Me too," Amy said.

Louisa then turned her eyes to Jim and smiled. "You believed, didn't you? You trusted God."

He nodded and swallowed the lump that was climbing his throat. "I did. But I learned something else that you taught me."

"I did?"

"You sure did. It's not magic, and it's not about me. It's about surrendering to God's will."

The smile left Louisa's face. "Not every prayer gets answered the way we want."

Jim knew she was thinking about her family and about Bob Appleton. "No, it doesn't. But that's why we leave it in God's hands, don't we?"

"Yes," she said. "He can handle it. We can't."

Her smile returned as she closed her eyes and fell back to sleep.

When Jim and Jake entered Miller's room, the police chief was sitting up in bed watching TV. A thick, gauzy bandage wrapped his neck in a makeshift collar. His hair was a mess, and dark circles shadowed his eyes. His wife sat next to his bed, her legs crossed, worry lines deepened across her forehead.

"Mornin'," Miller said as Jim entered. He clicked off the TV.

Jim dipped his chin. "Good morning, Chief, Mrs. Miller. How are you feeling?"

Miller shrugged. "Kinda like I just got shot."

"How bad is it?"

"Not as bad as it could have been. Caught me in the neck. Just missed the jugular."

"This your first time?" Jim said to Miller.

"I was shot at before, but this was the first time I was actually hit. And it'll be my last." He reached over and took his wife's hand. "I'm retiring as soon as we get the mystery with Louisa solved. I'd do it now, but I can't leave those ends hanging. I can't do that. Not to her."

Jake said, "Well, you may be retiring sooner than you think."

"She remembers everything," Jim said. "Well, almost everything." He continued on, telling Miller the remarkable story of Louisa's family and the house fire. When he finished, he leaned against the wall and crossed his arms. Jake put his hands in his pockets and rocked back and forth on his heels.

Miller didn't respond at first. He thumbed the buttons on the TV remote and stared at the blank screen on the wall. Glancing at his wife, he smiled and shook his head. "I've been in law enforcement a long time and seen and heard a lot of crazy things. Sad things. Women beat nearly to death by their husbands. Kids put out in the cold, nowhere to go. Car accidents that'd make your stomach turn inside out. I've wanted to quit almost on a weekly basis. Heard a lot of crazy stories over the years too. But this...this beats everything." Then to Jim he said, "You hear they found the body of that EnviroPride guy?"

Jim nodded. Investigators had found Cody Wisner's corpse buried in a shallow grave behind the farmhouse.

Miller was quiet for a stretch of seconds while he chewed his lower lip and thumbed the remote. Finally he shifted his eyes between Jim and Jake. "You believe her?"

"I have no reason not to," Jim said.

"And what about you?" Miller said to Jake.

"All I know, Chief, is that if it weren't for her, I wouldn't be here.

I don't know where she came from, and until someone can provide a better explanation, her story is as good as truth to me."

Jim pushed away from the wall. "She was put where she was needed. Jake, Audrey, Armand, Amy, and me—we all needed her."

Miller turned to his wife. "What do you think?"

She kissed his hand. "I think you need to check out Louisa's story."

"I can get someone else to do it."

She shook her head. "No. You need to do this. Get your mind off of..." She didn't say the name, but they all knew to whom she referred.

Miller looked at Jim and lowered his eyebrows. "You said she remembered *almost* everything."

"She's a little fuzzy on names," Jim said. "Can't remember her last name or the names of her parents or brother."

Miller's wife leaned close to him and kissed him on the cheek. "You can do it, Doug. Find this girl's family."

Chapter 58

WHEN MILLER CALLED and told Jim they needed to talk, Jim suggested they meet at the Red Wing Diner. After arranging for Jake to sit with Louisa, he and Amy drove to the Red Wing and found Miller in a booth, sipping coffee. A week later he still had a gauze bandage wrapped around his neck. The toil the ordeal had taken on his body was evident by his sunken eyes and slightly hollowed cheeks.

"Mornin', folks," Miller said. He did not smile, but there was a look of satisfaction in his eyes.

Jim and Amy sat across from Miller and held hands. "You have news about Louisa?"

They'd all assumed her family perished in the fire, but it was still a mystery why no one had come looking for her.

Miller nodded. "Her last name is Cartwright. Her father's name was Alfred, her mother was Crystal, her brother, Thomas. He was six."

Amy squeezed Jim's hand but kept her eyes on Miller. "Was."

"Yes, was." Miller sighed. "They all died in the fire. In fact, the house was so totally destroyed only partial remains of her mother and father were found. The officials assumed the rest of the family had died too. Including Louisa."

"Assumptions are dangerous things to make," Amy said. "They can have catastrophic consequences."

"Which explains why nobody came looking for her," Jim said. "But where was this fire?"

"Colorado."

Both Jim and Amy exhaled and sat back. It was too much for

Jim to take in, too much to think about at once. His emotions ran so high, he nearly burst into tears right there in front of Miller.

"And what date was the fire that took Louisa's family?" Jim probed, hardly daring to hear the answer.

"Same night as Jake's."

Jim shot a look at Amy, and the shock he saw there likely mirrored his own.

"How did Louisa get here?" Amy said. "How could she suddenly appear in Jake's house?"

Miller shrugged. "Who knows?" he said. "What are the chances of any of this happening?"

"We're not even in the realm of chance," Jim said.

"But it happened, didn't it? So doesn't that make it possible?" Amy said, leaning forward.

"Possible? Sure." Then, after taking another sip of his coffee, Miller said, "After all of this, I'm a big believer in anything being possible."

"So what happens to Louisa now?" Jim said.

"Well, that's the bulk of why I wanted to meet you. Seems she only has a few living relatives. Her mother had one sister; she lives in Germany and apparently wants nothing to do with the family. Her father was an only child. Both the maternal grandparents are dead, killed in a car accident two years ago. Her paternal grandfather has late-stage Alzheimer's and is cared for at home by his wife. She was contacted, the situation here was explained to her, and she feels she simply can't care for Louisa and her husband at the same time. So…"

"So that leaves Louisa a ward of the state," Jim said.

Miller nodded. "Yeah, it does."

Still holding Amy's hand, he looked at her and nodded then turned to Miller. "We want to adopt her. Is that possible?"

For the first time during their discussion Miller smiled. "Not only possible, but in the works. I thought you'd feel that way, so I took the liberty of contacting the folks in Colorado. A hearing is scheduled for next week. In Colorado. You need to be there for it, and if all goes well and the judge agrees, you'll get custody of her, and then you can begin the official adoption process."

Jim looked at Amy again. Tears rolled down her cheeks and caught in the corner of her wide smile. His tears were flowing freely now too.

"Are you interested?" Miller asked, smiling earlobe to earlobe.

Through her tears Amy laughed. "Do rabbits have big ears?"

Louisa sat propped with several pillows in her bed, nestled in like a single chick in a nest. She'd been sent home with an immobilizer on her hip and orders of no weight bearing on the right leg for six weeks. The covers were pulled up to her chest and turned down at the top, revealing the horse sheets Amy had bought her. One of the things the girl remembered was that she loved horses, was crazy about them.

Jim and Amy stood before her, holding hands. After almost four weeks of no news following the hearing, they'd just gotten word from the attorney's office in Colorado.

Louisa's eyes were wide and expectant. She'd taken the news of her family's demise as well as could be presumed when placing such weighty matters on a nine-year-old. But this was no ordinary nine-year-old. She was mature much beyond her years. Jim considered that she'd probably concluded on her own that her family hadn't made it out of the house alive. It was a weight she'd toted around for a whole week following the ordeal at the Appleton farm and her recollection of the fiery inferno that claimed the lives of her dearest.

"Louisa," Jim said, "we want you to know how much you mean to us."

"You're such a special little girl, you know?" Amy said. She glanced at Jim. "You've changed all of our lives."

Jim smiled and cleared his throat. "We love you, Louisa, and we have good news."

"Awesome news," Amy added.

"The judge gave us custody."

Louisa was quiet for a moment, her eyes shifting back and forth between Jim and Amy, her fingers pinching the folded edge of the sheet. Finally she said, "So I'm going to be your daughter?"

Jim nodded. "Unofficially for now. But as soon as we get all the adoption papers signed and approved, then it'll be official."

Louisa bowed her head then stretched her arms toward Jim and Amy. Amy approached her first, sat on the edge of the bed, and wrapped her arms around Louisa. Then Jim followed, rounding the bed and sitting on the opposite side. He joined in the hug. They stayed like that for a full minute, holding each other, relishing in the bond that held them together.

Eventually Louisa pulled away and looked up at Jim. "I'm glad I get to stay with you, Mr. Jim. I know you'll be a great dad."

Jim couldn't stop the tears that came, nor did he wipe them away. "Thanks, kiddo. That's because I'll have a great daughter."

"But the good news isn't over," Amy said.

"No?" Louisa smiled, and her eyes, those crystal blue eyes, flashed in the light of the sun coming through the window.

She knew; Jim knew she did. She'd known it since the first time she came into their bedroom and placed her hand on Amy's abdomen. She knew there was still life there.

Amy reached for Louisa's hand and placed it on her belly.

"Looks like we have to unpack the baby stuff," Louisa said.

They were all crying now, gushing tears like a park fountain.

"We have a lot of getting ready to do," Amy said. "Our family is growing."

"Everything's gonna be okay now, isn't it," Louisa said.

Jim hugged her tight. "You betcha, kiddo."

Chapter 1

THE NIGHT MARNY Toogood was born it rained axheads and hammer handles.

His grandfather made a prediction, said it was an omen of some sort, that it meant Marny's life would be stormy, full of rain clouds and lightning strikes. Wanting to prove her father wrong, Janie Toogood named her son Marnin, which means "one who brings joy," instead of the Mitchell she and her husband had agreed on.

But in spite of Janie's good intentions, and regardless of what his birth certificate said, Marny's grandfather was right.

At the exact time Marny was delivered into this world and his grandfather was portending a dark future, Marny's father was en route to the hospital from his job at Winden's Furniture Factory where he was stuck working the graveyard shift. He'd gotten the phone call that Janie was in labor, dropped his hammer, and run out of the plant. Fifteen minutes from the hospital his pickup hit standing water, hydroplaned, and tumbled down a steep embankment, landing in a stand of eastern white pines. The coroner said he experienced a quick death; he did not suffer.

One week after Marny's birth his grandfather died of a heart attack. He didn't suffer either.

Twenty-six years and a couple of lifetimes of hurt later, Marny found himself working at Condon's Gas 'n Go and living above the garage in a small studio apartment George Condon rented to him for two hundred bucks a month. It was nothing special, but it was a place to lay his head at night and dream about the dark cloud that stalked him.

But his mother had told him every day until the moment she

died that behind every rain cloud is the sun, just waiting to shine its light and dry the earth's tears.

Marny held on to that promise and thought about it every night before he succumbed to sleep and entered a world that was as unfriendly and frightening as any fairy tale forest, the place of his dreams, the only place more dark and foreboding than his life.

On the day reality collided with the world of Marny's nightmares, it was hotter than blazes, strange for a June day in Maine. The sun sat high in the sky, and waves of heat rolled over the asphalt lot at the Gas 'n Go. The weather kept everyone indoors, which meant business was slow for a Saturday. Marny sat in the garage bay waiting for Mr. Condon to take his turn in checkers and wiped the sweat from his brow.

"Man, it's hot."

Mr. Condon didn't look up from the checkerboard. "Ayuh. Wicked hot. Newsman said it could hit ninety."

"So it'll probably get up to ninety-five."

Mr. Condon rubbed at his white stubble. "Ayuh."

He was sixty-two and looked it. His leather-tough skin was creased with deep wrinkles. Lots of smile lines. Marny had worked for him for two years but had known the old mechanic his whole life.

Mr. Condon made his move then squinted at Marny. Behind him Ed Ricker's Dodge truck rested on the lift. The transmission had blown, and Mr. Condon should have been working on it instead of playing checkers. But old Condon kept his own schedule. His customers never complained. George Condon was the best, and cheapest, mechanic around. He'd been getting cars and trucks through one more Maine winter for forty years.

Marny studied the checkerboard, feeling the weight of Mr. Condon's dark eyes on him, and was about to make his move when the bell chimed, signaling someone had pulled up to the pump island. Condon's was the only full-service station left in the Down East, maybe in the whole state of Maine.

Despite the heat, Mr. Condon didn't have one droplet of sweat on his face. "Cah's waitin', son."

Marny glanced outside at the tendrils of heat wriggling above the lot, then at the checkerboard. "No cheating."

His opponent winked. "No promises."

Pushing back his chair, Marny stood and wiped more sweat from his brow, then headed outside.

The car at the pump was a 1990s model Ford Taurus, faded blue with a few rust spots around the wheel wells. The windows were rolled down, which probably meant the air-conditioning had quit working. This was normally not a big deal in Maine, but on a rare day like this, the driver had to be longing for cool air.

Marny had never seen the vehicle before. The driver was a large man, thick and broad. He had close-cropped hair and a smooth, round face. Marny had never seen him before either.

He approached the car and did his best to be friendly. "Mornin'. Hot one, isn't it?"

The driver neither smiled nor looked at him. "Fill it up. Regular."

Marny headed to the rear of the car and noticed a girl in the backseat. A woman, really, looked to be in her early twenties. She sat with her hands in her lap, head slightly bowed. As he passed the rear window she glanced at him, and there was something in her eyes that spoke of sorrow and doom. Marny recognized the look because he saw it in his own eyes every night in the mirror. He smiled, but she quickly diverted her gaze.

As he pumped the gas, Marny watched the girl, studied the back of her head. She was attractive in a plain way, a natural prettiness that didn't need any help from cosmetics. Her hair was rich brown and hung loosely around her shoulders. But it was her eyes that had captivated him. They were as blue as the summer sky, but so sad and empty. Marny wondered what the story was between the man and girl. He was certainly old enough to be her father. He looked stern and callous, maybe even cruel. Marny felt for her, for her unhappiness, her life.

He caught the man watching him in the side mirror and looked at the pump's gauge. A second later the nozzle clicked off, and he returned it to the pump. He walked back to the driver's window. "That'll be forty-two."

While the man fished around in his back pocket for his wallet, Marny glanced at the girl again, but she kept her eyes down on her hands.

"You folks local?" Marny said, trying to get the man to open up a little.

The driver handed Marny three twenties but said nothing.

Marny counted off eighteen dollars in change. "You new in the area? I don't think I've seen you around here before. Lately, seems more people have been moving out than in."

Still nothing. The man took the money and started the car. Before pulling out he nodded at Marny. There was something in the way he moved his head, the way his eyes sat in their sockets, the way his forehead wrinkled ever so slightly, that made Marny shiver despite the heat.

The car rolled away from the pump, asphalt sticking to the tires, and exited the lot. Marny watched until it was nearly out of sight, then turned to head back to the garage and Mr. Condon and the game of checkers. But a crumpled piece of paper on the ground where the Taurus had been parked caught his attention. He picked it up and unfurled it. Written in all capital letters was a message:

HE'S GOING TO KILL ME